Praise for Kate Gray's debut thriller,
The Honeymoon:

'An addictive, jaw-dropping read. I loved it'
Claire Douglas

'A nerve-jangling tale of tension, suspicion and betrayal'
T.M. Logan

'Secrets, lies and the mother of all cover-ups . . .
I was gripped by this twisty tale'
Louise Candlish

'Dark, devilish and deliciously addictive.
The Honeymoon hooked me from page one and delivered
twist after twist. The perfect summer thriller'
Chris Whitaker

'A page-turner full of secrets and
lies, this is a totally addictive read'
Heat

'Full of suspense and a whole load of secrets'
Prima

'I really loved this book. Gripping.
Atmospheric. Couldn't put it down'
Imran Mahmood

'Fantastically atmospheric and suspenseful . . . Set to be
one of the biggest sizzling reads of the summer!'
L.V. Matthews

'Brilliantly plotted, full of suspense and atmosphere, it had me
turning the pages long after I should have been asleep'
Lia Middleton

'Clever, twisty and tense'
Nicole Kennedy

'Tense, pacy, twisty and ingeniously plotted,
it's going to be HUGE this summer!'
Isabelle Broom

'A wonderful twisty thrill ride'
Crime Monthly

'This sizzling summer read is a breath-taking
exploration of obsession and betrayal'
S Magazine

ABOUT THE AUTHOR

© Johnny Ring

Kate Gray lives in North Yorkshire with her husband, two young children, and two rescue cats. She has also written six commercial women's fiction novels as Katy Colins. You can find out more about Kate and her writing on her website www.kategrayauthor.com

THE
SUMMER PARTY

KATE GRAY

First published in Great Britain in 2024 by
Mountain Leopard Press,
An imprint of HEADLINE PUBLISHING GROUP

1

Cataloguing in Publication Data is available from the British Library

ISBN 978 1 8027 9376 5 (Hardback)
ISBN 978 1 8027 9377 2 (Trade Paperback)

Typeset in 12/16.5 pt Sabon LT Pro by Jouve (UK), Milton Keynes

Printed and bound in Great Britain by Clays Ltd, Elcograf S.p.A.

HEADLINE PUBLISHING GROUP
An Hachette UK Company
Carmelite House
50 Victoria Embankment
London EC4Y 0DZ

www.headline.co.uk
www.hachette.co.uk

For my best friends, Jen and Jo.
May none of your office parties turn out like this.

PROLOGUE

Friday 21st June

They've found a body.

Concerned shouts come from up high, alerting others of the grim discovery.

The air is like something out of a horror film. That's why the rescuers have struggled to reach the isolated hotel until now, hampered by the smoke as thick as fog pinning everything in place.

A hazy glow of lights blink from the skyline like rows of eyes. Watching . . . judging.

As night bleeds into day, there is a deep bellow of a boat's horn, a heavy exhale as the approaching vessel's bright white lights slice through the fading darkness.

There are clangs of metal and loud grunts of effort as men use their might to lean across to hook their ropes to the pontoon and get access to Point Grey. They race up the hotel steps, praying they aren't too late. The stench of fire will cling to their skin and hair for days afterwards.

Panicked calls for backup ring out. This is worse than any

of the rescuers expected. The catastrophic scene will stay imprinted on their eyes forever.

Gritty flecks of dust and ash fall from the sky like confetti.

This was never meant to happen. This was supposed to be their annual summer party – a chance for the whole office to be together.

A celebration.

It should never have come to this.

The police will arrive soon and seal the hotel off as a crime scene. How long until they work out what's happened? There will be many questions and not enough answers.

Maybe this is the end of the nightmare.

Then again, maybe not.

After all, the dead body that the rescuers have found isn't the only one waiting to be discovered.

1

Friday 24th May

The email pings into everyone's inbox on a Friday afternoon. Within seconds of it landing, excitement tears through the digital creative agency like wildfire. There is very little work that will be done for the rest of the day. Messaging chats light up with childcare arrangements, potential outfit choices and shared links to online news sites showing which famous faces have stayed at Point Grey. But Mel misses all of this as she's too busy remembering how her colleagues take their tea and coffee.

She wobbles a tray teeming with different-sized mugs and various milk orders and carefully puts them on individual desks, catching snippets of chatter, including a mention of 'the iconic sea fort', knowing that *something* is happening, though she's not entirely sure *what*.

'Here you go.' She places the generous Sports Direct mug containing instant coffee, three teaspoons of sugar, and a glug of oat milk on the coaster on Amir's desk.

'Is it true? Are we really going to Point Grey?' she asks, breathless despite the short distance from the kitchen. 'The

3

junior designers were just saying that members of the Royal Family have stayed there!'

He taps to the headphones in his ears, frowning.

Realising he's on a Teams call, she blushes, dashing off to her desk, desperate to find out what the excitement is about and spilling scalding hot tea – milky English Breakfast, one sugar – on her desk in the process. She pulls a tissue from her drawer to wipe the drips, catching sight of the *'you don't have to be mad to work here, but it helps'* metal sign, from last year's not-so-secret Secret Santa. It used to be on show, but she had to take it down because of an anonymous complaint that it was 'offensive'.

There are ink stains on her fingers. As the only one who knows how to unjam the printer, she's spent the last painful hour wrestling with the stubborn machine. Time she should have spent working on a new recruitment policy, which means she'll be staying late tonight to finish it. Her chair squeaks as she leans closer to read the email everyone else has already seen, allowing herself to be swept up in the chatter and enthusiasm around her.

Her mood lifts with every exclamation mark on Zander's email.

Point Grey.

Tapping through to the website she reads:

Originally constructed as a sea fort in the middle of the Solent for naval defence in the late 19th Century, the imposing historical monument has been transformed into the hottest *luxury hotel on the South Coast, favoured by those who like the finer things in life. Its remoteness and quirky design make every stay here an unforgettable experience. Completely circular in construction, the hotel is sectioned off for an array of different uses. Guests will be wowed at supper in the Officers Mess – a moody, low-lit dining room, for up to sixty sit-down diners or enjoy happy hour at the luxurious bar full of dark panelled oak and vintage leather chairs. The eight bedrooms, accessed from a central corridor, leads out onto a cosy open-air courtyard. The real wow factor comes from the enormous roof terrace with 360-degree views of the sparkling Solent waters . . .*

'Looks fancy, hey, Mel?' Charlie says as he walks past her desk, nodding to her screen. All deep dimples and smiling brown eyes. She accidentally minimises the page in her fluster but he's gone before her brain has kicked in to come up with a witty reply.

Charlie King. Flavour's superstar Account Director who bought in the biggest retainer last year. Talented at what he does and loved by his clients for his cheeky charm. Also, the most handsome man that Mel has laid eyes on.

It takes a second or two for the sudden flush that's bloomed upon her chest to vanish.

She clears her throat and goes back to her screen to admire the glossy images of the hotel, which is all gleaming glass, polished marble, intimately lit bedrooms and state-of-the-art facilities that scream 'wealth'. She can imagine the sparkling sea and the caw of gulls, can picture her face tilted to the sun, the hem of her floaty floral dress wafting in the warm breeze as she shares a hilarious joke with Charlie before he asks if she wants to spend some time alone. Perhaps they wander through to the cocktail lounge or soak up the breathtaking views from the terrace . . .

From somewhere down the office a phone starts to ring. The trilling sound jolts her from her daydream and brings her crashing back to reality where, for one, she doesn't own a floaty floral dress, and two, apart from the odd pleasantry, Charlie King has no idea she exists. There's also three: she doesn't even know if she's able to go to the party because Leonora, her mum's carer, charges extra to stay past eight o'clock.

And four – Holly's pretty face rushes to the front of Mel's mind.

Uncertainty replaces the excitement that was there a moment ago. Of course, she wants to experience Point Grey. Lord knows she'd never be able to afford to visit the hotel herself, not when room rates start at over £350 per night and get booked up months in advance. But perhaps this year their annual summer party should be cancelled?

She lets out a deep sigh, summoning the energy to go and talk to Rohan about her concerns. Her limbs are heavy. Her head and her heart battle against one another as she plods across the open-plan office.

*

The CEO beckons her in from behind his hand-crafted oak desk, which she knows cost more than her monthly pay packet.

'Mel, come in. How's things?' Rohan offers her a broad, warm smile as she closes the door behind her, minimising whatever is on his laptop screen to give her his full attention.

He's in his mid-fifties but takes care of himself, as her mum would say, his penchant for going for seconds whenever cakes are brought into the office or a client sends thank-you doughnuts mitigated by the punishing schedule set by his personal trainer, which Mel's often heard him complain about.

'You get the invite?' he asks.

The cold air-con breathes down her neck, sending goose-bumps across her bare arms.

Mel clears her throat. 'That's what I wanted to talk about.'

'Uh oh . . . I've seen that look before.'

Mel doesn't like it but sometimes she has to be a party pooper. It's her role as HR & Operations Manager to be prac-tical and level-headed at all times, especially working under someone like Rohan with his impulsive ideas. He doesn't always see the bigger picture or that his actions have conse-quences.

'I know the invitations have been sent out but . . .' She takes a breath. 'Perhaps we should skip this year as a mark of respect?'

There is a pause.

'Ah, I see.' Rohan pulls out a nicotine replacement mint from a drawer and crunches down on it.

As she waits her eyes are drawn to the shelves behind him. The silver-framed photograph of Rohan and his glamorous wife Rumi, suited and booted at Buckingham Palace where he received his MBE earlier this year. He's in a tailored Savile Row suit and she's in a stunning designer cocktail dress, acces-sorised by the most beautiful teardrop necklace and sparkling pearl earrings. They look every inch the charitable, good-looking couple goals Mel can only dream of one day achieving. The light bounces off an array of awards beside the photo, freshly polished under the spotlights.

'You know, Mel, you always do such a fantastic job looking after the team's well-being, but Point Grey has offered us an incredibly generous rate because of the work we've done for them. We would be mad to give this opportunity a miss. We can't stop celebrating our successes.'

'It's bigger than that though.'

He leans back. 'I know what you're saying, but life moves on. People are still going to feel sad no matter when we have the party, and at least this way they can feel sad in a luxurious setting.'

Mel listens to his logic and bites her tongue.

He's always been more like a mentor than a manager, and she looks up to him in so many ways, but she's nervous that he's jumping the gun with this decision, as much as it pains her to have to try and oppose it.

But, then again, he's not the one who watered Holly's potted plant every day. He's not the one who remembered to clean out the last dregs of her milky coffee from her favourite mug – the one with the 'one in a million sister' on the side in faded font – so it wouldn't go mouldy.

He's not the one who held back the tears asking the cleaner to collect her things to send to her family. She had wanted to do it herself. She owed Holly that. But when it came to it, the sight of Holly's half-empty perfume bottle, the unopened box of protein bars and her personalised AirPods lying in her desk drawer set Mel off.

Thankfully, Bonnie had started her shift and kindly offered to take over and leave Holly's items on Mel's desk, giving the space a good clean to prepare it for the next employee.

The following morning, Mel had carefully wrapped Holly's meagre belongings in bubble wrap and posted them, along with a note expressing her deepest sympathy. Her pen dragged with every word.

Rohan's voice brings her back to the present.

'There's no timeline for when we're supposed to stop griev-ing and start living. As we've all sadly learnt recently, life is too short.'

Perhaps she's overreacting.

Mel has never worked anywhere where someone so young has died. She struggled to find advice on the protocols for managing such an event, despite scouring the internet. In the end, she'd handed a pamphlet to senior members of staff explaining how to deal with employees' heightened emotions, sent an agency-wide email with links to free bereavement hot-lines, informing them of the quiet space she'd set up in one of the downstairs meeting rooms for anyone to go and take time out if they felt overwhelmed, and an educational online video about night-time safety. She also persuaded Rohan to allow everyone time off to attend Holly's funeral if they wanted to pay their respects in person.

But that was months ago now and, as Rohan said, life moves on.

Shortly after that time they were nominated for a regional 'Creative Agency of the Year' award and won a pitch to rebrand a large health club chain, so what happened to Holly soon became old news. It wasn't long before the 'quiet space' was reclaimed as a meeting room – the fancy biscuits, tea bags and boxes of tissues that Mel had placed there vanishing, and Holly's name no longer mentioned in every hushed conversa-tion.

'I think the inquest has given us the chance to turn the page, as it were,' he adds.

She wants to reply that it's easier said than done.

A fortnight ago the judge delivered his verdict. What happened to Holly Mills was a tragic accident.

She's tried to block the events of *that* night from her mind, but the wine bottles piling up in her recycling every week tell a different story.

'Maybe you're right,' Mel says eventually.

'I appreciate your concern but think of it as a chance to put the past behind us.' His mobile phone lights up but he ignores it. 'I'm also hoping if we get everyone together it will remind the staff of the creativity that comes from collaboration. I know many places are pushing the flexi-hybrid method but the thing that makes Flavour great is the people. We need our family under one roof again.' He smiles.

There's a knock on the door. Zander, Rohan's PA, peers over the top of his trendy plastic glasses, beckoning him to wrap this up. Rohan signals through the glass that he'll be two minutes.

'I'm sorry to cut this short but I'm running late for my next meeting. Try not to worry, Mel.'

If everyone else can move on, then so can she.

Lightning doesn't strike twice, after all.

2

Friday 14th June

All Flavour employees are called to gather in the large meeting room for a special announcement. Mel slips in at the back, shivering under the air-conditioning. People around her clutch iced frappés and tropical smoothies in plastic takeaway cups with drooping paper straws.

Everyone has been talking non-stop about the summer party since Rohan announced it three weeks ago. Incredibly, aside from her own misgivings, there hasn't been a single complaint or suggestion that the party should be cancelled or postponed.

Clearly, Rohan is right; life moves on.

Mel smiles at the last few stragglers coming in and finding a place, some leaning against the 'inspiration wall' – another one of Rohan's ideas to spark creativity. He asked every member of staff to share the words of wisdom that motivated them. Mel had had to Google her suggestion.

The space has, over time, become full of candid Polaroid snaps of the team on socials, impressive press cuttings and framed quotes, such as 'Every day is a chance to be awesome when you're creative' and 'Design is the way we tell great stories.' Mel remembers the last time Rohan called everyone into this space to deliver the terrible news.

Many had already seen it online and worked out the reason for this sudden in-person meeting, but still, they filed in under the neon sign reading 'Live your best life', its message suddenly tacky and out of place. Someone was crying in the corner. Another sniffed loudly beside her as Rohan began.

'This is a dark day for the Flavour family,' Rohan had said, his laughter lines creased in a serious frown. 'On behalf of the company, I've offered my heartfelt and sincere condolences to Holly's family, but Mel has also set up a memory book in reception and arranged a card for everyone to sign so that you can express your own sympathies. We will stand together. We are here with you, and for you, during this devastating time.'

Mel blinks back the memory. There are no tears today, only excitement. She tries to follow what Rohan is saying.

'It's great to see you here again, thanks for making it in. As you know, we smashed the pitch we were given to rebrand Point Grey and, as a special thank you, they've offered eight employees the chance to stay over after the party next week.'

There's a dramatic 'ooh' from the huddle of colleagues.

'Staff at the hotel asked for everyone's names so they could pull the winners out of a hat and they have just this minute sent over the list of lucky VIPs. Now, I want to reiterate that this was all decided fairly by the Point Grey team and no one here had any involvement. So don't be grumbling if you don't win,' he laughs.

It's the first social event in forever that Charlie will be attending as a single man.

Mel crosses her fingers behind her back. If only both their names are drawn . . .

Rohan has called out the first name. 'Congratulations to . . . Wes Nelson.'

Wesley's face breaks out into a wide smile. The handsome twenty-something is jeered by the lads he shares a bank of desks with. He works as a Digital and Creative Lead and though Mel doesn't know *exactly* what he does, it involves a lot of time making noisy TikToks, talking about his impressive burpee reps at the gym and eating boiled eggs for lunch, which stinks out the communal fridge.

'Next up – Jonty Aspinall.'

Someone lets out a not-very-subtle groan. Jonty ignores it and ambles forward, all scrawny limbs and angles, to shake Rohan's hand as if accepting an award. He does the same job – Account Director – as Charlie but the men couldn't be more different in both looks and personality. He's in his late forties but his retro band T-shirt and drainpipe ripped jeans are more suited to someone ten years his junior. He gels his thinning hair into a peak above his forehead to try and appear younger, and no one has the heart to tell him that it only ages him.

He is also the constant thorn in Mel's side. She is repeatedly being dragged into meeting rooms to address complaints and deal with disputes concerning him. But nothing ever changes.

'Nicole Williams, congrats,' Rohan calls.

'Oh my God,' Nicole gasps, clutching her tanned chest with blood-red nails. She is the Head of Client Services and treats the office as a catwalk, showing off her clingy sweaters, skin-tight leather trousers and designer high heels. Mel craves that level of confidence.

Nicole's getting married in a couple of weeks' time, and it's impossible to miss the framed photo of her engagement shoot on her desk, arranged beside a zodiac diary and positive affirmation Post-it notes.

'She led the bloody rebrand campaign, no shock that she's been picked. Unless she magically *manifested* this whole thing,' Zander whispers scornfully behind his hand. Bringing in Point Grey as a new client is Nicole's most lucrative deal since she started at Flavour. 'She has to go over the top with her reaction as you can't tell from her face if she's surprised or not. What? You know it's true.'

Chloë, a junior graphic designer, giggles. Once she realises who she's stood next to though, she swiftly turns her laugh into a cough.

'Congrats, doll,' Zander claps as Nicole walks past.

'The next lucky winner is – Zander Sims,' Rohan calls out.

Zander lets out a dramatic whoop and performs an impromptu shimmy. He's larger than life in both stature and volume. Whenever Mel tries to make small talk with him, he has the knack of making her feel like she's getting the answer wrong, no matter the question. But as Rohan's PA, and the one who has to put up with Rohan's requests all day long, it's only fair that he has won a place.

'Next up is . . . Bonnie McCulloch.'

'Who?' someone calls out.

'Our hardworking cleaner,' Rohan clarifies. There's a badly hidden scoff from the back of the room. 'She's obviously not here right now. Err, Zander, can you make sure she's told she's won a place?'

Zander nods, writing it down on his notepad. The cleaner doesn't start her shift until later. Mel is pleased that Rohan remembered to make sure her name was included on the employee list given to Point Grey.

'Ok, so next name is . . . Charlie King.'

Mel straightens up as he wanders past smiling. *God, he is so handsome.* His aftershave trails behind him. A spicy oak smell that she may or may not have one time wandered down the fragrance aisle at Boots when she was picking up her mum's prescription, trying to find out exactly which one it was before realising how she was acting like a lovesick teen and gave up.

This changes everything.

There are two places left, Mel who was considering cancelling this office party is now praying her name gets called out. She crosses her fingers behind her back. She has as much chance as anyone else in this room. Out of fifty-two employees, why can't it be her? The next name is called.

'Dominique Sanchez.'

'A child-free night. Count me in,' Dominique laughs.

She is an elegant copywriter, originally from Argentina. She reminds Mel of the women who only exist in fashion magazines. Those who somehow manage to make shapeless dresses look chic, a style that would look like a potato sack on Mel. But then again, Dominique does have a personal stylist, a personal trainer and a very rich husband who works in tech.

'So . . .' Rohan clears his throat. 'One name to go.'

One last chance.

Mel swallows. She crosses her fingers even tighter.

'And . . . the . . . final . . . name . . . is . . .'

It's as if the whole room is holding its breath. Mel can't take her eyes off her boss, praying that he calls her name, at the same time, not knowing what she'll do or how she will react if he does. She mentally prepares herself for disappointment. Things like this don't happen to people like her.

Rohan's eyes slowly trail down the piece of folded paper in front of him. When he looks back up he is looking in her direction.

'. . . It's Melanie Robinson. Congrats, Mel.'

She can hear the smattering of applause over the blood rushing to her ears.

Me? Has he really said my name?

People are smiling, waiting for a reaction.

'I never win anything. Wow. Erm, t-t-thank you.' She stumbles over her words, her cheeks warm from the spotlight of the entire office.

The rest of the team disperse with a few grumbles about it being rigged and other people asking how much they'd be willing to sell their VIP ticket for, which Mel tries to pretend she doesn't hear. All she can think about is how she's going to get through the next few days, wishing the party was tomorrow and not a whole week away.

'Well done. You deserve it,' Tom from IT says as Mel floats down the corridor. The smile that had been fixed on her face falters at those simple words.

'Thanks,' she replies, suddenly wanting to be back at her desk, burrowed in her workload, away from everyone's gaze.

She doesn't deserve a night of luxury. But she can't admit the truth to anyone. So, she does what she's been doing ever since Holly died, which is smile and act like everything is completely fine.

3

Thursday 20th June

The chug-chug-chug of diesel motors on the water is drowned out by excitable chatter from the guests spread out around the Portsmouth quayside, waiting for the boat to take them over to Point Grey. Restless gulls swoop overhead. The early afternoon sun is beating down, and although the water doesn't sparkle exactly as Mel imagined it would, she knows this is going to be unforgettable.

Her colleagues are dressed in outfits fit for a day at the races or an English country garden party. Florals and silks, chinos and boat shoes. She fans her face with her hand. The entire office is here but not everyone has a golden ticket.

'Please could the VIP guests gather over here?' a beautiful woman in a Point Grey-branded uniform politely asks.

A whoop of jealous jeers from the other guests, all seemingly good-natured, ripples across the concourse as the chosen few step forward, easily recognised by the overnight bags and wheelie cases beside them.

Mel smiles at the others. She still can't believe her name was called out. Perhaps luck will be on her side from now on.

'Don't forget us now you're in the big league,' Tom calls out, making her laugh.

A glass of champagne is handed to her. She awkwardly grips the stem between her clammy fingers, terrified it's going to fall from her grip or spill down her dress.

It was such a hard decision to know what to wear.

She was supposed to be in a red satin spaghetti strap number. The dress was a stretch to afford but when she first saw it online, she knew it would be worth it. It was as if, with a slight squint, she could imagine her face where the model's was. Perhaps after a couple of strong drinks, she might have had the confidence to pull it off, but nerves got the better of her as she got ready this morning, and she changed her mind at the last minute, pulling out her old faithful pale green midi dress. The material is slightly bobbled under the armpits, and it's not clingy or skimming in any way, but it *is* comfortable and the thin cotton should help to keep her cool.

She'd left her house with a funny feeling in the pit of her stomach – excited butterflies, perhaps? – but she's not been able to shake off the sense it's something more than last-minute wardrobe wobbles.

A voice interrupts her thoughts. 'Hello, please can I take your name?'

With striking blonde hair, cascading down her slender back, the same length and the same glossy hue, it could be Holly standing there.

Mel's mouth runs dry.

She blinks.

'Melanie Robinson.'

The woman – *not Holly, definitely not Holly* – applies a

19

bright smile, her blue eyes crease. Mel holds on to the edge of the table, her fingers pressing hard into the wood, needing support. This shot of adrenaline has made her suddenly light-headed.

'Wonderful. Welcome, Ms Robinson. If I could ask you to please sign this waiver. We require overnight guests to complete this form. It will only take a minute.'

Mel glances at the detailed health and safety form, which relieves the hotel of any future claims, willing her heart to calm. *This is a legally binding document. Do not sign unless you wish to be bound by the terms*, she reads with a shiver. With a hasty scribble of her name, she ticks the box that says she takes full responsibility if anything happens during the crossings or her overnight stay.

'Hello, your name please?' the member of staff asks, once Mel has moved to the side.

'Bonnie McCulloch.'

Mel does a double-take when Bonnie steps forward. She is unrecognisable from the woman who turns up at half past five every evening in a blue tabard and stretch leggings. Usually make-up-free with her streaked chestnut-brown hair pulled tight in a ponytail, today that hair hangs loose, framing her face, soft waves bouncing on her shoulders. Her eye make-up is heavy beneath thick, brushed-up eyebrows that make her appear ever so slightly startled. She must be in her early forties. Faint lines around her thin glossy lips reveal she was once a smoker. She's shorter than Mel but judging from her toned upper arms looks as though she has double her strength.

'I bet she's thanking her lucky stars,' Zander says, pushing his trendy round sunglasses up his nose. He's wearing a shirt so loud, Mel can practically hear it. His husband is a talented sewer and handmakes most of his garish short-sleeved shirts. Still, she can't help but think of him as a frustrated kids' TV presenter, trapped in a middle-aged man's body.

Bonnie takes the pen, appearing not to have heard him, her signature scratches the paper.

'I reckon I could swim that easily.' Wesley gestures to the grey structure far away on the horizon as he hands back his form. His bottle green shirt is too small on purpose, buttons half undone to flash his tanned, hairless chest. 'How far away is it?'

'Around three nautical miles. Are you an experienced open-water swimmer, sir?' asks the member of staff.

'I'd love to see you try, mate,' Charlie laughs. He looks like he was made for boat life in his deck shoes, chinos and blue shirt open over a bright white T-shirt. Mel spies the edge of the tattoo on his upper arm, peeping from under his sleeve. A lion. Leo for his zodiac sign. As an Aries, she's already Googled how compatible they could be.

'I could, if I had to . . .' Wesley shrugs.

'I hope you've got some suncream with you?' Mel asks Jonty, noticing his nose turning pink by the second.

'I won't need it,' he says, bending down to tie the laces on his high-top trainers, which are almost as brightly coloured as Zander's shirt.

Mel, who made sure to liberally apply Factor 50, stares at him. 'Oh?'

'I heard there's going to be a thunderstorm later. It looks alright now but it's going to turn, mark my words.'

'Really?' The water couldn't be calmer and the sky is a perfect shade of cornflower blue. In fact, there isn't a single cloud above them. Mel exchanges a glance with Bonnie, stifling a laugh at Jonty's sudden apparent meteorological intuition.

'Yeah. The boat journey back after breakfast tomorrow will be a little rough. Don't say I didn't warn you.' He necks the rest of his glass and walks away.

'God, I hope he's wrong,' Mel says to Bonnie.

'Tsk, of course, he's wrong. Look.' She confidently extends an arm towards the view before them, adding, 'It's going to be fine,' in her soft Scottish burr.

Jonty must be winding them up for a bit of fun. There isn't a whisper of a breeze or any indication his claim will come true.

Once all the VIPs are signed in, they are each handed a black tote bag. Mel glances inside. There's a unisex polyester zip-up jacket with the bright lime green and cherry red of the Flavour logo embroidered across the chest. It reminds her of something you'd wear to the gym or for a yoga class; not that she does either but maybe she'll start. There's also a reusable eco-water bottle with her name on it, a couple of biros and a sealed envelope. Mel pulls it out, turning it over in her hands.

'I wouldn't get too excited. It's only a gift voucher for Mama B's Pizza House,' Charlie says, making her jump. She didn't realise he'd come up beside her, and immediately wishes she'd checked she didn't have anything in her teeth.

'Oh, right. W-w-well that's nice,' she stutters. 'I like pizza.'
I like pizza? For God's sake.

He pulls his lips into a sort of amused smile. It lights up his entire face, adorable lines creasing by his dark brown eyes. Heat rises across her. She is relieved when Nicole struts over.

'Zander wants us lined up for a group shot. Oh hey, Mel. I didn't recognise you. When did you get your hair cut?' She leans in for an air kiss and a strong floral perfume shoots up Mel's nose, her bottle blonde loose curls brushing Mel's cheeks.

Mel tries to ignore the desire to raise a hand and touch the gap where her hair once was. The last-minute haircut was a bad decision. The sharp bob is a lot shorter than what she had asked for and she'd left the salon in tears, cursing herself for trying to be too adventurous.

'Oh, I just fancied a change.' Mel lets out a laugh but it's forced from the back of her dry throat.

Nicole has a fixed smile on her glossy lips, her slightly narrowed eyes giving away what she's likely really thinking – that it looks like a dog's dinner.

Mel tells herself that her hair will grow back. It won't look this terrible forever.

'It . . . suits you.' Her engagement ring glints in the sunlight as she brushes down her bandage-style red dress.

Charlie's too busy peering in the complimentary tote bag to notice the flame-like heat reddening Mel's cheeks. She's about to say thanks but Nicole has already spun on her heel to walk away.

The eight VIPs awkwardly stand beside the company pop-up board. Mel swallows. She didn't know they were going to do this. She hates having her photo taken. She never knows what to do with her arms, or how best to smile to hide her slightly crooked front teeth. And she doesn't need a photo to remember this terrible haircut.

'Can everyone please put on the jackets from your goody bags? They're only thin. This heatwave wasn't predicted when

I ordered them,' Zander calls, thrusting a pale pink Polaroid camera at a member of staff. 'We need to look good, it's to go on the inspiration wall.'

The group groan about how hot it is.

'Fine, just hold them up then.'

'All squeeze in a little more, please. Perhaps put your arms around one another and smile?' the staff member says from behind the camera.

Without any hesitation Charlie places his arm across Mel's shoulders. She immediately has to remind herself to breathe.

This is already the best day of her life.

'Say "Team Flavour"!'

'Team Flavour,' they chorus.

4

The Daily News Online

Friday 21st June

HOTEL INFERNO

Published: 06.01, 21 June

FIREFIGHTERS are currently tackling a huge blaze at a five-star secluded hotel in the Solent. Emergency crews were called to Point Grey hotel at around 5.00am this morning (Friday) after billowing plumes of smoke were seen from the mainland.

The boutique hotel is based in a 150-year-old former sea fort off the coast of Portsmouth. The only way to access the remote venue is via boat and is dependent on the tide.

The cause of the blaze is not currently known.

A spokesperson for Hampshire Fire and Rescue confirmed: "We were alerted by the coastguard shortly before 05.00hrs to reports of a fire on the roof terrace at Point Grey Hotel. The fire is being treated as a serious ongoing incident with multiple crews dispatched, including Search and Rescue and HM Coastguard."

NewsOnline understands the venue had been hired out for a private function.

It is not yet understood if there are any casualties.

A spokesperson for Hampshire Police said: "Officers are currently at the scene following an emergency call. We will release further information when we are able."

The striking man-made island, surrounded by the Solent waters, was built in 1867 to protect Portsmouth Harbour from threats of a French invasion. The fort has been owned by luxury brand Cobalt Hotels Group for the past three years. Point Grey is a haunt favoured by the rich and famous because its isolated location affords maximum privacy. Celebrities known to have visited the hotel in recent years include younger members of the Royal family and Premier League footballers.

Comments:

MaureenC: So we don't know if the fire was started deliberately or not? I bet a faulty boiler or a discarded cigarette is to blame. Praying for all involved.

WiseGuy87: No one is surviving this.

JuliefromPortsmouth: It was so stormy last night too. I bet the wind made the fire spread. I can't imagine how those poor people trapped on the island are feeling, waiting for help!

- **BigBob:** I heard a rumour that no one at the hotel called for help. A passing fishing boat raised the alarm.

- **JuliefromPortsmouth:** What? Sounds dodgy.
- **BigBob:** [Comment deleted by admin]
- **JuliefromPortsmouth:** No one knows anything yet. Let's not speculate, especially when people's lives are at stake.

MrWhite: What if the hotel collapses? Has anyone thought of that? Wasn't there a famous pier that fell into the sea after a fire like this? Who knows how structurally unsafe it is? It could collapse at any moment. Those bricks must have some dampness in them, I mean it's over one hundred and fifty years old. God, I hope they manage to get the guests out before that happens.

- **BigBob:** That's if there are any survivors

The views expressed in the comments above are those of our users and do not necessarily reflect the views of News-Online.

5

Thursday 20th June

A forbidding, dark grey silhouette looms overhead, blocking the sun for a brief moment.

'Look at this place,' Dominique grins as the boat begins to slow. 'It's even better in real life.'

Point Grey.

A hush descends for the first time since leaving the dock, the party music turned down and conversations paused. Everyone cranes their necks, staring in awe as the captain steers them closer to the imposing circular granite building.

Mel's arms break out in goosebumps as they are swallowed up by the fort's dominating shadow. The breeze ruffles her hair. She couldn't appreciate how imposing the hotel is from online images. Rising solidly from the choppy waters of the Solent, the three-storeyed man-made island will be their home for the night. She squints, taking in the detail. No wonder celebrities hire this place to get away from the rest of the world. No paparazzo has any chance of sneaky shots out here. It's so remote. Once the boat leaves, there is no way to get on or off easily.

'This has got "James Bond's man cave" written all over it.

A lair used for nefarious doings.' Zander presses his palms together and lets out a dramatic cackle.

A member of the crew calls hello from the metal-framed pontoon, which is tacked to the base of the fort with chunky black screws. Another man with deep-set wrinkles wearing a Point Grey-branded polo shirt helps secure the boat, and invites everyone to 'go on up' the two flights of metal stairs.

There's a yell from the front of the line. Someone from the graphic design team has dropped his phone into the water. A member of staff tells him it's long gone, the Solent swallows everything that it takes.

Mel grips the rough railing and exhales slowly. The crossing was a lot bouncier than she expected.

She wishes she'd been able to eat something this morning but a mixture of nerves, adrenaline and excitement had been swirling in her stomach since she woke. The invitation said there would be canapés and cocktails on arrival, hopefully by then she'll have an appetite. She needs to line her stomach ahead of the free bar – if rumours are to be believed.

The main hotel entrance is through two huge oak doors. Five inches thick, the date '1870' is engraved into the keystone. A narrow passageway leads to an open courtyard in the middle of the fort. From there, stairs go up or descend to the lower deck. Mel follows the group up the stone steps. Soon they emerge into the open air of the 360-degree roof terrace.

There is a collection of gasps. A Hamptons-style beach bar is set up at one side, with plump sea-glass turquoise cushions on low whitewashed chairs on the other. Soft reeds in ceramic pots sway in the gentle breeze, emitting the fragrant scent of rosemary and fresh mint. Relaxing music from hidden speakers fills the space with stirring strings and calming classical piano. There's a circular fire pit, a sun deck, a wellness suite, and, randomly, a kitsch red and white painted replica lighthouse.

Mel squints. Bright sunlight bounces off the marble surfaces as if they are the first guests to ever step foot on board.

'Welcome to Point Grey – the only sea fort hotel in the UK,' a young member of staff in a smart branded polo shirt says. She is waiting beside a tall table with individual room keys neatly lined up. 'Please follow me and I will lead you to your room.'

Some of the VIPs have already gone to join the rest of the colleagues for the drinks reception, but Mel is too excited to see where she will be sleeping. It still hasn't sunk in that she will be spending the night here.

There is a braided rope barrier that's clipped across the top of the stairs to the bedrooms, a sign printed on an embossed card reading 'Overnight Guests Only'. A thrill zips through her as the polished gold clip hook is unclasped. She takes her welcome flute of champagne and steps down to the level below.

The inner courtyard is decorated with fat olive trees in rustic planters. Strings of unlit fairy lights are threaded above her head. It's going to be magical here once the sun sets. A couple of striped deckchairs have been placed a few metres away, next to a cool box full of ice and mini bottles of Prosecco. The Flavour logo is stamped on each one.

The layout of the guest accommodation follows the curve of the circular fort. From where she is standing, all eight bedroom doors, each painted in a soft feather grey, are visible. Beside every door, in satisfying uniformity, are black umbrellas in chrome umbrella stands in case it rains and guests need to make a dart from their bedrooms up the open-air stone steps.

'We hope you enjoy your stay. If there is anything you require, please don't hesitate to let us know,' the member of staff says, handing Mel a silver keycard. Her room number is embossed on the metal. It's only when she walks off that she remembers she should have asked about the Wi-Fi. She'd like to check that her mum is ok.

Mel opens the heavy bedroom door, disorientated for a second. The room is pitch black. The lights must be on a sensor but despite Mel waving her arms nothing happens.

'Come on.'

She tries again.

Eventually, chrome spotlights turn on, illuminating the room with a warm glow.

It's incredible.

The king-sized bed appears miniature in the enormous space. The baroque-style headboard with gilded edges looks like something out of a French palace. Her feet sink into the plush grey carpet, leaving footprints as she pads across to a polished walnut dressing table. Large light bulbs frame the antique-looking mirror, as though she's backstage at a theatre. There's a sleek kettle and expensive tea and coffee bags in polished glass canisters, bottled mineral water from the fort's very own well, and individually wrapped homemade shortbread biscuits.

Her case has already been delivered and placed on a golden luggage rack beside the door. She draws back the blackout curtain covering the porthole window to be greeted with endless waves. She catches herself smiling at her luck.

There is a clunk and a whir and suddenly a blast of icy cold air shoots down the back of her neck. The air-con must be super high-tech, and motion-sensored. She looks around for the remote to turn it down. Her eyes fall on a folded information card. *Point Grey prides itself on marrying history and cutting-edge technology to create a quintessentially British hotel with a twist.* It goes on to say that *the hotel is full of hidden gadgets and features designed to enhance the client's stay.* She wonders who the copywriter was, Nicole? Dominique?

Unusual shadows catch her eye, drawing her to the black metal hooks in the ceiling, placed between thick iron rivets. According to the information card, these hooks once held up the sailors' hammocks. There is also an exposed pipe that runs along the wall beside the bedroom door that was used to store ammunition but *'designers opted to retain these features as a sympathetic nod to the hotel's incredible maritime history'.* It looks like a piece of contemporary art.

A box of luxury chocolates, tied with a red velvet ribbon, is nestled against the many plump cushions on the bed. A sudden pang hits. She wishes that she could share this moment with someone special. Not that Mel has anyone to bring. In fact, she deleted her dating apps after a string of bad apples. Why is it so hard to weed out the good ones? Are there any left in the world? Her mind goes straight to Charlie. He was in a long-term relationship and then, at the start of this year, she heard rumours it was over. She's been building up the courage to talk to him ever since.

Her efforts to show him how she feels have evidently been too subtle. She always makes sure his favourite brand of coffee is stocked, even though it's over budget. Once she rearranged the office foliage so she could see more of him – after all, his handsome face shouldn't be hidden behind drooping oversized cheese plant leaves. She would never admit this to anyone but sometimes she keeps the discarded notes he leaves in the meeting room because she can't bear to throw away his doodles. She knows it's utterly pathetic, but there is just something about him.

And he has no idea that she exists.

Until tonight.

Tonight is about making him notice her, no matter what. For the first time in a long time, she is going to put herself centre stage.

She shivers and tries to look for the panel that controls the air-conditioning.

Mel can't see how to change the temperature. There's nothing in the welcome book about how to adjust the settings. At first, the blast of cold air was what she needed. There's been a heatwave in England for the past few days and she's forgotten what it's like to not be constantly sweating. But this room is now glacial. She'll freeze if she sleeps with it like this.

Holly's face rushes to the front of her mind.

Goosebumps cover her arms and her stomach flips at the memory of her colleague.

Mel needs to hurry, she's missing the drinks reception but first, she has to call for help. A beautiful vintage telephone sits on the bedside table, a teal-coloured bakelite. The receiver automatically connects to reception. She only has to wait two rings until a friendly male voice answers.

'Point Grey, Edward speaking, how may I help?'

'Oh, hi, I wondered if someone could have a look at the air-conditioning in my room, please? It's so cold in here.'

'Of course. I'm sorry to hear this. We wouldn't want you to freeze to death. Can you please confirm which room you're in?'

Her grip on the phone tightens. *We wouldn't want you to freeze to death.* She tells herself to stop being so sensitive.

'Room four.'

'I'll speak to maintenance to have a look at it right away. Is there anything else I can help with?'

Mel swallows and pulls herself together. 'No. I mean, no thank you.'

The bright lights in the ensuite bounce off the polished tiles. She catches sight of herself in the large circular mirror, her cheeks are flushed and her mascara has already flecked under her eyes. Beside the sink, in a sleek wooden box, is a selection of complimentary toiletries. Miniature high-end beauty products, premium body wash, bamboo cotton buds, and a small gold-plated vial of perfume. She absently sprays it. The fruity fresh scent is a smell she knows from somewhere.

It stops her in her tracks.

Holly's perfume.

Holly once accidentally spritzed Mel with it in the work bathroom.

An unexpected rush of emotion clutches her chest. What are the chances? The bottle has no label on it. It's probably some bespoke, heady mix. But no, she's certain it's the exact same berry notes that always clouded Holly's desk. It smells of youth and endless possibilities. Mel grabs a tissue and dabs her eyes.

She needs to pull herself together and remind herself that no one here knows what she did.

6

Thursday 20th June

The drinks reception is in full swing on the roof terrace. The sun beats down and there's barely a whisper of a sea breeze to move the cloying air. Guests in dark sunglasses are fanning their faces and using napkins to discreetly wipe sweat from their foreheads. Silent staff hover on the fringes holding perspiring bottles of Prosecco. Gleaming trays of minuscule hors d'oeuvres pass through the bustling space. Mel wishes she'd brought a wide-brimmed hat. It won't be long before her hair starts to frizz in this humidity. And here she thought it couldn't look any worse.

Her head pulsates, it's not only the heat but the unexpected scent of Holly's perfume that has made her feel so strange.

Threatened.

Mel sees Tom and Rohan standing together, their heads bent close. She can't hear what they're talking about, but it looks serious. Rohan is wringing his hands together and Tom appears deep in thought. She moves closer, the classical music flowing from the speakers drowning out the sound of her heels on the stone floor.

Rohan's jaw is tense, eyes fixed on Tom. Something is definitely up.

As soon as they see her, they straighten as if they have been caught doing something they shouldn't have.

Rohan clears his throat loudly. 'So, yes, as I was saying . . . Oh hello, Mel. Didn't see you there.'

Tom plasters a strange tight smile on his face. He's usually so laid back. It's odd to see a deep frown on his forehead. He works in IT and is a stereotypical geek – skinny jeans, thick-rim glasses, a checked cotton shirt which must have come straight from a fresh packet judging by the creases running down his chest, and wild black curls that spring in every direction.

'Hi, Mel, excuse me. I'll leave you to it. But listen, Rohan, don't worry yeah. I'll make sure everything is taken care of,' he says, striding away as fast as he can.

'Everything ok?' Mel asks the moment he's gone.

'Yeah, all good.' Rohan leans to give her a kiss on the cheek. His skin is clammy. 'How is your mum? Did you manage to speak to my contact at Silverdale?'

'Yes, thanks so much for putting me in touch with them. She's on the waiting list for now, but thanks,' she mumbles. 'A carer is staying over with her tonight.'

'I'll try and pull some strings, see if we can get you some longer-term respite. I hate to think of you suffering alone. You're a good daughter, Mel. She's lucky to have you.'

'It's what family does.'

'Doesn't mean it's easy though. Oh, so I was—'

A shriek from nearby slices the air and interrupts what Rohan is about to say.

'What – there's no signal! How am I going to update my

insta stories?' a girl from accounts moans, flashing her phone in the air.

'You're here to get away from it all,' Rohan calls, his eyes creasing with laughter lines. 'It won't be long till you'll return to the real world. Enjoy yourselves.'

Mel didn't think about the fact that Leonora wouldn't be able to get in touch with her in case anything goes wrong. Though if anyone needs her, there's nothing she can do from the middle of the sea, hours away from home. And besides, Leonora told Mel to let her hair down and blank out any guilt at having this small window of respite. She looked her straight in the eyes and ordered Mel to relax and enjoy herself.

Still, a flutter of anxiety makes Mel's heart race. Despite being an ancient building, this is a modern hotel. There must be some signal or a way to connect to the outside world, surely?

Not picking up on her wave of panic, Rohan strolls away to say hello to other guests. She surreptitiously places her complimentary flute of champagne on a tall table, wanting to keep a clear head for as long as possible.

Charlie is on the other side of the terrace, slipping on a pair of Ray-Bans. For days she's been running through possible topics of conversation in her head. All of them are meant to make her appear effortless and much cooler than she actually feels whenever she's around him. He glances over. Can he sense her eyes on him? Mel quickly looks away.

She rubs her warm palms against her dress, praying that sweat patches aren't blooming under her armpits in this heat. When she next dares to look up, her heart races. Charlie is coming towards her. The pre-rehearsed small talk immediately vanishes from her mind.

She builds up the courage to raise a clammy hand and give him a wave. Charlie smiles and comes closer.

Her mouth runs dry.

Perhaps she should have drunk more? Lubricated a little. Some of her younger colleagues were passing around a bottle of tequila on the boat, necking shots. Why didn't she boldly invite herself into their pre-drink party? She clears her throat. His hands are in his pockets, a picture of confidence.

Oh gosh. Right. Okay, stay calm.

'Not keen?' Jonty's nasally voice comes from behind her.

'Erm, sorry?' she asks, flustered.

Charlie walks straight past her. Her arm plummets to her side as if it doesn't belong to her. Jonty nods to Mel's abandoned glass of fizz as he hastily lights up a cigarette.

'I'm trying to pace myself,' Mel replies curtly.

Normally he parades around the office as if he is the one in charge, but there is a tightness to him today, a sheen on his pale face and an anxious fidget that even the cigarette isn't helping to ease.

'Mind if I . . .' He reaches past her and picks up her glass, tipping it into his mouth before she gets the chance to reply. He finishes her drink in one, letting out an obnoxious burp before walking off.

Mel stares daggers at Jonty's back.

She spies Charlie out of the corner of her eye, laughing and joking with Nicole and Wesley.

Some of her younger colleagues are in short, revealing dresses, their hands clamped to their sides to stop the scant pieces of material from lifting in the occasional gust off the sea. Even when Mel was their age she never had the courage to expose so much of her body like that. If she could turn back the clock, she wonders if she would do things differently, be bolder and braver. Care less about what people think.

Mel peers over the stone wall to the sea. Her stomach pulls at how high up she is. Leaves and seaweed swirl, carried on frothy brown crests of waves. There is a lifeboat fixed to the bricks further along, held up by a series of pulleys and ropes. She imagines how scary it would be being dropped to the water from this height. She pushes the thought away.

For a short while, she stands on the edge of the party, watching the hubbub play out around her.

She glances around, praying to find someone else on their own who she can maybe spark up a conversation with, but people have already migrated into their usual cliques.

The creatives. The designers. The youngsters. The senior directors.

She hovers awkwardly near the content specialists who give her tight polite smiles, their conversation abruptly trailing off. One of them makes an excuse to use the bathroom. The others proclaim they also suddenly need it too, leaving Mel on her own once more.

7

Thursday 20th June

Mel swallows down the bubble of emotion that rises inside her. Her colleagues must find it awkward to socialise with her because of her role in the agency. As the office co-ordinator she's involved in recruitment and retention, approving leave requests, and generally being super organised.

It's never been anything personal.

They're not avoiding you, you're seeing things that don't exist.

Her role is simply a lot less creative than those around her. Mel's mother used to say that her daughter coloured inside the lines. Always following the rules.

Working at Flavour means she gets to hang out with the cool crowd, play Spotify roulette in the communal kitchen, and celebrate their wins. But in the end she always retreats, alone, to her spreadsheets and PowerPoint presentations and policies. It's fine, she tells herself, except in situations like this when it's obvious that she doesn't have her own group to hang out with.

Mel chews her lip. Just then she sees Bonnie, who is also on her own, and makes a beeline over to her.

'Warm, isn't it?' Mel says. *If in doubt, talk about the weather.*

Bonnie fans her face, the movement brings a rush of digestive biscuit-like fake tan. It's a relief to smell something new. Mel still can't shake how disconcerting it is that, out of all the smells in the world, Holly's exact perfume is in her ensuite. She keeps catching wafts of the aroma, which has settled in the fabric of her dress, releasing in waves as she moves. It's as if Holly is here, walking alongside her.

'Aye, you're telling me, hen. Although, I'd prefer to be too warm than too cold. Talking of which, have you been to your bedroom yet? Jesus. Mine was like going down the freezer aisle of Morrisons. Not that I'm complaining, mind you,' she adds hurriedly.

'Is your room cold too?' Mel says.

'Arctic more like. It was set to minus three or something. I didn't even know you could turn it that cold.'

Minus three. The temperature you start to freeze.

'They must be overcompensating for the heatwave,' she continues, not picking up on how Mel has stiffened beside her.

'I called the front desk, they're sending someone to look at my room,' Mel says.

'Ah good. I think I managed to fix mine at the control panel thing. Hopefully, yours'll be sorted soon,' Bonnie says. 'I really like your dress, by the way.'

'This? Oh, it was only cheap, I've had it for years.' Mel shifts, wishing she could accept a compliment more easily. 'I like yours too.'

'It's got pockets,' Bonnie beams. 'Are you going to join the tour of the fort? One is starting soon.' She glances at a group of employees walking away from the bar. Mel spots Charlie amongst them. 'If you're into history or hearing stories about haunted hotels . . .'

'This place is haunted?' Mel asks, her stomach flips.

'Depends if you believe in ghosts, hen,' Bonnie laughs softly at the look on Mel's face.

'Oh, hang on,' Mel says quietly. There's a label sticking out of Bonnie's dress. She carefully tucks it back in and as she does she spots a tattoo hiding near the straps. 'Who's Dylan?'

'Thank you. He's my wee boy.' Bonnie's face lights up. 'I got it not long after he was born. It's faded a bit now.'

'How old is he?'

'Almost twenty-three. Not so wee anymore.'

Mel blinks. She doesn't look old enough to have a twenty-three-year-old. 'Wow, what does he do?'

Bonnie gulps her drink. 'Erm, he's working in Italy. He teaches sport at a school out there.'

'That's amazing, you must be so proud. Whereabouts in Italy is he?'

'Hmm? Oh, the north.'

A waiter walks past with a bottle of Prosecco and offers them a top-up. As he's pouring the fizz into their glasses, Mel can't help but glance over at Charlie.

'You like him? Don't you?' Bonnie nudges her.

'You might want to make it a little less obvious,' Dominique says joining them.

'Sorry?' Mel freezes, she hadn't realised she'd been listening in to their conversation.

'You, staring at Charlie like a schoolgirl with a crush.' She tilts her head. 'We all know you fancy him. It's so obvious.'

Her cheeks burn under their amused half-smiles.

'I don't know what you're talking about,' Mel says quickly.

'Hmm, really? You're both staying over tonight so who knows what could happen . . .' Dominique winks. 'What goes on at sea, stays at sea. Or something like that, isn't that right?'

'No! I mean, I'd like to but . . .' Mel takes a deep breath, trying to stop babbling. 'Hang on, if you both know then . . .' She lowers her voice. 'I mean, do you think *he* knows?'

'Nah, men, they're all the same.' Bonnie chuckles.

'They don't see what's in front of them half the time,' Dominique laughs. 'But if you do want him to notice you then you need to do something about it. Fortune favours the bold and all that. God, I'm starving. I hope it's not long before they serve dinner. These canapés aren't even touching the sides.'

Bonnie excuses herself to use the bathroom. Mel wants to follow Charlie, even if that means joining the ghost tour, but Dominique is blocking her path.

'Don't you think it's a bit weird?' she asks, adjusting her designer tortoise-shell sunglasses.

'What?'

'I don't know,' she sighs, 'it's not right that we're here laughing and joking as if nothing happened. I mean, the last time we were all together . . . well, it's a little insensitive.'

Mel brings her glass to her lips and gulps. 'Perhaps everyone needs the chance to let their hair down?'

'Yeah, maybe. I don't know.' Dominique tries to catch the attention of a passing waiter for another top-up. 'I still don't understand. Holly was fine when I left that night. Who could have imagined what would happen hours later.'

There's a whoop as a champagne cork is popped further down the roof terrace.

'God, don't you just love that sound?' Dominique smiles, flashing perfectly straight white teeth.

There's an awkward pause.

'You must know something?' Dominique moves closer; the smile slips.

'Me? Why?' Mel coughs.

'Well not *you* personally, but I'd have thought the whole of the office who were out that night would have been pulled for an interview. I suppose the police don't have the resources but surely someone knows something. I mean, the fact that she was so close to home was heartbreaking. Did they ever speak to you?'

'It was an accident, they don't need to interrogate her colleagues.' Mel stiffens.

'I still can't get my head around it.' There's a deep sigh. 'As her line manager, I wonder if I should have done more. You can't help but feel a little responsible, you know? Perhaps that's just me?' Dominique isn't looking at Mel. Her gaze is on the horizon, her thoughts clearly somewhere far away from the party.

'It was a tragic accident,' Mel says in a low voice as a sudden warm breeze moves Holly's scent around them.

Dominique continues as if she's not heard her. 'I'm sure she wasn't even that drunk when I left. There are so many unanswered questions. Even after the inquest.'

'Like what?'

'Well, how did she get from the hotel to the woods? No way she could have got there alone. Also . . . where was her coat? She was definitely wearing one when she arrived. Had this black fluffy hood. I remember because I asked if it was faux fur. That's never been discovered. Isn't that strange to you?'

Mel's heartbeat thrums faster.

'Someone knows more than they're letting on.' Dominique gives a half-shrug, tipping her glass to her lips. Leaving a kiss of blood red lipstick behind.

Mel doesn't trust herself to speak.

'Don't hold me to it. It's only a theory.'

A waitress appears holding a tray dotted with small healthy-looking salad bowls. 'Can I interest anyone in a canapé?'

'Oooh.' Dominique's face lights up. 'Is it vegan?'

Mel can't stomach anything.

'You ok?' Dominique frowns, pulling her sunglasses down to peer at Mel. Her hazel eyes sharp and trained on her.

'Fine. I just need to get out of the sun.'

The older man who welcomed them to the hotel claps his hands and loudly calls for everyone's attention. 'Ladies and gentlemen, if you would like to join in a tour of the fort, we will be starting in five minutes.'

'Screw that. I'm off to the bar.' Dominique is soon lost in the crowd without a backward glance.

8

Thursday 20th June

'Good afternoon, my name's Gus and I'm the general man-ager here,' Gus says, spreading his arms wide to gesture towards the stunning panoramic views. The high vantage point, the miles of sea and bobbing sailboats beyond. 'I like to say I have the best view from my office.'

He reminds Mel of a kindly old sailor from a fish fingers advert.

'My colleague, Eddie, is also around and he will be looking after those lucky guests staying the night.' He smiles to reveal a row of yellowing teeth. 'Some fun facts: The fort is one hun-dred and fifty years old – almost as old as me,' he chuckles. 'The granite walls are fifteen feet thick and with no neighbours to offend, you can make as much noise as you want here.'

'Alternatively, no one will hear you scream,' Jason, in graphic design, says with a wink.

Gus continues unfazed, regaling them with the history of the hotel.

'Point Grey was built to protect Portsmouth dockyards. At that time there had been years of unrest and there was little trust in the French. As such, the construction included space in the walls for seven-inch rifled muzzle-loading naval and coast defence guns, which you may have seen as you entered. It took fifteen years to build, and by the time it was ready, the threat of invasion had already subsided. It was officially declared surplus to requirements in 1962. It's now the successful hotel and event space you see before you. We take pride in being the custodians of such a fascinating piece of history.'

'They take pride in it, alright. This place is so clean, you could eat your dinner off the floor. Maybe Bonnie could pick up some tips . . .' Jonty says loudly.

Mel rolls her eyes, remembering another of his complaints that she had to deal with. If Jonty had his way he would have fired the cleaner on the spot due to an incident where he claims tea was spilled into his desk drawer. He argued at the time that he would never leave it open, so the fact that it *had* been open meant that she must have been snooping. Mel spoke to Bonnie about it and she insisted it wasn't her job to clean *inside* drawers, so it must have been left ajar and some cold tea happened to leak through when she knocked his mug by accident. Thankfully nothing was reported missing or damaged, apart from some Post-it notes getting soggy, and Mel could mark the incident off as just another time-wasting exercise. But, considering this all happened a few months ago, he's still not ready to let it go. She sighs.

Thankfully, Bonnie doesn't appear to have heard Jonty's dig, as something in the water has caught her attention.

Gus continues: 'The designers have kept as much of the fort's original features as possible. The bathrooms contain the wash basins from the Victorian times and you'll find rifle racks dotted about. The lucky VIP guests will spot iron hooks for hammocks and metal trackings previously used for the cannons in their bedrooms. You might have also noticed the replica lighthouse? It's modelled after the original lighthouse that is no longer in operation. Of course there are some modern features too. Every room has state of the art intelligent systems installed for guest comfort. We also have a spa area on the roof terrace, a wine cellar and a games room. Oh, and we're licensed for weddings.'

'God, don't get this one started on weddings,' Laura in marketing calls out, nudging Nicole.

'Well, our packages are very competitively priced.' He winks. 'Follow me.'

Gus leads the group down to the third and lowest level of the fort. The light changes the deeper they move, the space growing increasingly claustrophobic. Gone is the bright hot daylight, instead, gloomy shadows press around them. Clunks and thumps echo with their footsteps. As someone not entirely comfortable in enclosed spaces, Mel makes a conscious effort to take slow, measured breaths.

'As you may expect in a building of this age, many have reported spooky goings-on. I don't want to alarm anyone but rumour is we've even got a ghost,' Gus says, rubbing his liver-spotted hands together.

Someone makes an eerie moaning noise.

Mel tries to edge closer to Charlie but he's too far back.

'Guests and members of staff have reported the sensation of a hand on a shoulder, a sense of being watched, and the sound of ghostly footsteps, as if someone is behind them but when they've turned there's no one there . . .'

Mel would like to get out of here now. She inhales sharply as a chill passes through her. There is something off about this place. But then don't all ancient buildings, in the right light, with brittle air, feel haunted? She tells herself that ghosts aren't real. They don't exist.

Your mind plays tricks on you, that's all.

'They say that his soul is trapped here because of what happened to him.' He pauses for dramatic effect. 'Back when it was used by the military there were around one hundred and fifty men stationed here. And the conditions were awful; nothing like the luxury you are enjoying today. There were high rates of infection. The soldiers were forced to drink half a pint of Gunpowder Pussers daily, a 109 per cent proof rum, to help ease the suffering.'

'Well, that doesn't sound so tough,' someone calls from further down the narrow, windowless corridor.

Gus shakes his head. 'Admiral Nawton was the man in charge. He was lauded with respect and highly decorated but in reality, he was a cruel boss. He purposely took care to select men who couldn't swim, so there was no danger of them making a break for it, effectively capturing them under his control.'

Mel shivers in the damp air.

'Despite never engaging in warfare activity, there were plenty of drills to make sure the equipment, and the men themselves, were up to the task if duty called. Sadly, during one of these drills, a gun backfired and the man behind it – George Coaker – was instantly blown apart. He was due to be sent home and marry his sweetheart the following week.' Gus lowers his voice before continuing. 'He was killed in 1910 and it's been reported that he's haunted the lower levels of the building ever since.' He pauses. 'And the place where he took his last breath . . . is exactly where you are standing right now.'

Just then, Mel hears a sound so deafening it reverberates up through her feet.

A heavy honk of a sea siren.

The call for help.

A few people try to hide their amusement at how they leapt out of their skin at the perfect timing.

Gus tells them to follow him. 'Don't worry, it's not a real alarm. That's to let you know that dinner is almost ready.'

They start walking back the way they've come. Mel wills her racing heart to calm down, wiping the sweat from her clammy hands against her dress without anyone seeing. She thinks of those 150 men, unable to swim, trapped here with no escape. The rough brick walls close in even more.

'What's down there?' Wesley asks, pointing to a corridor. Mel bites down the irritation that this question is stalling their rise to fresh air and cocktails and sensible people who didn't join this stupid tour.

'That's the staff quarters,' Gus replies. 'To save on the costs of hiring boats, the waiting staff arrive and leave with the day guests. After ten o'clock, the only residents on the island are the night manager and the overnight guests. If I'm honest, I would live here all the time if I could. You'll have the best sleep of your life. Guaranteed. Not only are the beds fantastic but the peace and quiet is unparalleled, and sea air does wonders for you.'

'What about through there?' Charlie points to a closed door marked 'Private'.

Gus clears his throat. 'Ah, this is the bolt passage, a circular secret corridor that runs the whole way around the fort. We believe it was used for the men stationed here to access in an emergency. They might also have used it to make a quick dash to the soldiers' latrines, located on the other side,' he says, as a polite ripple of laughter echoes.

'Cool. Can we go all the way round?' someone asks.

'I'm afraid it's just for staff. And even then it's only for the nimble ones as most of the space has become a bit of a dumping ground . . . but don't tell my boss I said that,' Gus chuckles.

Eventually, they climb up to the middle deck and move through to the lounge area, which is like stepping into the pages of a luxury interior design magazine compared to where they've just been: warm, welcoming and high-end comfort.

Mel can breathe again.

There are quirky original features that have been enhanced by the designers amongst the gilt-framed portraits, elaborately patterned rugs, a Farrow and Ball-hued ceiling and dark wooden trims. The group starts to disperse but Mel hangs back as something has caught her eye.

High up on the wall above the cast iron mantelpiece a display of two antique guns – Victorian pocket pistols – are fastened to the exposed brick. Between them there is a mark on the paint. She takes a step closer. Her forehead creases.

Small black metal hooks are fixed into the plaster, identical to the ones holding the other guns, but these stand empty.

A shiver dances across her arms at what this means.

One of the guns is missing.

9

The Daily News Online

Friday 21st June

TRAGEDY AT SEA

Friday 21st June. 16.00

SEVERAL bodies have been discovered after a deadly fire broke out on Point Grey sea fort early this morning (21 June) in a 'distressing and tragic incident'.

A spokesperson for Hampshire Police at a press conference, said: 'This is a challenging and highly complex ongoing incident. Sadly, there is evidence of several casualties but we are not in a position yet to confirm official numbers while our investigations are in the very early stages. We're following a number of lines of inquiry. I understand the news of this incident will be shocking and we will release more information as soon as we can.'

When asked what might have caused the blaze, the spokesperson said: 'We are ruling nothing out. Our current focus is the search for survivors.'

It is understood that at least seven guests were staying overnight at the £350-a-night luxury hotel in the Solent estuary, off the coast of Portsmouth.

A spokesperson for Flavour, a Buckinghamshire-based creative design agency, which had hired the venue said: 'We are distraught by the news and will be working closely with the rescue services.'

The investigation is being jointly led by detectives from the Hampshire Major Investigations Team and Fire and Rescue who have stressed the inquiry is in its 'early stages.'

Comments:

Man_U_Dad: Very upsetting. What must their families be going through? Tragic

PreacherMan: Call themselves a creative design agency. Their logo is sh*t.

Beverley63: I wouldn't be surprised if paranormal activity is to blame. Isn't it one of the most haunted places in England?

- **GeorgeS:** I heard that the police suspect arson.

- **Beverley63:** I can't believe someone would do this deliberately. Praying for the #PointGreyVictims

Kathrynnnnnn: As time goes on, the less likely it is that we hear any good news if anyone survived. All we can do is wait and pray 🙏

The views expressed in the comments above are those of our users and do not necessarily reflect the views of News-Online.

10

Thursday 20th June

Dark shadows creep across the brick walls as waiting staff glide in and out of the packed dining room. The opulent space is crypt-like, thanks to the exposed bricks curving inwards. The large stone chamber is filled with circular tables, each one dressed in a cream tablecloth and laid with heavy polished silver cutlery and Point Grey-branded dinner plates. Swooping strings of bejewelled chandeliers hang above their heads casting miniature rainbows against the array of crystal glassware. Corks are popped and relaxed laughter carries on the warm garlic-scented air.

Mel finds her name on the seating chart, spotting Charlie on the other side of the room, his back to her. Nicole, beside him, rearranges her dress. It's very low cut. Mel looks down at her own outfit. Perhaps she should have worn something a bit more risqué?

She takes her seat and smiles hello to the others at her table. Looking around, she can tell those who have already had a bit too much to drink or caught the sun. Noisy chatter and excitement bounces off the low ceiling.

'Ah, Mel. Here she is, the VIP. Everyone is talking about how amazing this place is. People want a look around the bedrooms. Are they as crazy as this room? I mean, what's with all the hooks?' Amir asks.

'Yeah, they're certainly unique,' Mel says, spreading salted butter across her seeded roll.

'You jammy cow.' The woman to her left – Lisa from reception – says. She's buried under layers of brightly coloured necklaces and bold feather earrings that dangle to her jaw.

Silent staff appear and lay pressed white napkins, stiff like a thick card, on everyone's lap, before executing a synchronised delivery of the starter. Oysters with a caviar foam. Mobile phones are pulled out to capture the moment.

'The chef has a Michelin star you know,' someone on the table says, as their phone's camera shutter clicks.

As they eat, Mel tries to follow the various conversations going on around her, but her mind is stuck on the missing gun. She waited behind after the tour had ended to ask Gus about it. He told her not to worry.

'That? Oh. Erm, we think a previous guest took it as a souvenir and we've not got around to replacing it yet. Rest assured, they are display only and completely disarmed,' he said with a cheery corporate smile.

But there was a flash of something in his eyes. Confusion. It was as if he was trying to bluff his answer. She didn't get the chance to ask anything else before he was called away, scuttling off with a hurried backwards glance at the empty space on the wall.

There's a tinkle of metal against glass. The room falls into a respectful silence as Rohan stands up and clears his throat.

He pats his shirt pocket, pulling out a folded piece of paper, followed by a pair of stylish designer reading glasses. A sign of his ageing Mel knows he hates.

'Welcome, everyone.'

There is the standard cheer across the room.

'I hope you're all fed and watered and ready for a great night. First, I want to say a huge thank you to the waiting staff team for their impeccable service. Now, I'll keep it brief. You've not crossed the Solent to hear me witter on.' A couple of polite chuckles ensue. 'I'd like to say a special thank you to Nicole for winning the pitch and doing a phenomenal job on the rebranding of this incredible place. The team at Point Grey are clearly impressed by the hard work given that they've laid on tonight for us. I know she's played a blinder so I want her to take the credit she deserves.'

Nicole blushes when she realises the room is looking at her, but quickly sits up and raises her half-empty glass in Rohan's direction.

'I want to say how immensely proud I am of you all for working so hard despite the challenging economic backdrop we find ourselves in. As some of you know, I started Flavour with nothing more than a simple idea and a strong belief in the power of creative minds. I could never have predicted the path from poverty to success we have taken. Receiving an MBE was, of course, a life goal, but honestly, the thing I'm most proud of is this.' He stops and looks around the room. 'I am proud of every single person here. We are more than a team. We lift one another, support one another and don't turn our backs on one another. We are a family.'

Mel thinks about how a lot of other managers could do

with taking note of the way Rohan gets the best out of people by playing to their strengths and inspiring them to work hard. He's always encouraging his staff to think outside the box.

'In fact, I thought this would be the perfect place to announce some changes at Flavour. There's someone who I work closely with who has demonstrated over the past difficult six months how loyal they are to the Flavour family. I want to thank them for all they do and also ask you to join me in congratulating them as they rise up the ranks.'

Promotions? There's going to be a promotion? Mel knows nothing of this. A zip of confusion and annoyance tears through her. Rohan looks over his glasses to the smiling crowd, and the delicate blueberry panna cotta that she's just finished expands and turns in her stomach. What is he doing?

As wonderful as her boss is, he also has an impulsive risk-taking attitude. Many a time he's said yes without thinking through the consequences. Is this another one of his 'act first, think second' tendencies? Mel grits her teeth, trying not to let her irritation show to those around her. There are policies to follow. He can't hand out promotions on a whim, he's undermining her role in front of the entire room. She picks up her water glass, and a thin slice of cold lemon bashes her teeth as she takes a gulp. Rohan should know better.

She scrunches up the napkin on her lap, wanting to stand up and tell him he can't offer promotions without consulting HR first when something hits her.

What if she's the one about to get a promotion?

Perhaps that's why she's been kept in the dark about it.

It's about time. She's been at the company for seven years

and not once had a pay rise. Rohan has been so kind and genuinely concerned about her mum's care but an increase in her wage would make a real difference. Her annoyance simmers slightly. What if she has to say something in response? In front of all these people? She wipes the sweat from the back of her neck as discreetly as she can, praying the fabric of her dress will not let her down and reveal unsightly sweat marks when she stands to thank him. The thought of everyone facing her and clapping for her makes her want to run but the acknowledgement would make it worthwhile.

Rohan clears his throat. The music has been turned down. She takes a deep breath.

'. . . I'd like to take this moment to congratulate Jonty Aspinall.'

Mel's stomach lurches.

'I am pleased to announce that he is stepping up to the position of Senior Account Director.'

Jonty raises his wine glass in the air. There's a brief moment of silence before a smattering of weak applause.

What? Why would Rohan promote *him*? Of all people. The one person in the entire company who's caused her so many headaches, and problems that she is legally bound to keep confidential. Mel's head spins. It's like rewarding a naughty child for their terrible behaviour.

He doesn't even need the money. He's not shy about revealing the financial gains he's walking away with following a bitter divorce settlement. Mel sympathises with his ex-wife for putting up with him for all those years.

'Great. Just what this company needs. Let's give this arrogant man even more power,' Lisa says dryly, interrupting Mel's thoughts. She's not the only one surprised by this sudden announcement.

'That's bullshit,' Charlie says before being told to shush by someone on his table.

Mel can see him out of the corner of her eye, shaking his head. He and Jonty were on an equal pay grade but with this promotion, Jonty is now effectively his boss. A man who will waste no time in trying to get rid of Charlie – or use him, stealing his best ideas. This impulsive decision is going to cause her a real headache at work next week.

Rohan clears his throat, giving Jonty a tight smile as if to tell him to stop lapping it up. He shifts on his feet. 'I also want us to remember those who can no longer be with us. As you know, we lost a valuable colleague. Holly wasn't with the company for long but I'm sure none of us will forget her bright smile and the way she lit up any room. I'd like to ask you to raise your glasses in a toast to Holly.'

'To Holly,' everyone choruses sombrely.

Mel quickly takes a sip of water.

There's a clatter from the far side of the room. One of the waiting staff has dropped a plate or a glass, which shatters against the stone floor, breaking the awkward silence following Rohan's words.

Rohan looks flustered. 'Okay, let me wrap this up. I hope you all have a wonderful night, and I know that being here is an experience that none of us will forget, but remember, this doesn't mean that every office party will be in such a spectacular setting.' There's a light ripple of laughter. 'So, make the most of it. For now, please raise your glass to another successful year for Flavour. Thank you, each and every one of you for your hard work.'

There's a whoop, a burst of applause and the clink of glasses. Voices rise alongside the jazz music above their heads. Mel catches Charlie finishing his drink in one, his eyes still firmly fixed on Jonty.

Conversations go on effortlessly around her, no one making a move to include her. She needs to talk to Rohan, make him understand how undermining this rash decision was.

Perhaps this shock promotion is a sign that she needs to do something different. Stop hoping that her talent will be rewarded and go out there and find a new job. A bigger pay packet would mean she could afford to give her mum the help she deserves rather than this haphazard way of living, which isn't good for either of them.

Leaving would feel disloyal, especially when Rohan has been so good to her, especially with her mum's needs, but she deserves more respect. However, it will have to wait, this party isn't the right place to speak to him about her concerns.

'So, how did you *really* wangle a night's stay?' Amir asks, nudging her back to the present.

Mel turns and faces him. 'Sorry?'

'I know Rohan said the VIPs' names were drawn from a hat, it was done fairly but that's not what I heard. Apparently, the draw was fixed. You were all chosen for a reason.' He gulps his lager.

'I heard that too. I mean, the bloody cleaner gets to stay over! How's that fair? Not that we're bitter, or anything,' the man on her right says.

Amir leans closer. 'I mean, Nicole rebranded the place, of

course, she would get "picked",' he says, making inverted commas with his fingers, 'but what about you? Has there been bribery in HR?'

'Ignore them,' Lisa nudges Mel with a kind smile. 'You enjoy it. People can go on all they want about the draw being fixed but they're sore losers. If I was lucky enough to get the chance to sleep over in a place like this then I wouldn't give two hoots about what anyone else thinks or how I ended up here. The important thing is that *you're* one of the chosen ones. Make the most of it. Everyone else would kill to be in your position.'

11

Thursday 20th June

The after-dinner entertainment is in full swing on the roof terrace. An enthusiastic DJ plays loud nineties dance hits from a cabana-style booth over on the far side. It's just gone eight o'clock but the sun continues to beat down. Mel's thighs stick together in the muggy heat.

'Forget what those two said about the VIP winner list being fixed,' Lisa says yet again, walking over to join her.

'Oh, yeah, I have, don't worry,' Mel replies, pleased to have some company.

'Good. It's like Rohan said, we need to make the most of this . . . especially as it's never happening again. The summer party, I mean.'

'Oh? Why?'

'Because of what he's going through. Didn't you hear that Rohan's getting divorced?'

'Rumi and Rohan? What? No.' Mel raises her eyebrows. 'Why would they be getting divorced? I thought they were solid.' The beautiful framed photo of them in his office leaps to the front of her mind. They looked so happy. She had no idea.

'Infidelity? – that's what normally happens. He's punching with his misses. God knows how she has the energy for an affair though. It was enough of an effort to shave my legs to come here, let alone hunt for a newer model.' She lets out a trademark cackle. 'That's what I've heard through the grapevine anyway. Apparently, someone saw him crying in the men's bathroom and did you see what he posted on his Instagram the other day? He's got really into mental health all of a sudden.' She gives a knowing nod as if this explains it all. 'Plus, he's cut up about Holly, feeling responsible that something like that could happen to one of his employees. I mean, I guess everyone who was there that night has a role to play.'

'What do you mean?'

'Come on, don't give me that innocent look. Have you never asked yourself why she was left to wander the streets, drunk and alone? Why was there no level of care for the poor thing? I know it's easy for me to say given I'm probably one of the oldest here, but these young ones think they're invincible.' She points out Scarlett, the newest Flavour employee, a slip of a thing in her early twenties. She looks drunk, laughing loudly at something Wesley is saying, flailing an arm over his, teetering on her glittering heels. Mel remembers being that age, thinking she knew everything, with no idea how little she actually knew about the world. About life.

Lisa starts talking again before Mel can say anything. She has a habit of doing that.

'I think that's why this place is a better option. We all arrive together and leave together. Safety in numbers, unlike that last party.'

Mel hadn't thought of it that way.

'I feel sorry for Rohan in a way. He's got a lot on his shoulders, *plus* now a failed marriage. If you ask me, I think that's why he promoted Jonty. He's lining up his successor, mark my words.'

Mel shudders. Jonty being in charge of the whole business would be a disaster.

'But what's that got to do with the summer party?'

'The company's at risk.' Lisa purses her lips, highlighting the plum lipstick that has bled into the fine lines around her mouth. It's as if Lisa has forgotten who she's speaking to. Mel is about to tell her that gossip like this is inappropriate but Lisa talks over her. 'If they get divorced she's going to want a payout. Rumi owns half the business, remember.'

'No, that's not going to happen. Rohan wouldn't let anything happen to Flavour,' Mel shakes her head firmly.

'I don't know. This OTT lavish party is a front, if you ask me. He's got very expensive divorce lawyers to pay for and the money has to come from somewhere. We need to ask that cleaner, whatshername . . .'

'Bonnie.'

'Yeah, her. She must see and hear it all. I bet she knows something . . .' Without even finishing her thought, Lisa calls for Bonnie. The warm smile that was on Bonnie's face starts to falter slightly as Lisa repeats what she told Mel.

Mel bites her lip. She should be shutting this conversation down but after what Rohan did with the unexpected promotion, she's too tired to care. Perhaps she can be part of the speculation for once.

'You think Flavour is in trouble?' Bonnie's eyes widen. 'I need this job. I need the money for my son.'

'To visit him, you mean?' Mel asks. Bonnie catches herself and the troubled expression that was there a second ago fades. She nods.

'He lives in Italy,' Mel explains to Lisa.

'Oh, I love Italy. I've been loads. Whereabouts?' Lisa asks.

Bonnie looks off to the side, as if racking her brain. 'I can't remember exactly. Near Rome . . . Sorry, but will you excuse me? I'm desperate for the loo.'

'I hope I've not worried her, clearly she hasn't heard anything,' Lisa pulls a face, once she's gone. 'Hopefully it's just another rumour.'

12

Thursday 20th June

A couple of young waiters weave through the crowd, carrying silver trays with a selection of drinks. Mel takes a glass of chilled white wine, beads of perspiration run down the stem. Her high heels pinch her toes so she sits at an empty table, resting her feet for a moment. She wishes the tightness in her shoes was the only thing bothering her.

Her mind runs over what Lisa told her before she wandered off to find someone who will give her a cigarette.

Surely she's misread things? Do all her colleagues think the agency will be closing down? She needs to put an end to this rumour. Flavour won't be closing down. But, then again, Rohan did keep her in the dark about Jonty's promotion. A flutter of panic dances through Mel's chest. Even though the pay isn't great, she needs this job. She doesn't know what else she'd do.

There's a long queue at the bar where Charlie is still deep in conversation with Nicole. He's doing a remarkable job of keeping his eyes above her pushed-up breasts. The words of Dominique and Bonnie are ringing in Mel's ears. They're right. If she doesn't make the most of this opportunity when else will she get this chance? She wishes she knew how other people go about dating colleagues. How do you pick up on signals if you're not sure they exist? She kicks herself for not asking the women whether they think Charlie might like her back.

'Anyone sitting here?' A male voice pulls her attention.

She looks up to see Tom, pointing to the empty chair beside her.

'Oh, no. I mean, sit down if you'd like.'

'Thanks. God, I'm so hot.' He coughs. 'I mean in a temperature sense.'

Mel smiles.

'Having a good night?' he asks. Whatever he was talking about with Rohan earlier must have been resolved as there isn't a hint of tension on his flushed cheeks.

'Erm . . .' How does she answer that? 'Yes. You?'

'Yeah. Shocked by the announcement, like many.' Tom nods to Jonty. 'I heard he's now on six-figures plus commission but look at him.'

Mel follows Tom's gaze to where Jonty stands slightly away from the party. She thought it was because he was thinking of others and not wanting to poison them with his smoke, but perhaps Tom is right. The stooped shoulders and the perpetually nervous inhalations are not the actions of a man on a high. More like a man on the edge. What does he have to be stressed about?

The sight of him annoys her. She turns her back and tries to focus on Tom.

'If it's any consolation, I'm as shocked as everyone else. And that's coming from the guy who's seen what's in his spam filter. Viagra pills,' he mouths, making her smile.

'You have access to everyone's emails?' she asks, mentally

running through the shopping websites she's been on, the many Rightmove properties that she can't afford but lusted over during her lunch break, the occasional indulgent clicks on the *Daily Mail*'s sidebar of shame . . .

'Only if things are flagged on the system.' He takes a sip of his cider. 'Usually, if they breach the company's policy on swearing or hatred or violence or porn; that sort of thing. Don't worry, I can't snoop into everyone's inboxes.'

She thinks back to the chat he was having with Rohan. 'Everything ok?' she asks, changing the topic. 'You looked a bit tense when we arrived.'

'Oh, yeah. It's nothing. I'm sure Rohan'll tell you when he's able to. It's confidential at the moment.'

'That sounds worrying . . .'

He swallows and signals for her to step out of earshot of other guests. 'You're going to hear sooner or later, but *please* act surprised when he tells you.'

'Tells me about what?'

The bright smile has faded from Tom's lips.

'This morning we received an anonymous email that alleges fraudulent activity in the company.'

Her stomach drops at that word 'fraudulent'.

'Sorry?'

'Stealing. I can't share exactly what it said but I managed to trace it to the original sender. And this is where things get weird.' He rubs the back of his neck.

'Weird?'

Tom nods. His unruly curls bounce with the movement. 'Yeah, see, this email was sent from Holly.'

Mel gawps at him.

'I know. It freaked me out too. I was just telling Rohan about it when you came over.'

An accusation of fraud is more than enough to try and wrap her head around. There will have to be disciplinary meetings, policies to follow, and an investigation. Trade unions will get involved . . . But the fact that it has come from their dead colleague? She's starting to believe Holly is haunting her.

'Holly's dead. She's not sending emails,' she says firmly.

'Yeah, I know. I've not had time to figure out how the hell it's possible yet.'

'What did Rohan say? And do you think it's true? The accusation I mean?' Mel is suddenly very warm.

He shrugs. 'Rohan was confused, like I was. He told me to keep it to myself until we can do some digging but it's got to be a hoax. I mean, an email from Holly Mills. It's probably someone messing about.'

'What did the email say exactly? I promise I won't utter a word to anyone.'

'Even though you work in HR, I trust you.' He flashes a genuine warm smile. Mel tries not to take it personally. 'Holly . . . I mean, whoever sent it from Holly's account, alleged that at least two members of staff are stealing from the company. I can't remember exactly but there was stuff about how these employees are fiddling expenses, taking backhanders from suppliers, and even that one of our clients isn't real.'

'A fake client. What?'

'I guess they think if they create a fake client then they can hide expense receipts for this fictitious company.' He frowns. 'This is the tip of the iceberg, apparently. Oh I remember, there was a line about how company ideas may have been sold too.'

Mel stares at him. 'But who would do this?'

'I don't know. If this is true then it's explosive stuff. But it doesn't make sense. Not to mention, dead people don't send emails.' He drops his voice as Zander glances over. 'Freaked me out anyway.'

'Yeah. I bet. So, hang on, what happened to her email account?'

'It's an automatic process. The system deleted it, the same as when anyone quits or retires. No different when someone dies. The employee number and associated accounts are wiped. Which is why this can't have come from her.'

'So you can't access any of her messages?'

'No, not anymore. Why?'

'She wanted to speak to me about something before she died. I never knew what it was and always wondered. My hunch at the time was that it was to do with Jonty.' Mel shakes her head. She needs to act more graciously about his unexpected promotion rather than look for things that probably don't exist. 'Never mind. Don't worry about it,' she says.

'Sorry. Anyway, I'm sure Rohan will flag it with you next week. I'll be at my desk first thing tomorrow trying to figure this out, not all of us are lucky enough to have the morning off work,' he teases, breaking the tension.

'And I thought IT was about turning it off and back on again,' she replies with a grin.

'Oi, there's a lot more to it than that,' he laughs. 'You have to hold the button on the router down for at *least* three seconds. But yeah, like I said, not a word of this to Rohan. You have to act surprised when he tells you.'

Mel mimes sealing her lips. She would know if employees

were stealing, wouldn't she? But then if there was anything suspicious, people would be unlikely to share gossip with HR. There must be a sensible reason behind this. Out of the corner of her eye, she spots Charlie. One of the junior designers is threading her arm through his, whispering in his ear.

'Mel?' Tom's voice pulls her back. He gently waves a hand in front of her eyes and she realises she's completely zoned out to what he has been saying.

'Sorry. I was miles away.'

'Ah, yeah. I thought you were,' Tom says. He pushes his curls out of his eyes. 'I, err, just asked if you fancied coming for a dance? With me?'

In this light, Mel can see how nice his eyes are, a soft hazel colour.

He's waiting for her to say something and as lovely as he is, she only wants to dance with Charlie. But she can't say that so she tells him how she's got two left feet.

'You can't be worse than me. I was once chucked out of an indie nightclub as the bouncer thought I'd taken something, judging by my dodgy moves!' he says, quickly downing the rest of his bottle.

Mel laughs. 'Ok, you win the worst dancer.'

An awkward pause stretches out between them.

'Right, I'm going to head to the bar, can I get you anything?' he asks.

'I'm all good, thank you.'

Tom slips into the crowd. She glances around to find Charlie but he's nowhere to be seen.

13

Thursday 20th June

The DJ is playing a trendy house mix from the rooftop terrace. Judging by everyone moving in time to the beat around her, Mel's the only one not to have heard this song before. Scarlett is twirling without a care in the world. She's got her arms outstretched, a cocktail glass in her hand sloshing as she moves, a deep stain seeping down the front of her low-cut top. She probably hasn't even noticed. Other colleagues – those ten or so years younger than Mel – are moving in sync as if rehearsing for a music video. The effects of daytime drinking in the sunshine are clearly starting to hit.

Clusters of people have congregated around the unlit fire pit on the far side. Rohan is holding the group's attention with some elaborate story judging by his hand gestures. Charlie's there talking to Wesley, but Mel can only see snatched glimmers of them through the flurry of dancers in front of her. There's a game of beer pong taking place near the replica lighthouse. Shrieks of laughter carry on the thick air every so often. Mel wanders around like a spare part, unsure where to go and how to join in. Out of habit, she pulls out her phone

71

to call Leonora to check in, cursing at the no signal notification.

Gus is leading a demonstration of how to open a bottle of champagne with a ceremonial sword and the party piece has attracted a small crowd on the other side of the roof terrace. Is Charlie heading over? She suddenly makes a beeline in that direction.

'Would anyone like to try it themselves?' Gus asks.

'Mel, I dare you to have a go . . .' Nicole nudges her. Her previously bouncy blonde curls have dropped slightly and her eyeliner has smudged.

'Yeah right. It's probably against HR policy,' Amir scoffs, putting on a pretentious voice that makes the others laugh.

Heat washes over Mel. Are they mocking her?

'Can I not tempt anyone to have a go?' Gus asks again.

A few months ago Wesley had persuaded her to be involved in a TikTok. She didn't know what it was about but he told her that it was a way to attract new clients to the agency. She felt a bit foolish shimmying down the corridor to Taylor Swift but it made people smile and she even caught Charlie's eye. It must not have achieved the views or shares that Wes was after as she was never asked to get involved again.

'I'll do it.' Mel raises her hand and steps forward with a confidence she doesn't possess. What was it Dominique said about needing to do something to get Charlie to notice her?

Today is about fresh starts and new experiences.

Amir and Nicole swap surprised wide-eyed glances. A group of maybe ten or so of her colleagues have emerged from the dining room and are coming over to see what's going on. Charlie steps closer.

Before she knows it she's being handed a heavy, solid silver sword with intricate embellishments on the handle. There's something about the weight of it, the sudden power she's been bestowed with. She shivers and clutches it tighter in her right hand.

'You simply hold the neck at an angle, like so,' Gus instructs, holding a full bottle of champagne in one hand.

Her palms are sweating, making it difficult to get a good grip on the sword.

'Has anyone been injured doing this?' she asks, staring at the sharp blade.

'No, we only use sober guests,' he says and winks. 'Right, Nelle—'

'It's Mel.'

'Sorry, Mel. All ready?'

Gus explains what she needs to do but before he's even finished it's already jumbled up in her mind. All she can think about is getting the bottle open and not embarrassing herself. She can't fail. Not with this many pairs of eyes on her. As the seconds trickle on and more of a crowd builds, she wishes she'd never agreed to this. What was she thinking? Is it too late to change her mind? Someone begins a slow clap. She's not sure if it's supposed to be encouraging or mocking.

It's too late to back out now.

'Go on, Mel,' someone shouts.

She swallows and tightens her clammy grip on the heavy bottle Gus has handed her. She needs to show that everything is fine. Even if everything is *not* fine.

'So, now you've been shown what to do, I need to check . . .' Gus pauses for dramatic effect. 'Have you been drinking?'

She shakes her head.

'Anyone here wants to contest this?'

There is a mumble amongst the audience. Some have grown bored at her hesitation and walked off for a smoke, and others have jostled to get a better view. Despite the disappearing audience, the clapping continues. That's when she realises Charlie is nowhere to be seen. He must have wandered off. She wants to stop but she's too far in now.

'Ok. You remember what I showed you?'

She can't find her words so blindly nods. Another lie.

Gus turns to face the crowd. 'On the count of three. One . . .'

She angles the bottle a little more. Why did she agree to this? How can she make it stop?

'Two.'

The sword is too heavy, her wrists are trembling under the weight.

Come on. Don't mess this up.

'Three!'

Someone screams.

The knife slices clean through the bottleneck . . . and the skin on top of her left arm. Silence flows through the crowd of horrified faces.

Gus's thick eyebrows shoot up in horror.

Mel woozily stares at the blood-splattered sword, which fell from her right hand and clanged on the floor. Black spots rush to the edges of her vision.

'The first aid kit is in the office. Quick, come with me, please,' Gus orders.

Mel is briskly led away, past the whispers and curious alarmed eyes of the crowd, her left arm raised in the air. Blood trickling down to her elbow from the gash on her bare wrist.

14

Hampshire Constabulary: Interview started at 20.45

Officer O'Neal: For the purposes of the tape, please can you state your full name and job title?

Witness: (Clears throat). Yes. It's erm. It's Magnus Raynor. Gus. I'm the erm . . . (Inaudible)

Officer O'Neal: Please speak up.

Witness: I said I'm Gus Raynor, I'm the general manager of Point Grey. Sorry, I'm still in shock. I turned on the radio as I got myself ready this morning – it was my day off – when I heard the bulletin about the fire. I've been glued to the news ever since. I . . . I . . . I can't believe it. The papers say there are 'several casualties' but what does that even mean? Is anyone seriously injured? Oh god. No-one's *died* have they?

OON: I'm afraid we're not able to say at this early stage.

Detective Hutchinson: Inspector We're trying to piece together a timeline of events, and we would appreciate it if you could tell us how your final shift started. From the beginning.

GR: Yesterday, Thursday, was busy. When a corporate takes over the entire place it's all hands to the deck.

75

My staff worked exceptionally hard, especially in the heat, to offer our usual impeccable service from the moment the guests arrived. To be honest with you, I knew there was going to be trouble. I could never in a million years have imagined this.

OON: What made you think there would be trouble?

GR: At my age, and with my years of experience, I get a feel for people. Some guests are utterly charming and others could do with a slap. Corporate functions are the worst. Honestly, some people lose their minds when they embark, it must be something to do with the sea air. (Clears throat). A fun game I like to play is to try and work out who will be handing in their notice by the end of the night. It's always the ones you least expect. The quiet ones. Guests turn up suited and booted but any shred of professionalism vanishes the moment the free bar opens. I've seen it all. Strip teases, topless hot tub parties, extra-marital affairs, punch-ups on the dance floor and the telltale white powder dusting the toilet cisterns. It amazes me that people put their careers on the line for one hedonistic night. They let rip, acting as if their jobs don't matter. We only get to see one side of the story but I imagine many p45s are handed out the next day. So far no one has been sacked on the spot, not as far as I've witnessed, at least.

OON: I see.

GR: You'd be surprised how the place comes to life after dark. Part of my job is to look the other way. Discreet is my middle name. So I say nothing about the number of guests who bed-hop, about the terrified calls to housekeeping claiming that their wedding rings have vanished after they took them off to 'wash their hands'. But apart from all that, it's a great place to work. Of course, there's always leaks to fix, holes to patch up and small repairs to turn my hand to. Not unusual for a nineteenth-century building, but despite the flaws, I have an affinity for the place. Something about how old and solid it is. Despite surviving two world wars, the fort is still steadfastly standing tall. But perhaps not after this fire . . .

OON: Right, so, back to the night in question. Did any guests give you cause for concern?

GR: Are you asking if I know who started the fire? People are speculating that it's arson but I can't believe anyone would do such a thing deliberately. However, there was one woman who stood out. I'm not blaming her! I'm simply saying that she was always slightly removed from the others. She accidentally injured herself during the champagne sabrage and–

OON: – Sorry. The what?

GR: The champagne sabrage. It's something we do for corporate parties and weddings. Basically, we show how to open a bottle of champagne with a ceremonial cavalry sword. People love it and we always get the best online reviews from those who've seen it performed. It's a sort of team bonding activity.

DIH: Sounds dangerous.

GR: Well, yes, I suppose it could be, but I'm highly trained.

OON: So you perform this stunt?

GR: Yes.

OON: The guests watch?

GR: (Silence)

DIH: Mr Raynor?

GR: (Pause) Normally, yes. This time, I decided to let this one guest have a go. She had these sad eyes, like a dog that's been kicked about. She promised me she was sober. It wasn't my fault.

OON: What happened?

GR: She was holding the sword. She must have slipped or something, I don't know. One moment she was in control, the next, there was blood everywhere. I could see the headlines: 'Partygoer injures themselves at sea'. 'Drunks handling dangerous weapons as a novelty act'. Head office wouldn't be happy. The lady who hurt herself, well . . . she was so calm, almost zen. We cleaned her up and bandaged her wrist. Thankfully it was only superficial so the blood stopped quickly. Actually, come to think of it, she was one of the overnight guests . . . Do you know if she survived?

OON: We are unable to confirm those details right now, I'm afraid.

DIH: Is there anything else that stands out from the night?

GR: There was another guest, a man, who attracted my attention. I'm not sure of his name. Tall, skinny. Had this air of superiority, as if he knew better than anyone. He was involved in a scuffle on the dance floor. Not that unusual to see a drunken fight though, not when there's a free bar. And this lot were putting it away. He'd had a skinful. He was also staying over . . .

DIH   So they were the only things out of the ordinary that happened at the party before you left?

GR: Erm (Pause) Yes. That's all. I mean, that's all I can remember.

OON: Are you sure? You looked as if you were about to say something?

GR: (Mumbles)

DIH: Mr Raynor?

GR: Nothing else happened. Excuse me, I'm just in shock. I don't have anything else to tell you. I wish I could help more. My team and I performed the usual brief end-of-night clean-up and then I left on the ten o'clock boat to escort the rest of the partygoers back to the quayside.

OON: Leaving how many guests to remain at Point Grey overnight?

GR: Eight. No. Sorry, there were only seven guests in the end, as one of the VIPs returned on the boat with myself and the others.

OON: And how many members of staff remained?

GR: One. The night manager. Please can you tell me if he's okay, at least?

OOR: Like I said, I'm afraid I'm not able to reveal anything at this moment in time.

GR: (Sniffs) This is a literal nightmare.

DIH: Let me get this straight, there was one person to look after the needs of these seven VIP guests?

GR: Yes. (Clears throat). Only one member of staff needs to stay at the hotel overnight. Company policy. It used to be two of us that would stay but you know how it is, cost-cutting measures brought in by head office.

OON: The Flavour Agency who had booked the venue, had recently done some work for Point Grey, isn't that right?

GR: I believe so. Designed a nice new logo for us. Cost quite a bit to get everything updated, seemed a waste of time to me.

DIH: Did you know these people?

GR: Me? No, I never met them before. I oversee the day-to-day stuff at the hotel, the corporate executive decisions come from higher up.

OON: I see. Because of this recent redesign work, Flavour employees were told eight VIP guests would get to stay overnight. Apparently, staff at Point Grey picked these names from a hat. Can you tell me who was involved in that decision?

GR: Oh? I've not heard of this. They said *we* picked the names?

OON: Yes. We've spoken to your head office and they have no knowledge of this. They told us that you would know.

GR: That's weird. Nothing to do with us. We don't know who is staying until the confirmation comes through. (Pause) Hang on. These people, the ones trapped in the fire, you're telling me they were chosen specifically? But why?

OON: Well, Mr Raynor, that's what we're trying to find out.

15

Thursday 20th June

Mel is escorted down the corridor, away from the shocked faces.

'My colleague, Eddie, has gone to get the first aid kit. Wh-wh-what happened?' Gus repeats as he rushes her to the reception area. 'Did it slip? This has never happened before. You must have drawn the sword back too far, causing it to catch your skin as you swung upwards towards the neck of the bottle . . .'

With every second that passes the woozier she gets. Her wrist is throbbing as quickly as her heart is racing.

'Here, sit down here.'

She's gently led to a dark green leather sofa opposite the reception desk. A framed aerial view print of Point Grey hangs beside a year-at-a-view calendar tacked to the pale grey wall. An empty plush office chair sits before a wide-screen iMac, a sleek chrome landline phone, and a neat collection of stationery perfectly lined up, as if just for show. A sun-bleached globe stands tilted on its axis on a shelf beside an antique sand hourglass.

'You told me you hadn't been drinking,' Gus says.

Did he? She can't remember him asking her that.

Her colleagues are all still outside. No one has come to check on her. She's relieved that Charlie missed what happened now.

'This is Eddie – Edward – he's the night manager.'

Edward joins them. His sandy red hair is cut short and he has serious-looking light blue eyes. He's probably in his late twenties or early thirties.

He smiles politely, says a quick hello and doesn't recoil at the sight of the blood. 'We'll get you sorted in no time. Let me get some bandages and clean it up.' She can hear him saying something further, about filling in forms and logging this incident. Perhaps he's older than she first thought, he's calm and collected, telling Gus he should go and take a break, which he refuses.

Her head thumps from the adrenaline and the alcohol rushing through her. She winces as his cold hands touch her skin.

'Thankfully it's superficial,' Edward says, moving efficiently. Now he's wiped away the blood, it's clear she's only nicked the surface. 'You won't need stitches but maybe go and get it checked out with the GP when you get back home.'

He works out, judging by the clearly defined muscles beneath his tight light grey button-down polo shirt. There is the slightest stubble on his slim cheeks. A small scar to the left of his freckled nose. His gold name badge says 'Edward: Happy To Help'.

A strange sense of déjà vu washes over her. It's as though they've met before.

She shakes it off. She doesn't know any Edwards.

'Thank you. I feel so silly,' Mel says, wanting to fill the silence as he gently applies the antiseptic cream. She wishes someone would come and see if she was ok, come and at least pretend that they care about her. An unexpected rush of emotion clogs the back of her throat.

'Oh, sorry. I've bled on your shirt. That's going to be a nightmare to clean.'

'It's fine, please don't worry about me. I can change. I'll ask one of the team to get you a Coke, full fat. You'll need some sugar in you for the shock. Where does it hurt?' Edward asks, not taking his eyes off her.

The funny thing is that she doesn't feel a thing.

A sudden longing for human touch washes over her.

'You've got a career in medicine if hospitality goes to pot, Doctor Ed.' She nods to her neat bandage, letting out a girlish laugh that takes her by surprise.

Is she flirting with him? It's the adrenaline coursing through her. The unexpectedly good-looking man beside her, his knee touching hers, that's brought this on. She's not been this close to anyone for so long.

He flashes a kind smile. She lets herself imagine he's concerned about her. But in all probability, he must simply be worried that she's planning on suing the hotel for negligence. Not that she would. It was her fault. She wasn't paying attention, her hands were shaking and her head was too full to concentrate on what she was supposed to be doing.

It could have been really nasty, she realises, the blade of the knife could have sliced deep veins. She just had a dance with death.

Tears appear out of nowhere.

'Hey, don't cry.' Edward shifts, a fleeting expression on his face that she can't read.

'Oh God, excuse me. I'm not usually like this. In fact, I'm not like this at all.' She takes the tissue he hands her and wipes her eyes. 'For some stupid reason I foolishly let myself believe things would be different tonight. I even convinced myself I might be up for a promotion. Life's been a bit fraught at home and we lost one of our colleagues not that long ago and . . .' She's been so focused on looking ahead, not stopping to accept how the past few months have affected her. Tonight was supposed to be a distraction but they're kidding themselves. 'I know that none of us know how we're going to go but this was especially awful as she was so young and I feel like I'm responsible. I guess it's got on top of me . . .' She blows her nose.

I am responsible.

A rush of heat washes over her. She scrunches her eyes tight for a second, willing the unwanted voice at the back of her mind to go away.

Keep it together, Mel.

'Sorry, I'm going off-topic. I can't stop thinking about her. I barely knew her so I can't imagine what her loved ones are going through.'

'You're probably in shock.'

'Sorry.'

'Stop saying sorry.' He smiles, glancing up from the first aid kit he's packing away.

He's got a lovely smile, straight white teeth and perfectly plump lips . . . She stops herself – what is she doing? Mel straightens, thankful that he can't read her mind.

'Thank you for being so nice to me.'

'No problem, I'm glad you're ok.' He glances at her bandaged wrist. 'Are you ready to rejoin the party? Your friends will be wondering where you've gone.'

He stands to leave without waiting for her answer. There's a pocket of cold air when he suddenly moves and she wishes he would stay a little longer.

16

Thursday 20th June

Soft pools of light lead the way back to the party, blinking on as Mel passes the sensor, as though someone is watching her and guiding her. Tom came to find her to see how she was. His eyes widening at her bandage. He said he heard from Amir about what had happened, checking if there was anything he could do to help.

She tried to laugh it off as nothing, saying it was 'only a nick' and 'it looked worse than it felt', but under her dressing her wrist throbs like hell. Most of the guests are pretty lubricated now. She tells herself no one will remember in the morning. What goes on in Point Grey stays in Point Grey.

Her heels echo on the parquet floor. Eventually, she locates the ladies' bathroom, needing some time and space on her own. It's like entering a Gatsby-inspired New York jazz club. The deep blush pink walls are covered in antique gilded picture frames. A low velvet chaise longue sits under a sparkling chandelier near the golden hand-dryer. She walks across the black and white chequered mosaic tiles to get to the bank of original ceramic sinks and runs her hands under the tap. The cold water instantly cools her. Once in the cubicle, with the door locked, she tries to work out what to do now. After seeing her reflection, maybe she should go back to her bedroom and freshen up, a perk of having all her things with her. A burst of music filters in as the door to the bathroom opens. There is a clatter of heels and laughter.

'Did you see what happened with the sword? I bet she did that on purpose. It was clearly, like the *most* obvious, cry for attention.'

'Oh my God. Definitely.'

Mel freezes. They're talking about her. She can't make out who these voices belong to. They sound young, perhaps from the junior account management team? She holds her breath to try and hear better, not moving an inch.

'Like, I'm sorry but there's no way he'd give her a second glance. It's kind of pathetic to watch but that's what Mel's like, always leeching on to everyone, silently begging them to like her. You'd have thought at her age she wouldn't be so bloody desperate all the time.'

Mel bites her lip. What do they mean 'at her age' – she's only thirty-two, not that much older than them! She wishes she had the courage to boldly stride out of this cubicle and see their faces drop, but another part of her wants to listen and hear more. Her heart thrums in her chest at this dangerous eavesdropping. She tilts her head, pressing it against the closed toilet door.

'She may as well wear a massive sticker on her forehead announcing that she fancies Charlie.'

'Isn't he leaving anyway?'

'Charlie?'

What? He's leaving?

'Mmm hmm. That's what I heard. I mean, something's been going on with him. You know he lost two client pitches in a row? Even that dog food company didn't take it to the final round. I worked so hard on those concepts too. I was fuming. When I asked him what had happened he just brushed it off. Here, try this one. It's lush.'

There's the sound of plastic lids popping open. They must be putting on make-up. The tap runs and Mel misses a bit about what one of them says.

'Ooh yeah this is nice, it's giving Tilbury. God, I had no idea he was leaving. Wonder where he's going. I bet he's been headhunted.'

'Dunno. If you ask me he's been distracted for a while now.'

'Must be because of Holly. Apparently, they were very close. Like, *inappropriately* close.'

'No way. She was younger than us and he's got to be thirty-five. At least. Eww.'

'Tell me about it. Grim. Well that's what I heard anyway. She was savvy, maybe she was planning on using him to climb the ladder, you know how obsessed she was with her job, remember all that note-taking she did?'

'You've got to admit it's weird without her here, isn't it?'

A sniff.

'Yeah.'

'Well, whatever's going on with Charlie, maybe it's for the best he moved on.'

'Or maybe he simply needs to get under someone to get over them.'

'God. Don't tell Mel. She'll be all over him.' They break into a cackle of laughter.

Pins and needles run up Mel's legs but she doesn't dare move a muscle until she's heard the click of heels and the door creaking shut behind them. Charlie's leaving? Charlie had a thing with Holly? They think she's pathetic?

Her brain is trying to process it all as she rushes to the taps and clings on to the basin, taking some deep breaths.

'They all talk about you behind your back, like, all the time,' a female voice says, bouncing off the tiles around her. A different voice to the ones who were there a moment ago.

Mel thought she was in here alone. 'Sorry?'

It's coming from the next cubicle. The door creaks open to reveal Scarlett hugging the porcelain between her bare knees. Her dress is hitched up, showing her black lace knickers and a floral tattoo across her slim thigh.

'Scarlett? Are you ok?'

Scarlett ignores the question.

'They say mean things about Sad Mel but I think you're alright,' she says, a strand of spit catching the light as it trails down her chin.

Sad Mel?

'Mean things. Like what?'

'You're so desperate. Always forcing people to do stuff they don't want to do. Ramming "fun" down their throats. Not cool.'

Mel thought they appreciated all she does. She organises the Grand National syndicate every year, keeps a list of team birthdays, she sorts out the office-wide Secret Santa arrangements, she is the fire safety marshal. What more can she do? And to think they think she hurt herself on purpose to get Charlie's attention . . . Her mind is whirring. She's had to shut down gossip in the past, but she's never had it be about her.

'People also think you're weird about whatsername,' Scarlett slurs.

'Who?'

'That girl who died. Holly.'

The booming bass of the DJ reverberates through the brick walls.

'What do you mean?'

'Something about how you went OTT with flowers, making sure everyone signed some massive sympathy card. I mean, I wasn't even here so maybe don't listen to me . . . I just heard you like to stick your nose in other people's business.'

Mel bites her tongue. Her job in HR is literally to be in people's business.

'I guess they saw it as if you were overcompensating for something.'

'What? Overcompensating for what?'

Mel braces herself for whatever Scarlett is about to say next. Her heart beats wildly in her chest.

You know what you've been overcompensating for.

The guilt that you've carried all this time.

The pause lasts an eternity.

'Scarlett?'

But she doesn't answer. Instead, Scarlett turns and violently retches into the toilet bowl. Mel dashes forwards to hold her hair back.

She knows she's not everyone's best friend, but she had no idea that people hated her.

She knows so much about these people and they know nothing about her.

17

Saturday 22nd June

Hampshire Constabulary: Interview started at 08.00

Officer O'Neal: Thanks for speaking to us, Ms Sanchez. As I said, we're trying to gain an understanding from key witnesses to help us piece together what happened at Point Grey in the early hours of yesterday morning. We've managed to locate the guest list and your name was listed as a VIP overnight guest.

Dominique Sanchez: Someone was looking down on me, that's for sure. (crying softly) I just can't believe it. I've been fixed to my phone, scrolling through these unbelievable images, reading the speculation on social media. I mean. Technically I should have still been there. Please tell me everyone is going to be ok? No-one's giving me any answers. Who are the survivors? Are there any?

OON: Unfortunately, due to the severity of the situation and the ongoing recovery operation, we're unable to release that sort of information. But please trust that we're doing all we can to get to the bottom of things.

Detective Inspector Hutchinson: Can you start by explaining to us why you didn't stay overnight, as was the plan?

DS: Because I was told I had to leave. Our CEO, Rohan – you probably already know that – well, he ordered me to go. I told Mel – Melanie Robinson, our HR lady – that I didn't want to spend a second longer on the fort but that was a lie. It was pure bravado. In fact, I was gutted, I wanted to stay overnight so much, I mean, it's Point Grey, who wouldn't. But now . . . God.

DIH: Help yourself to a tissue if you need one.

DS: Thank you.

OON: Did something happen for Rohan to ask you to leave?

DS: (Pause) I got a little vocal at the party, let's say. I'd had a few drinks. We all had. It was honestly nothing more than the booze talking, but basically, I gave an impromptu speech and said a few things I now wished I hadn't.

DIH: Did something provoke you to do this?

DS: Rohan said something at dinner that annoyed me. About us being a tight family but in my opinion, we're more dysfunctional. Rohan is deluded if he thinks we all get on. People are never happy. There's always bitchy comments about colleagues not pulling their weight or those doing too much and smothering you. But perhaps I should have kept these opinions to myself. I definitely said too much. Now, in the cold light of day, I could cringe thinking about how I must have come across, especially after what's happened.

DIH: Do you remember what you said?

DS: Something along the lines of how fake everyone is. How terrible we were to be having fun so soon after what happened to Holly.

OON: Holly? (Sound of papers being shuffled)

DS: Yes. Holly Mills. You won't have her listed on the guest list. She used to work at Flavour but she died . . .

OON: She tragically died of hypothermia, is that correct?

DS: Depends on who you ask. Some say her death is suspicious and that certain employees knew more than they were letting on about what happened to her. Let's just say that since Holly's death I've become a lot warier of my colleagues.

OON: Was there anyone on the fort in particular who you had concerns about?

DS: Everyone? (Long pause) I'm only half serious about that. Like, we don't properly know one another, especially since we started working remotely a lot more.

DIH: Did you pick up on anyone acting differently to how they normally do?

DS: No, not really. Everyone let their hair down, did shots, danced, and acted nicey-nicey, not like they are behind other people's backs. I knew there were going to be plenty of sore heads the next day. I didn't know it would end the way it did. (Sniffs)

OON: Would you say there is a lot of back-stabbing that goes on?

DS: Yes. Oh, there's always gossip flying around. It's exhausting trying to keep up with it all. You never know who or what to believe. Thinking about it now, there *was* a weird atmosphere from the moment we arrived. Then add the heatwave . . . Jesus, we were melting. Things were bound to erupt.

18

Thursday 20th June

With Bonnie's help, Mel manages to get Scarlett out of the bathroom and into the fresh air on the roof terrace. It's almost half past nine and the sun is slowly setting. The horizon has erupted with stunning golden orange strips. The light will fade quickly now. There's not much of a cool breeze but if Scarlett is going to be sick again she can at least turn around and throw up over the wall into the sea.

'I'll go and grab her a bottle of water. Do you mind sitting with her, please?' Mel asks.

'Sure.' Bonnie rubs Scarlett's back like a worried mother.

The two gossiping women's words repeat in Mel's mind. Things have started to make sense now. She thinks about the times that conversations in the kitchen tapered out whenever she was around or the tight smiles when it's her turn to present at the weekly department meeting. She remembers those raised eyebrows and knowing smirks seen out of the corner of her eye whenever she passed Charlie's desk. Deep down, at work, she's always had this feeling of being late to the party. It's as if she hears the punchline but never the build-up, and laughs along anyway.

Now she knows they were laughing at her.

She wishes she could stand in the middle of the heaving dance floor with her arms outstretched, all the attention on her for once, and demand to know what she's done wrong, why they won't be her friends. Instead, she tries to blot those unkind truths from her mind as she swerves past the drunks in front of her. Scarlett needs her right now.

The beat of the bassline is giving her a headache. People are necking back shots of clear liquid. Conversations happen around her but she is removed from it all. She pictures the guests whispering maliciously, hands pressed to the sides of their mouths, talking about her whenever her back is turned. She walks in a daze. The disco lights pick up a flash of white from the bandage on her wrist.

'Want one?' A shot glass is thrust in her face.

'No thanks.'

'C'mon, lighten up for once,' they jeer.

The smell turns her stomach. She weaves through the throng of dancing bodies, arms and limbs jerking to the repetitive dance tune she's never heard before. Wesley is sweating, reaching his arms to the sky, revealing damp sweat patches under each armpit. She swiftly dodges an elbow. Mel can't remember the last time she was in a nightclub. The festival scene wasn't her cup of tea and her university days were tame to say the least. She's never been good with packed crowds of drunk people. Something to do with the uncertainty, the low-level anxiety that anything could happen in a blink of an eye. She knows how quickly life can change in an instant.

An ear-splitting twang of static booms across the dance floor.

'Hello. Is this thing on?'

Dominique has stepped up to the DJ box and taken the microphone off the DJ.

'Can you hear me? I wanna say a few words in memory of Holly . . .'

What's going on? Mel has never seen Dominique look so drunk. She's sweated most of her make-up off, her normally sleek black hair has frizzed in the heat and there is a stain down her chic dress, which is now crumpled and dishevelled.

'She was such an amazing young woman.' Her lips are too close to the mic. She ignores the static that is making others wince and carries on talking. Her loud voice travels across the open space. 'She had her whole life ahead of her. How can you be enjoying yourselves when the last time we were all together someone died?'

The rest of the crowd hush. Thankfully, she's pulled the microphone away to a comfortable distance. Every party-goer has stopped dancing and is giving this impromptu speech their full attention, ignoring the spectacular sunset lighting up the horizon. A ripple of unease spreads. Talking about what happened at the Christmas party in front of everyone is breaking an unspoken rule.

'Holly was a truly wonderful, beautiful young lady. I'm so honoured that I got to be her manager, and to spend time with her, even for a short while.' Dominique clears her throat. Tears have sprung to her red-rimmed eyes. 'She was full of incredible ideas, she worked her magic on clients and was a real team player. A lovely person inside and out . . .' Her voice crackles with rich, thick emotion.

Mel had no idea Dominique was taking Holly's death so badly. By the looks on the faces around her, neither did anyone else. She should have done more to prepare for an outburst like this. First thing on Monday she'll schedule a meeting, perhaps discuss some counselling options.

'. . . You should be very blessed that she touched our lives.'

Mel hears Zander's voice in her ear, and realises he's talking to the person behind her.

'She's only saying this because she was so rude to her when she was alive. Once a bitch, always a bitch, now she's got to live with the guilt. I wouldn't be surprised if she knows more than she's letting on about what happened that night.'

Mel turns to look at him.

He has his eyes fixed on Dominique, one hand on his hip. 'She's always like this when she's had a few drinks. Some people get teary, some are fighters and some are hungry for attention, making it all about them.'

Dominique moves an arm, splashing wine on her designer heels. '. . . Everyone here acts like this poor girl didn't exist. You've all moved on and it's so fucked up.' She wobbles precariously. 'I can't stand this fakeness. None of you are true friends.'

Her tone has changed. Instead of a moving memorial, there is now an edge to her words. The microphone whines as she staggers nearer to the power source. It's like a car crash on the opposite side of the motorway. You know you shouldn't look but you can't help yourself.

Mel's natural urge is to step over and gently take the microphone off Dominique, guide her to a quiet area and check she's okay. Or even take her straight to her hotel room and encourage her to drink a bottle of water and take a couple of painkillers for the mother of all hangovers that will be waiting in the morning. She knows she should do these things, but truthfully, she's tired and fed up of looking after everyone. Especially when it's never reciprocated.

The words of those mean girls in the toilet come back to her. Perhaps it's time she let someone else deal with it for once. They're all grown adults. This isn't the office, she's technically 'off the clock'. They're not her responsibility. Just like Holly wasn't.

'Holly worked hard for this company and now she's dead. She literally died on a social with us! But still no one here cares. So much for this being a "family",' Dominique makes quotation marks with her slender fingers. 'It's such bollocks.'

Charlie walks over to Dominique, arms outstretched as if trying to placate a hostage taker. He says something but Mel can't hear what, his words drowned out by Dominique launching into a rant about how fickle everyone is at the agency. How they need to watch their back.

Mel spots Rohan saying something to Jonty. He steps forward, blocking Charlie who glares at him behind his back.

Jonty bellows over Dominique, stopping her in her tracks. 'Alright, I think it's time you handed the mic back. You're killing the vibe here. This is supposed to be a party.'

'You,' Dominique wildly pivots to face him. Sloshing more wine. 'You're the worst. I missed out on my son's first birthday as I was working all goddamn weekend preparing slides, slides that YOU never used, alleging I formatted them wrong. Don't you come anywhere near me!'

The whole office can't tear their eyes away. It's as if everyone is holding their breath. Waiting for another colleague to jump in. But no one does.

Someone coughs.

'Get down, love. Don't ruin the night because you can't handle your drink. It's pathetic,' he sneers.

Hushed whispers and awkward laughter fill the bewildering silence. Further back someone has their camera phone raised in the air – its bright white light trained on the uncomfortable scene.

'Don't you dare tell me what to do,' Dominique screeches.

Jonty moves forward to take the microphone from her hands but Dominique suddenly pulls away. The almost empty glass of wine slips through her fingers and smashes on the concrete. In the blink of an eye, she swings her right arm forward and lets out a grunt of frustration.

All anyone can hear is a deep reverberating boom as the microphone cracks into the side of Jonty's skull.

19

Colourful disco lights flash into the night sky. Balearic dance music is playing but no one is dancing.

'She's assaulted him!'

'He shouldn't have intimidated her.'

Conflicting opinions wash over Mel as she tries to process what she's just witnessed. Dominique has wobbled off the podium and is being steered away, still ranting about how 'everyone has blood on their hands after what happened to Holly'. Streaks of mascara trail down her tanned cheeks. Jonty is clutching the side of his head. Blood gushes from his nose onto his shirt. The alarmed-looking DJ is trying to get the party atmosphere back as quickly as he can.

'Alright folks, the show's over,' Rohan says as brightly as he can muster, turning to face the cluster of rubber necks. Eventually, chatter and movement fill the space once more.

Jonty is led to a nearby table. It's not long before he's sitting with tissues shoved up each nostril. His nose looks swollen and sore. The emerging purple bruises under each eye are getting deeper by the second. The alcohol in his system is probably keeping most of the pain at bay for now.

'You need to be checked over by the first aider,' Mel says, crouching down to his level. 'Then we'll get this incident written up. It may be wise for you to get the boat home and head to A&E to check that nothing is broken.'

'Oh bore off with your rules, Mel.' Jonty sniffs. She can smell the booze on his breath. 'I'm fine. I'm not taking it any further. You don't need to take my statement or whatever box-ticking exercise you love to do. Seriously. It's a scratch.'

She's not sure if he's trying to hide his embarrassment or if he actually is ok.

Thankfully, the bleeding has stopped.

She clenches her jaw. She can't force him to listen to her. 'Fine, you're the boss.'

Mel picks up the bloodied tissues and puts them in the nearest bin. She's not sure where Dominique is but she wants to go and talk to her. It is so out of character for her to have done this. She will have to be pulled in for a disciplinary meeting on Monday. Of course, grief works in funny ways, but that doesn't make what she said about the company acceptable and especially not assaulting a colleague, even if it was by accident.

Mel needs a minute to herself. Already speculation is building that Dominique did it on purpose. Others believe it was a case of drunken clumsiness and bad timing, claiming he walked into the microphone. Mel's not sure exactly what she saw. But karma has been served. She spots the night manager, Edward, helping Wesley down the steps towards the bedrooms. Judging from Wesley's unbalanced state it's clear he's had a few. What's happening? One moment everyone was having fun and the next it's complete disarray. Clearly it's time the party comes to an end.

'Jesus. I didn't think this would happen,' Rohan says, running his hands through his hair. She jumps. She hadn't heard him come up beside her. 'I'd hoped that we could come away and start to look to the future but perhaps I've rushed things. Now, please don't tell me you told me so.'

'It's still so raw,' Mel says, as tactfully as she can.

'Yeah. I guess I just didn't appreciate how raw.' He wrings his hands together. 'At least no one is badly hurt. Everyone's had too much to drink to think about getting to the bottom of it now.' His jaw tenses. 'Will you please see if there's room on the boat for Dominique? I've already told her to get her things together.'

'But surely she can sleep it off . . .'

'I can't have someone rewarded for an outburst like that. One rotten apple ruins the bunch.'

Mel stutters. 'Well no, I mean . . .'

She wants to tell Rohan that he's called this wrong but she doesn't. He's the boss after all. Still, her cheeks ache from biting her tongue with all the things she wishes she could say to him.

'I'd feel a lot happier if Jonty left too. I think he needs to have a medical professional give him a once over,' she says. Plus, selfishly, she can't bear to think of how he's going to be at breakfast or on the boat ride home tomorrow morning. She's already reached her Jonty limit.

'Jonty's fine.' Rohan holds her gaze, speaking softly. 'He's tougher than he looks. The bleeding has stopped and Bonnie says she doesn't mind sitting with him for a short while until the dizziness goes.'

Mel glances over, poor Bonnie, she has no idea who she's helping. If only she knew how little he respects her. But at least someone is looking after him and that someone is not Mel.

Jonty is like a cat with nine lives. That or a cockroach. Invincible.

'Right, well.' Rohan's watch screen lights up. 'It's almost ten, thank God the party is nearly over. I'm too old for these things.' He rubs his face. Exhaustion is etched in every wrinkle.

A cheer from the revellers as the DJ plays one last song.

'I'd better go and get ready for the boat. Cheers, Mel, I appreciate your help.' He lightly places a hand on her arm. 'I'm so grateful to have you on the team, you know.'

She smiles weakly.

He goes to leave but she draws a breath.

'I didn't realise we were handing out promotions without going through the correct channels, Rohan.'

He turns. 'Pardon?'

'I wasn't going to say anything but you know people have issues with Jonty. It's not a good thing to put him in a position of power, it doesn't give the right message – especially to the women in the company.'

Rohan glances around as if someone is going to overhear. But everyone is too far away, dancing to the last song of the night, arms in the air, murdering the chorus of 'Mr Brightside' without a care in the world.

'None of those complaints were proven. And you, out of everyone, should know that that is confidential information.'

He gives her a strong look. 'Let's talk about this on Monday, shall we.' It's a statement, not a question.

An announcement by the DJ tells the guests to drink up as the boat back to dry land will arrive in a few minutes.

She wants to ask Rohan whether they should address what Dominique said in her speech, if everything is ok with the business, if the rumours of his divorce are true, and what about this allegation of fraud sent from Holly but she can't. She promised Tom she'd not say a thing. Next week she will arrange a meeting and raise her concerns in a less direct manner. Right now, she doesn't want to think about work anymore.

20

The Daily News Online

Saturday 22nd June

ARSON ATTACK

Published: 10.13am, 22 June

A DEADLY fire which broke out on Point Grey, a luxury hotel based on a remote sea fort on Friday (21 June) was started deliberately, fire crews today revealed.

Fire crews are said to suspect the blaze was started on the rooftop terrace but spread throughout the marine landmark. Thick smoke billowing from the resort could be seen from the mainland.

The fire has claimed the lives of 'several guests' according to Hampshire Police. A number of bodies have reportedly been recovered.

The search continues for survivors with forensic investigators seen combing for clues at the 150-year-old fort.

Detective Inspector Stephanie Hutchinson from Hampshire Police said: "We have carried out a preliminary joint assessment with Hampshire Fire and Rescue Service who believe the fire was started deliberately and, as such, we are now treating the incident as arson."

The isolated maritime building was transformed into a boutique hotel three years ago and is regularly exclusively hired out for company away-days, weddings and wellness retreats.

Flavour, a creative agency based in Marlow, Buckinghamshire, confirmed members of its staff had been on the fort at the time of the blaze. Chief Executive Rohan Ali said: "We are aware of an incident overnight at Point Grey hotel, where seven members of staff were staying over following our annual summer party. We are cooperating fully with police and cannot comment any further at this time."

According to Flavour's website, the company has a "fifty-plus team of professional, hard-working kick ass innovators."

Comments:

Man_U_Dad: Arson? My money's on an insurance scam. Owners probably wanted to get a quick sale. Unbelievable to think they did this whilst they had guests staying!

John: If it wasn't a freak accident then it must have been started deliberately.

- **Hugz63:** Yeah. That's what the word arson means.
- **John:** Alright, smart ar*e.

Kathrynnnnnn: I mean, you go to a work party and you expect to get home safe. You don't expect to die. But this isn't the first time this has happened. Why has no-one mentioned #HollyMills?

The views expressed in the comments above are those of our users and do not necessarily reflect the views of News-Online.

21

Thursday 20th June

The VIP guests are standing on the rooftop terrace. Down below, the boat taking their colleagues back to Portsmouth quays is waiting to set sail.

'Bye! Don't be too jel,' Wesley jeers, his voice snatched by the warm breeze.

Mel spots Tom laughing with others as he is welcomed on board. She enjoyed their chat tonight, maybe she has been too hasty to judge a book by its cover.

The large boat dips and rises as it moves alongside the pontoon. Mel hopes there are plenty of sick bags on board for Scarlett. She asked Lisa to keep an eye on her and make sure she got back to the hotel room ok. If she had any phone signal, she would be asking Scarlett herself to let her know when she gets in safely. A pang for her mum washes over Mel. She can't remember the last time she didn't say goodnight to her. A rush of longing to hear her voice makes her wobble.

Nicole leans precariously over the grey stone and yells, 'See you, losers.'

The boat pulls away, letting out a jaunty toot of the horn,

making them laugh. A strange moment of silence falls once the boat has sailed away. The chatter of her colleagues fades until there is nothing but the sound of the waves.

Everyone is going to be talking about this party for a long time.

Jonty's standing away from the small group of VIPs. Ever since 'Microphone-Gate' he's been slightly removed, brushing off any concern and acting like it was no big deal. The smell of his cigarette carries on the night air. Mel can taste it at the back of her throat.

'I can't believe how quiet it is without the DJ,' Bonnie says, her voice low, interrupting Mel's thoughts.

She's right. The roof terrace that had held fifty-plus colleagues a short while ago is now a silent, empty space. The speed of the clean-up was impressive. The waiting staff cleared the detritus of the party in a matter of moments. There's not a half-empty abandoned glass of wine or scrunched-up napkin to be seen. It's as though it didn't even happen.

Mel hears the heavy clunk of the wooden doors leading to the pontoon. She pictures the night manager sliding a decades-old lock into place across the sea-salt warped wood. What is he locking out? Or locking in?

'How's your arm? Someone told me what happened,' Bonnie asks Mel.

Mel's left wrist is throbbing slightly under the bandage. She should probably take some painkillers.

'Oh, erm yeah. I'm fine thanks. Did you have a good night?'

Bonnie smiles. 'I'm not going to lie, it was a little awkward at times. Everyone is such good friends here and it's hard to fit in, especially with the trendy youngsters. But still, it was nice to put faces to names, especially those I remember from the Christmas night out. Coming here is a real treat. This sort of thing doesn't happen to people like me.' Mel is about to jump in and tell her that she has every right to be here but Bonnie has turned her head to nod at Jonty. 'Someone's recovered.'

He has his back facing them, looking out over the seawall on the other side of the terrace. Strings of fairy lights hauntingly flutter above his head.

'Yeah. That was kind of you to sit with him, I hope it wasn't too painful.'

'Painful?' Bonnie looks quizzical. 'No, it was fine. My son's had a few injuries in his day so I knew what to look out for. He's a nice man, we had quite a pleasant chat.'

Pleasant? Jonty? He is such a two-faced liar, it's no secret he accused Bonnie of snooping in his desk behind her back, but to her face is being polite. Mel hasn't the heart to tell her the truth about that man.

'And then there were seven.' She jumps as Charlie comes up beside them.

'Och, you gave me a fright,' Bonnie laughs.

Mel wishes she'd found some mints and freshened up slightly. His body close to hers, his aftershave intoxicating.

The glow from the string of festoon lights casts him in a golden shade. Her stomach flips with a mixture of adrenaline and longing. He apologises to Bonnie with a wry wink and looks out over the water. The sky is dark and still oppressively hot given it's gone ten o'clock.

'Are you thinking what I'm thinking?' Charlie asks.

'What? That we're all alone until the morning. No way of escape.' Mel lets out a shrill laugh.

He looks at her, a strange smile fixed on his lips. 'No, I wasn't thinking that. I was thinking more about the fact that we could have another drink. The party can really get started now.'

'Oh, right, yes, of course.' Mel flushes. Her mouth is dry.

'But now you put it like that, yeah, I guess it is mad to think we're all the way out here, alone,' he says, looking across the murky water.

'Come on, let's open a bottle and raise a toast to us lucky ones,' Nicole whoops loudly, coming over to join them, placing her arm across Mel's shoulders as if they are best friends.

'Now the real fun and games begin,' Zander says, rubbing his hands together.

'Speaking of getting the party started. How about we get it going with a bang?' Wesley rummages in his shirt pocket and pulls out a spliff.

Mel blinks. The shock of seeing what he's holding momentarily overtakes her annoyance that everyone is staying up instead of going to bed, leaving her and Charlie alone. There's no way she can dust off her chat-up lines and attempt to flirt with an audience.

'Don't look at me like that,' Wesley laughs. 'You don't always have to be so straight-laced, Mel. There's no one here. No cameras, no police, no big boss. We're off-duty. And we're adults.' He's smiling but there is a hardness to his words. 'Maybe you should let your hair down for once?'

Mel has the injury on her wrist to prove what happens when she lets her hair down.

Wes turns to Bonnie. 'Bonz? What you sayin'?'

Bonnie's jaw tenses. 'Is that what I think it is? I don't want you smoking that anywhere near me, thanks.'

This is the first time Mel has seen an edge to Bonnie. Wesley doesn't appear to have registered her brusque reply.

'Alright, no drama.' Wesley turns. 'Zander, my man?'

'God, if I had any of that I'd be fast asleep,' Zander laughs. 'Drugs are for mugs anyway.'

'Charles?'

'Nah, I'm all good, man.'

'Come on. No one's goin' to join me?' he asks, realising that he's not found the fellow lawbreakers he thought he would. 'Stop trying to impress the ladies,' Wesley taunts Charlie. 'I remember what you were like at the Christmas party. Or is it only class A's that get you goin'?' Wesley laughs meanly at his 'joke'.

Charlie stiffens. 'Leave it, alright?'

Wesley backs off with his arms in the air. 'Fine, fine. Just a bit of banter, mate. It's all good. Peace and love, yeah?'

He walks off, whistling. Charlie mutters something under his breath but Mel doesn't catch it. Zander has broken into a painfully off-key rendition of a song about getting high.

'Right, well, as nice as it is out here, I'm going to find out how to get another drink,' Nicole says, wiggling in her tight red dress.

'Good idea. Mel, you coming?' Charlie calls as he starts to move away.

'Sure,' she says, as nonchalantly as she can, ignoring the hundreds of butterflies somersaulting inside her.

*

'Ladies first.' Charlie holds the door open to the cocktail lounge that Mel had seen pictures of on the website.

A brass plaque against the wooden frame reads 'Residents

Lounge'. The small oak-panelled room still manages to boast a baby grand piano and an impressive selection of leather-bound books filling the floor-to-ceiling line of bookshelves stretching across an entire wall. The scent of apple brandy and old money hangs in the air. There's a bar at the back of the room. Glass decanters hold amber liquid that twinkles in the low, golden glow of the Tiffany lamps.

'Wow, this is gorgeous.' Bonnie smiles at Mel. 'I'm only staying up for one more drink though. My pyjamas are calling. I just hope my bedroom's warmer than when we arrived.'

'God, me too,' Mel replies. The lounge is lovely and cool after the sultry outside temperatures.

'Ah, I think we're without a barman,' Charlie says. 'Can we help ourselves?'

From where she's standing Mel can see a small under-the-counter wine fridge holding bottles of lager, white wine and mixers. Two bottles of red wine stand on an oak console table beside polished glassware in neat, uniform rows.

'I think we should wait for the night manager,' Mel says. There was no mention of complimentary drinks for overnight guests and, without a price list, she can only begin to imagine how much a drink at hotel prices will set her back.

'Let me go and see if I can find him,' Zander says, wandering off. He staggers into the doorframe as if not expecting it to be there.

'I still can't believe Dominique's had to go home,' Nicole says, sitting opposite Mel on a tanned leather armchair with chunky copper studs running down the side seams. She crosses a slender leg, giving the room an eyeful of her thigh.

'I think she decided she wanted to go back and see her kids,' Mel lies.

She had been bracing herself for a difficult conversation to tell Dominique that she needed to leave but thankfully Dominique said she didn't want to spend another minute here in this 'crappy hotel'. She had already packed her bag and was ready to go when the boat arrived.

'Bollocks,' Nicole laughs. 'She left because she didn't want to have breakfast with Jonty. She hates him. She definitely hit him on purpose.'

Mel doesn't know what to say to that. There are going to have to be some serious mediations happening next week. A headache threatens to start if she thinks about it too much so she dismisses it for now.

'That was the highlight of the night for me, watching Jonty getting whacked,' Nicole grins.

'Did anyone see where he went?' Charlie says, looking up from the selection of spirits.

'I think he was still smoking on the roof terrace,' Bonnie says, her hands clasped on her lap. She appears to be consciously taking up the least amount of space possible. Mel hopes she manages to relax. She's got every right to be here, the same as the rest of them.

'He probably got the message that we didn't want him to join us,' Nicole replies. 'Hopefully he won't reappear until late in the morning. I don't want to have to look at his smug face over my eggs benedict. I have to say that Dominique did make some good points though. Before the assault.'

'Like what?' Bonnie asks.

'Maybe this isn't one big happy family that Rohan likes to believe it is. We give so much of ourselves to this company and for what? Only the chosen few get to make the big bucks, look at Jonty,' Nicole says, picking at her blood red nails. 'She was saying some mad stuff about Holly, wasn't she? What did you think, Charlie?'

He runs a hand through his hair, mussing up the normally neat style. 'I mean, honestly? Lock Dominique in an empty room and she'd come out with some drama. It follows her around. That's the type of person she is. She wasn't friends with Holly. In fact, I heard she was a bit of a cow to her. But, I guess you don't *really* know someone just because you work with them.'

Mel remembers what Zander said about Dominique. How her emotional out-of-character public outburst was fuelled by guilt.

She shakes her head. 'She was drunk and upset. She probably won't remember half of it in the morning—'

Nicole speaks over her. 'Fine. But come on. It's not like we properly knew Holly, any of us. Yeah, it's sad especially as she was so young, but what did anyone even know about her?'

She doesn't get to finish her point as Zander bounds back into the room.

'Guess what? I can do better than another drink in the bar . . .' He has an excitable look on his flushed plump face. 'I've just bumped into that night manager dude who said the hot tub is ready for us. Hot tub, baby!'

Mel's stomach tightens. The invites for overnight guests said to bring swimwear but she thought it might be for a spa treatment tomorrow morning. She certainly doesn't plan on getting undressed in front of her colleagues. She has to work with these people every day. Her plain one-piece may be modest but it would still feel like being in her underwear.

'Where's the hot tub?' Nicole asks, grinning at the idea. 'I've not seen one?'

Zander's getting more animated by the second. 'He said it's up by the lighthouse. They've had a cover on it all evening as it's reserved for the hotel guests. VIPs only. He's set up complimentary champagne and towels. It sounds fabulous. Come on.'

'I wouldn't want to scare you so I'm going to skip this,' Bonnie says, getting to her feet and brushing imaginary crumbs off her lap. 'In fact, I'm going to call it a night. Sleep well.'

Nicole, Zander and Charlie all say they're up for a hot tub and turn, waiting for Mel's decision.

It's on the tip of her tongue to say she's also going to head to her bedroom, but this is her chance. She can't bail now. She's learnt, in her thirty-two years, that nothing good comes from being timid.

'Count me in.'

22

Thursday 20th June

Mel fumbles with her bedroom key, not entirely sure whether she's doing the right thing. She hates stepping out of her comfort zone but she needs to if she wants things to change in her life.

The air-conditioning in her room has thankfully been fixed. The icy cold air has dissipated but a shiver still runs over her. Her eyes dart around at the enormous space. Nothing appears to have been touched or moved but something feels off.

She looks up at the hooks on the ceiling. The black metal glints at her. A large, framed painting hangs behind the bed, which she hadn't noticed before. A haunting scene of a lashing ocean, all blues and greys and wild sea spray smeared in oil paints. She thinks it's an abstract print, but moving closer, she can see that in the bottom right-hand corner there is what looks like a concrete pier. At the edge of the pier, too close for comfort, is a small figure staring out at the storm. One wave would sweep them to their death. It's probably worth a lot of money and is painted by some famous artist, but it gives Mel the creeps.

The wooden wardrobe door creaks loudly as she opens it. It smells of stale trapped air and untreated wood. No one is inside. She drops to her hands and knees and lifts up the valance sheet on the bed. The white cotton flutters between her fingertips as it moves. No one under there, either.

Standing up, trying to push down the sense of unease, she tells herself to stop being silly. But then she notices something that sends a rush of goosebumps across her skin.

Now the air-conditioning is at an acceptable level, it's easier to smell Holly's perfume. It hangs in the air, as if the ghost of her colleague has been in this room while Mel's been upstairs at the party.

She hurries to get out of her dress, avoiding her reflection in the floor length mirror. Her navy swimming costume is a little snug but she covers up with one of the fluffy hotel robes, pulling the tie cord tight. She's still unsure if this is a good idea or not. The only time she's been in a hot tub was on holiday about ten years ago. It felt like she was sitting in human soup. The jets kneading her back were so powerful they left a mark. She found the whole thing pretty uncomfortable. But the others are so excited and this is an opportunity to talk to Charlie.

Mel takes some deep breaths. Her hands press against the cold marble basin. It's still relatively early – it must not be even eleven o'clock – but she is exhausted after the emotion and revelations of the evening.

'You are brave, you are strong, you are confident,' she says under her breath, before quickly wiping away a few flecks of dried mascara from under her eyes and managing to pull her shorter hair into a ponytail. Unsure whether it looks better or worse tied up. She shuts the bedroom door and makes sure it's locked behind her.

Out in the courtyard, she hears the tell-tale click of a lighter. Her stomach drops. The smell of Jonty's cigarettes wafts over her. He looks her up and down. He makes her skin crawl.

'We're getting in the hot tub,' she explains, pulling her robe tighter across her body to ensure that not an inch of flesh is on show, wanting to hurry to join the others up on the roof terrace.

'Right. Sounds fun,' he says, sarcastically.

'I thought you'd be fast asleep after what happened with Dominique,' she says. It's hard to see in this light but his nose still looks red and swollen from being struck by the microphone. The bruises under each eye have calmed somewhat since she saw him right after the incident. Now, they could be mistaken for tiredness.

'That. Pfft.' He blows out smoke as he lets out a wheeze of a laugh. 'That was nothing. Some people don't know how to handle themselves when they're drinking.'

Mel thinks of the many emails she's sent Rohan about Jonty, all the times she tried to get her boss to listen to her. His reply was always along the lines of it being 'better to have your enemies pissing out than pissing in'. But she knows the real reason Rohan looks the other way. Jonty knows too much about the company. If they fire him, not only would he likely launch an expensive tribunal, but he also could easily poach clients given he knows their list backwards and forwards. So, he stays.

Still, Mel pictures those interns and graduates whose complaints were dismissed because his word was always taken over theirs. She thinks of Holly, and the grievance that never came, even though Mel knows it was on its way.

'Anyway, aren't you going to congratulate me on the promotion?' Jonty's nasal tones bring Mel back to the present.

'Well done. I hope you're happy,' she says through gritted teeth.

'You could try and make that sound a little more genuine.'

Her blood pressure rises at the smirk on his face, always looking like the cat who got the cream.

'You know what? Fine. I'm not happy for you.' She folds her arms. 'Don't think I don't know all about you. Just watch out, your card is marked.'

'Oh, really? Well, I'll tell you this for nothing – you're looking in the wrong direction.' He inhales sharply. A dark and forbidding look steals over his features. 'That cleaner needs to be careful.'

'Bonnie?' Mel rolls her eyes. *Here we go again.*

She'd hoped that Bonnie's kindness in sitting beside him after what happened with Dominique on the dance floor, might have changed his mind and shown him how she's a genuine person. Clearly not.

'Yeah. She's always snooping around. When I've confronted her in the past she came up with some bullshit excuse but I could tell from the way she started sweating that she'd been caught. Stealing, no doubt.'

Mel sighs. She's never received any official complaints about things going missing in the office.

'Anyway,' he exhales, 'now I've been promoted she needs to watch out. Let's just say, I'll be speaking to Rohan to look at us outsourcing the cleaning.'

Mel doesn't know whether to believe him or not. It makes her wonder, what if he tries to outsource her job too?

'You may have persuaded Rohan to keep you but we both know you're not the innocent party that you make out. Holly knew that too,' Mel says, crossing her arms.

'What?'

'She had your card marked.'

Mel's suddenly back at the Christmas party. The dance floor was heaving, the familiar opening bars to The Pogues' 'Fairytale of New York' was starting. She remembers because it's her favourite.

'Do you have a minute?' Holly asked Mel, her eyes flashing over to Jonty, standing at the bar with Charlie and Wesley.

Mel remembers his garish light-up reindeer Christmas jumper and the obnoxious way he demanded an expensive bottle of Merlot from a young barman, without saying thank you.

'I've been trying to get some space in your diary,' Holly said.

Mel had rearranged the meeting a few times. Her mum was going through a rough patch so everything in her diary had to be rescheduled.

Holly chewed her bottom lip. She had said previously that it was urgent but wouldn't give Mel any details, simply saying that she needed to speak to her in private. It had to be confidential.

'I promise, first thing on Monday I'll make sure to clear some time for us to speak,' Mel had reassured her.

But Holly never made it to Monday. She didn't even make it home that night.

'Me?' Jonty says, incredulously, pulling Mel from the memory.

'Why would Holly want to talk about me? I don't think I had more than two conversations with her.' Jonty drops his cigarette and stamps it into the ground under his gaudy high-top trainers. He hasn't changed his bloodied shirt. It's going to be impossible to wash out the dried red stain.

Mel falters. The truth was, she didn't know for sure what Holly had wanted to say to her. Based on history, and the way Holly had been acting at the party, Mel had always been fairly certain she knew what Holly had wanted to discuss in their confidential meeting – another terrible experience with Jonty – but judging by the genuinely confused look on Jonty's face, perhaps she had jumped to conclusions?

'I don't know what you're talking about,' Jonty repeats. 'But a word of advice? Maybe drop the hard act; it doesn't suit you. I know you don't like me but Rohan does. And he has a right to make his own decisions about what's best for this company.' He suddenly lets out a hacking cough, waving a hand through his plume of smoke.

She turns on her heel and walks away, hearing him muttering something under his breath.

She might be wrong but it sounds like he's telling her not to trust anyone.

23

Saturday 22nd June

Hampshire Constabulary: Interview started at 12.00

Officer O'Neal: For the purpose of the tape please give your full name.

Witness: Tom Beckett.

OON: Thanks for taking the time to come and see us, Mr Beckett. Anything you know which may have happened at the party or before the event – anything, no matter how small – might help give us a valuable insight.

TB: I can't believe it. Arson. (voice breaks slightly) When I left they were lapping up the luxury. Things couldn't have been better.

Detective Inspector Hutchinson: Nothing out of the ordinary?

TB: No. The only real drama was when one of my colleagues, Dominique, pulled the mic off the DJ to give an emotional speech. It ended with her whacking this guy called Jonty in the face, which we all agreed he deserved. Oh, God. Sorry. I mean, do you know if he survived? When will you release the names of

122

those who have died? Please tell me Mel is ok? Melanie Robinson? She was staying over too. I've heard rumours . . .

OON: I'm afraid we're not yet able to release any details to the public until we have informed immediate family.

TB: (Swears quietly)

DIH: We are aware of the incident regarding Ms Sanchez and Mr Aspinall during the party –

TB: – I'm sure Jonty won't have had anything to do with it, if you're thinking the fight was some sort of motivation to commit arson. He would have been embarrassed but not bent on revenge.

OON: You told one of my colleagues that you wanted to speak to us about something you feel might be relevant?

TB: Erm, yes. But it wasn't to do with what happened between Jonty and Dominique (Sound of chair squeaking). It might have nothing to do with what happened whatsoever . . . have you spoken to Rohan yet? Rohan Ali? He's the CEO.

OON: He's on the list of people we still need to speak to.

TB: Well, he'll probably mention it to you too. So, I look after the IT and maintenance for Flavour – I'm 'the tech guy' – and on the morning of the party, we received an anonymous email, which alleged fraudulent activity in the company. It had been routed through several servers but I managed to trace it to the original sender. And what I found didn't make sense. It had come from Holly's company account.

OON: Holly Mills? The graduate who died?

TB: Yes.

OON: So someone hacked into her account?

TB: No, it shouldn't be possible. The system wiped her account after she died and there's no way for anyone to have reinstated it. But there it was, a message with severe consequences if true, coming from beyond the grave.
(External noise)

OON: Excuse me. We're in the middle of an interview here. (Muffled voices). No, I booked the room. Yep, thanks. (Chair scraping.) So sorry about that.

TB: It's fine.

OON: So, where were we? There was an accusation of fraud?

TB: (Lengthy inhale) I told Rohan as soon as we got to Point Grey. He was shocked, as you can imagine. Obviously, there are procedures to go through with any sort of accusation like this, but the fact it came from someone who has sadly died, made it tricky to work out what to do. He agreed that we couldn't act too hastily. I mean, there was nothing we could do at the party. He planned for us to pick it up in a meeting yesterday – Friday – but with the fire . . . (sniffs) I came here to tell you this as Holly's email was legit.

OON: And how do you know this?

TB: We've recently been having some problems with the website – we upgraded it and I won't bore you with details but it has caused me no end of headaches trying to fix all the resulting glitches. (Clears throat). Anyway, basically, the bugs led me to execute an internal reset of our systems – a bit like unclogging the toilet – which finished on Thursday morning. And because of this reset, files and data have come to light which had previously been stuck. Including Holly's email. She sent it before she'd died but it must have got trapped, blocked up as it were, and it's only by running this new software that it's been freed.

OON: How serious did you think this allegation was?

TB: Well, erm, I don't know. (Pause). The email was dated in December, it seems Holly had originally tried to send it to HR but obviously it was never received by our HR lady in December. No-one else has alleged anything like this since.

OON: And who did she believe was behind this *fraud*?

TB: According to Holly, one of Flavour's clients doesn't exist. It's not a real company. It's been invented purely as a way for these thieving employees to bury their excessive expense claims under 'client entertaining'. I've made a start verifying this and alarmingly there is one client's name who appears on our books again and again.

DIH: So Holly was effectively a whistleblower to this crime?

TB: Yes. I think so. And, well, strangely enough, those she accused - our colleagues who work for this fictional client – were staying overnight at Point Grey. And, if these rumours are true, then they are all dead.

24

Charlie is sitting alone on a bench near the hot tub. The lid is still on, keeping the heat in. Apart from a rhythmic gurgle and hum, the only other sound is the waves slapping the bricks of the fort.

'Where are the others?' Mel asks, glancing around.

A bottle of champagne stands in a gleaming ice bucket. Tea lights have been lit. It is very romantic. Mel wonders if he's noticed. This would be an amazing first date.

'Dunno, I didn't realise I would be so quick,' He laughs. He lifts open a wicker basket full of fuzzy cashmere folded blankets and passes her one to sit on.

'Well, you snooze, you lose, right?' he says, popping open the champagne, and handing her a flute. 'How's your wrist by the way? I heard what happened.'

'Oh, yeah, I'm so clumsy. It's fine,' she says. The bandage is hidden by the sleeve of her robe. She wonders what he heard. Those bitching girls in the toilet believed she did it to grab his attention. Should she tell him that it wasn't like that, or would that only bring his attention to the fact others gossip about her behind her back?

'Cheers, anyway. You know, we've never had the chance to hang out,' he says, interrupting her thoughts.

'Yeah, I know.' Her hands are sweaty, she tightens her grip on the glass.

'We should drink up. This bottle won't last long once the rest of them join us.'

For a brief moment, she'd forgotten that there was anyone else staying over.

'Maybe we could see if the wine cellar is open,' Mel says, surprising herself. 'Didn't that Gus guy say they had several hundred bottles stored here, or something?'

Most of the facts from the tour of the fort went over her head. She was too focused on trying not to panic whilst down the dark, creepy narrow corridors to listen to the history lesson, well, apart from the ghost story. That has stayed with her, unfortunately.

Charlie draws back in amazement. 'Melanie Robinson, well I never. Here I was thinking you were a teacher's pet all the time and now you're suggesting we could break into the wine cellar?'

'I didn't say that.' Heat rushes to her cheeks. 'Is that what you think of me?'

'Well, you know. You're usually a bit . . . corporate. It's nice to see you relax a little. I'd love to know more about you. Like, what's the set-up? You never have your camera on during Zoom calls.'

Only Rohan knows what she's going through at home and even then, she's lied about how bad it can be. She's overheard the wild guesses about why her video is always off during online meetings. She lets her colleagues come up with their own theories that it's because her house is a mess, she's having building work done, the internet connection isn't strong enough . . . when really it's because she's terrified that at any minute her sixty-one-year-old mother will wander in wearing only her nightdress and start shouting profanities.

Everyone thinks Mel lives alone. She did, once upon a time. Then her mum got worse and the carers got more expensive. So, until that pay rise happens, she's staying put. Moving back home to help take care of her mum wasn't the worst thing in the world. No, it's watching her decline and being helpless to stop it that's almost killed her. She glances down at her phone, not sure why she's carrying it around when she can't use it. Habit, probably.

'Oh, well. I moved into my mum's house to help as she was going through some . . . stuff, and it's quite small and cluttered so it's easier to keep the camera off. But, erm, what about you?' She doesn't want to dwell on her living situation right now. It'll only put him off her.

'Me? There's not much to say. It's just me and my cat. I'm pretty boring.' He smiles, flashing his deep dimples. There's an awkward pause. She's waiting for him to expand. From a bit of earwigging and social media stalking, she knows that he lives in the newly built flats by the station, loves snowboarding, and went to Berlin with some mates at Easter. He also recently broke up with his girlfriend.

'I can't get over how cool this place is.' He sits back and lets out a contented sigh. 'Have you heard the rumour that we were chosen to stay for a *reason*?' He uses his fingers to make air quotes. 'Loads of people are jealous. I mean, if only they could see us now.' He stretches his arms out towards the full sky, the twinkling lights on the distant horizon.

'Erm, well I suppose people will say anything when they're jealous in order to make themselves feel better,' she says. All the rumours she's heard about this company this evening swim to the front of her mind. 'I've never understood why people need to tear others down in order to build themselves up.'

'Deep.' He grins. 'Jonty's promotion certainly rubbed a lot of people the wrong way. I heard he was thinking of leaving.'

'What? Jonty? Leaving?'

He takes a large swig. 'Yeah, I bet that's how Rohan got him to stay. Throw some more cash at him and hand out a new job title. He was bad enough before but now, with this promotion, he's going to be unbearable.'

Mel's surprised to hear Charlie say this. 'I thought you got on with him?'

'Me? With that posh twat? No. I can't stand him.'

'Oh.' They're always friendly in the office, never any hint of bad blood between them.

'I guess it's a case of keeping your friends close and enemies closer.' He falls silent, turning his lips into a wry smile. 'Or something like that. He screwed me over with a client a year or so ago, and took credit for something I'd worked my arse off for.'

'Really?'

'Yeah. I was fuming. He gave me some lame apology that he was *sorry for the way I was feeling*. Complete bullshit. He would step on anyone's toes to get to the top. Even Rohan needs to watch his back. Anyway, I've forgiven but never forgotten, you know. It's annoying that I have to work so closely on certain accounts with him. I try not to let it get to me. One day he'll get his comeuppance.'

'My mum likes to say that it'll all come out in the wash.'

'Hmm, I hope she's right.' Charlie is looking out across the horizon. 'I guess his leaving was just another rumour. You know how Flavour is full of them.'

'Speaking of which . . .' She sits up straighter. 'I heard you were thinking of leaving?'

Her breath catches in her throat as she waits for him to answer, praying it's not true. It takes forever for him to reply.

He groans. 'God, the rumour mill in this place is ridiculous.' He shakes his head. 'I'm not going anywhere. Don't believe everything you hear.'

She lets out a sigh of relief as subtly as she can and looks out at the starry sky above their heads. 'Jonty said there was going to be a storm later.'

'He's winding you up. That's his speciality.'

'It's also what gets him into trouble.' Mel purses her lips. 'You should see the file of complaints I have about him.'

'Oh yeah? Who else hates him?'

Heat rushes to her cheeks. The alcohol is making her tongue loose. 'I can't name names . . .'

'Go on . . . I won't tell.'

'Erm, well, this is between us, right?'

He lifts his right hand into a mock salute. 'Promise.'

This conversation is veering into dangerous territory. Confidentiality is the number one rule in HR. She chews her lip. Charlie smiles at her, waiting. She's cross with Jonty, and

Rohan in a way, she feels like her professionalism has been disrespected tonight. So, after a beat of hesitation, she tells him about how many interns and graduates – all female – lodge complaints after working with Jonty. How he struggles to get along with junior members of the team but bats off any criticism by making out that it's *their* fault. According to Jonty, it's always a clash of personalities, nothing he did or said was wrong, and Rohan always believes him. Mel, on the other hand, is less forgiving.

'If he's had so many complaints then why hasn't he been fired?' Charlie asks.

Mel shrugs. 'He's clever. None of them have been severe enough to warrant dismissal, only a rap on the knuckles. I was hopeful that I might be able to build up a strong case with one person, there was even a meeting in the diary, but . . .'

'But what? What happened?'

'Let's just say we didn't get to take her complaint any further.'

'What does that mean— oh. You're talking about Holly?'

'I can't get into details. I shouldn't have even told you as much as I have.' Mel takes a deep breath. She's divulged too much. She prays she can trust him. 'The strange thing is that when I spoke to him about it, literally ten minutes ago, he acted like he had no idea what I was talking about.'

His jaw tenses. 'He's a good actor.'

Mel can't ask Charlie what he means as there is the sound of footsteps.

'Hey, sorry, we got lost,' Zander calls out. Nicole is following behind, both of them in their robes. Mel's stomach falls.

There goes her and Charlie's 'date'. She tries to hide her disappointment, kicking herself that she wasted this perfect opportunity to get to know Charlie by talking about Jonty. Idiot. At least their arrival allows her to catch her tongue. A sickly sensation swirls in her stomach, she really shouldn't have told him all of that confidential information.

'Ah, here you are. We got started without you, sorry.' Charlie lifts his half-empty glass. 'Where are the others?'

'I don't know where Wesley is.' Nicole shrugs. 'Bonnie's gone to bed.'

'I wouldn't be surprised if he got the munchies and is getting the night manager dude to make him a sandwich,' Zander says, picking up the bottle of champagne and pouring himself a flute. 'Is this all the booze we've got?'

He tops up everyone's glasses until the bottle is empty.

'Mel was talking about breaking into the wine cellar,' Charlie says.

'Oh well, n-not breaking in,' she stutters. 'That's not what I meant.'

'I'll go and grab us another bottle,' Zander offers. 'There were more bubbles in the residents' lounge, right?'

'If not then try the wine cellar,' Charlie suggests, winking at Mel.

'You all jump in if you want, just make sure to leave room for a little one,' Zander says.

'Oh, see where the night manager is? If he's not making Wesley a snack, ask if he could put some music on or something?' Nicole calls after him.

'Beyoncé coming right up.'

'Right, are we getting in?' Nicole gestures to the hot tub.

She takes off her robe with a confidence that Mel can only dream of. She's in a red bikini. Her body looks like it's been modelled on Barbie. Mel pulls her own robe tighter.

'Charlie, will you help me take the lid off?' Nicole asks.

Charlie glances up from where he'd been staring intently at the label on the champagne bottle. He clearly doesn't know where to look. 'Erm, sure.'

He heaves open the heavy lid, steam covering his face. There is a strong smell of chlorine. 'Man, this is hot.'

'No shit.' Nicole laughs. She doesn't wait a second before stepping a foot in then letting out an ear-piercing scream. 'Jesus Christ. It's scalding.'

'I told you it was hot.'

'Yeah, not that it was literally lava. Oww.' She's holding her right foot and wincing.

'There's a shower over there,' Mel says, pointing to the opposite wall covered in tiny mosaic tiles. 'Maybe run cold water over it?'

Nicole turns and hobbles towards the shower. 'I'm going to sue. There's no way it should be that hot. Literally, that's burnt my skin. Oh my God, it's gone all red. Look.'

'Maybe we need to leave the lid off and let it cool down slightly?' Mel suggests.

Nicole is muttering loudly about how much compensation she could ask for if this leaves a mark. She glances back to see if they're listening to her. The sudden twist of movement sends her off balance.

It happens so fast.

Her left foot goes from underneath her. She tries to steady herself, flailing her arms to grab purchase. But it's no use. The alcohol has made her sluggish and the floor tiles are slippery. Water must have splashed out when Charlie lifted the lid off. No one noticed the large puddle on the ground. One minute she's fine and the next she's on the floor in a heap.

'Oh my God, Nic, are you ok?' Charlie asks, jogging over to her.

Mel watches as Charlie gently helps Nicole sit up. She screams out in pain, the sound slices through the silence.

Her shoulders judder and short gasps of breath escape her lips.

'My arm.' Mascara drips down her cheeks. 'It's broken!'

25

Thursday 20th June

Mel wraps Nicole's robe around her juddering shoulders, wanting to keep her warm for when the shock of the fall kicks in, and gently leads her towards the residents' lounge. Her left arm appears to be swelling before their eyes.

'What's going on? I was just coming to find you guys,' Zander asks, looking confused. He's clutching two bottles of white wine in his arms.

'Nicole's had a fall by the hot tub. She slipped on the wet floor,' Mel explains.

Charlie is crouched down, talking to Nicole crying on the sofa.

'Can you do this?' He has his own arm outstretched and is turning it palm up to palm down.

Nicole shakes her head. Pain and panic line her scrunched-up pale face. 'No, it hurts so much. It's broken, I'm sure of it. Oww.'

'I think we need to get her to a hospital.' Charlie turns to Zander and Mel. 'I once had a rugby injury that looked like that and it needed pins in.'

'What's going on? I thought I heard screaming,' Bonnie says, appearing from the corridor. She's not had time to change out of her dress and into her pyjamas but she's washed the make-up off her face.

Mel quickly tells her what's happened. How it was so sudden, the wet floor, the scalding hot tub.

'Oh my gosh, how scary.'

'We need to find the first aid kit and get it in a sling if you can't move it,' Charlie says, pulling himself to his full height.

'I know where it is.' Mel raises her bandaged wrist in the air.

'This place is cursed. First you and now Nic,' Zander says. 'What if it's the ghost? George?'

Mel doesn't know if he's trying to lighten the mood but it's not helping.

'Ghosts don't exist,' Charlie pulls a face, 'and you can't blame phantom spirits on someone slipping over. It was an accident.'

'The hot tub being a million degrees was no accident. Some-one must have changed the settings on purpose. There's no way it should have been that hot,' Nicole snaps.

'I've got some painkillers in my room,' Bonnie suggests.

'I don't think a fucking paracetamol is going to help a broken arm,' Nicole replies through clenched teeth. 'I need an ambulance.'

Mel pulls an apologetic face at Bonnie; she's only trying to help. 'Ok, I know it hurts but you need to stay calm. We don't know if it's broken yet. Hopefully, it's a nasty sprain.'

It looks red and is swelling more and more by the second but thankfully there are no bones sticking out.

'I'm getting married in two weeks. I can't walk down the aisle with a great big ugly cast.' Nicole bursts into tears again.

Charlie passes Nicole a tissue. 'Come on, stay positive, Nic. First of all, we need to find the first aid kit—'

'And then the night manager. I know this place is big, but I presumed he'd be hanging around, waiting to leap into action and satisfy our every need, like some personal butler,' Zander butts in. 'On the plus side, it means we can raid the bar without him noticing.'

Nicole sniffs the tears away. 'I don't even know what he looks like.'

Mel's stomach twists, remembering how she flirted with him after her accident. 'He's tall. Has light reddish hair, a sort of boyish face.' *Very handsome.* She coughs. 'Maybe in his early thirties. His name is Edward.'

'When did anyone last see him?' Charlie asks.

Mel looks around the residents' lounge for a telephone or a bell to call to get the night manager's attention. 'Zander, you said you saw him? He told you about the hot tub.'

'Yeah, he said he'd come and check on us in a bit.'

'Well, where is he?' Nicole whines.

Mel's about to tell her that she'll go and look for the first aid kit when the door handle turns. It swings wide open. Wesley staggers into the room.

'Were you playin' hide and seek? Where have youse been? I thought you'd vanished. Proper freaky,' he says, his arms outstretched, unsteady on his feet, stinking of weed. 'Woah, what's with the vibe in here?'

'Nicole's hurt herself.' Charlie stands up.

Wesley peers at Nicole on the sofa, roaming his eyes over her bikini, and the tanned skin that's on show.

'Have you seen the night manager?' Zander asks him.

Wesley shakes his head. 'Me? Nope.'

'Let's go and find the first aid kit,' Mel says, getting to her feet. 'Then we can use the phone on reception to call for help.'

'What? Are you expecting an ambulance to come out here? And how do you think that will work?' Zander scoffs.

'No, but perhaps a medical professional can tell us what to do. Ideally, she needs to get her arm treated in a hospital. Can't you see how it's swelling up?' Mel replies, biting down the frustration at how dismissive he is.

Wesley makes a wet noise between his lips. His eyes are bloodshot and wide. 'Of course it'd be Nicole. The drama queen.'

He wobbles and falls against a tall cabinet. The movement makes a vase full of white lilies topple over. The noise echoes.

'Careful. Don't step on the broken glass,' Bonnie says, crouching to the floor to pick up the pieces. 'It wasn't some Ming vase or anything, was it? You wouldn't know in this posh place.'

Wesley's tight trousers got splashed as the vase fell. It looks like he's wet himself.

Mel realises he's not moving. 'Wesley?' she asks. 'Are you ok?'

He stands motionless, staring at a picture on the wall. What was previously hidden behind the bouquet is a photo of the night manager in a gold gilt frame with 'Employee of the month: Edward' typed in thick bold letters underneath.

'That's what the night manager looks like,' Zander says. 'Pretty fit if you ask me.'

'This dude,' Wesley lifts his hand ever so slowly, frowning, 'I've seen him before.'

'No. Really?' Zander says, rolling his eyes. 'He's been around at the party all night.'

'I didn't mean that, fam,' Wesley throws him a look. 'I mean, I've seen him hangin' around our office.'

Bonnie glances up from the floor where she's carefully picking up the pieces of the vase and moving them out of the way so no one gets hurt. Mel turns to face him.

'Yeah, it was a few weeks ago. He was outside, lookin' as if he was waitin' for someone. And I saw him again the following night. He had a proper bad cough. Thought he was chucking a lung up at one stage. That's mad. Small world, huh?'

Mel thought she recognised Edward when he was treating her wrist. Perhaps she'd also seen him hanging around outside the office, but hadn't registered it.

Nicole lets out a moan of pain, clutching her arm and clenching her eyes shut. 'I don't care where you saw him. Can someone just go and bloody find him!'

*

Charlie has taken Wesley to his bedroom. Mel doesn't know if he's drunk or stoned or both, but he was winding the others up, especially Nicole. They could hear Wesley chanting football songs the entire way down the corridor. Mel wants to get changed but she said she'd wait with Nicole.

There is an angry red patch across Nicole's bare toes from when she dipped her foot in the hot tub. The skin looks puckered and scalded. Surely there should be a sign warning guests that the water gets seriously hot? It must be faulty. Mel understands Nicole wants someone to blame but accusing someone of tampering with it is extreme. She remembers the waiver they signed on the quayside, all that intimidating legal jargon, Point Grey will have covered their backs if anything was to go wrong here.

Nicole is crying. Bonnie softly shushes her and tells her help won't be long.

But they are miles from a hospital. Who knows how long it will take for help to arrive? Mel's about to ask Bonnie if she thinks Nicole could be airlifted out of here when the door to the residents' lounge opens.

'Here,' Zander pants, handing over a green first aid kit. He's changed back into his garish patterned shirt and suit trousers.

'Thanks. Did you manage to find the night manager?' Mel asks, glancing up from the assortment of plasters and antiseptic cream to try and find something to use as a makeshift sling.

'No. There's no sign of him.' He shakes his head.

'I thought this place was meant to be five-star luxury. Where the hell are all the members of staff?' Nicole asks, cradling her arm. 'Did you call for help?'

There's silence.

Mel's stomach tightens at the expression on Zander's face. 'Zander, are you ok?'

His thick neck is flushed.

'Zander?' Mel repeats.

'There's a problem . . .' He pauses, trying to catch his breath. Beads of perspiration glisten on his forehead.

'What do you mean?' Bonnie asks, picking up on the sudden change of atmosphere in the room.

Zander's eyes are magnified behind the lenses of his glasses, giving him this comical appearance. But this isn't a joke. And no one is laughing. Mel is so used to seeing him unflappable, in control and obnoxiously confident, but right now he looks afraid.

He swallows. 'The phone lines are down.'

26

The landline stands on the main desk in the reception. A sleek chrome thing with plastic tabs next to raised buttons – presumably a direct dial to the kitchen, the staff area or other spaces. Mel holds the heavy handset to her ear with her right hand, aware of the slight tremble in her wrist.

Zander's right. There's not a dial tone. Nothing. A black void. Despite this she jabs at the buttons, pressing them in no order, hoping something will happen.

Nothing does.

'You ok?' Charlie asks, joining her. He's back in his chinos and short sleeved navy shirt, holding a bag of frozen peas. 'I went to get these, figured it might help with the swelling.'

Mel smiles at how thoughtful he is. 'That's kind.'

He shrugs away the compliment. 'Are you ok? You look stressed?'

'Zander said the phones aren't working,' Mel says, tucking a strand of hair behind her ear, wishing she was dressed in her normal clothes and not this robe covering her swimming costume.

Charlie frowns and picks up the receiver as if he doesn't believe her.

'Ah well, that's probably where the night manager is, fixing the problem with the phone line. God knows how ancient the wiring is in this place.'

Mel wishes he'd hurry up. 'Did Wesley go to his room ok?'

'Yeah. He was talking nonsense and kept saying he felt ill. I told him it was mixing the weed along with everything else he knocked back. He caned the free drinks. Wouldn't surprise me if he cracked open the minibar too.'

There's definitely going to be some sore heads in the morning.

'What should we do now? I'm worried about Nicole's arm. She's in a lot of pain. Bonnie has made a temporary sling but there's no way she'll be able to sleep tonight. It needs an X-ray.'

'Nic's tough. She'll be in shock but it's not life-threatening. This manager guy will show up soon and he can deal with it.' Charlie leans against the desk, crossing his ankles. 'Well, that kind of ruined things outside, didn't it?'

'Yeah,' she replies, her heart thrumming under the look he is giving her.

'It's a shame, I was enjoying hanging out with you.'

Mel can't hide the smile that erupts on her face. 'Me too.'

He has such deep and inviting brown eyes. She has to remind herself to breathe.

He smiles, then looks away. 'I'm sure this guy will be back soon.'

'Do you really think he's gone to fix the phones?' she asks, absently picking up a paperweight and running her fingers over the cold glass, wishing her heart would calm down.

'I don't know, I hope so.' He pauses. 'I mean, where else would he be?'

She puts the paperweight back and as she does so she nudges the imposing iMac to life. The artificial glow of the screen makes her blink. It shows what looks like an Excel spreadsheet. She pushes a plush office chair out of the way – it screeches on its rubber wheels – to get a better look.

It's a list of guest bookings. Flavour is highlighted in bold red font. Mel takes a step closer. On the right-hand side of the table is tomorrow's date. Mel reads the words again. An icy chill dances through her.

'You ok?' Charlie asks.

'I thought we were being picked up at ten o'clock tomorrow morning?' Mel frowns.

'We are.'

'Not according to this.'

They both lean in to re-read the spreadsheet. Her fingers tremble on the mouse pad, moving the cursor down. Every day for the next week has been scored out. Not one single booking or reservation.

It's as if someone has planned for no one else to come on board.

'They probably haven't updated it,' Charlie suggests, letting out a yawn.

First, Nicole's injury, then the phone lines are down and now this. Mel takes a deep breath and tells herself that there's an innocent explanation. However, the whispering voice at the back of her mind says something completely different.

Someone here knows what you did.

27

The Daily News Online

Sunday 24th June

SHOOTING AT SEA

<u>**Published: 10.55, 24 June**</u>

POLICE have launched a murder inquiry following the fatal Point Grey hotel fire after detectives revealed evidence of a shooting.

Hampshire Police said a "number of bodies" had now been recovered from the remote sea hotel, in the Solent estuary.

In an update posted on its website, the force said there appeared to be evidence that some of the victims – who have not been named – suffered "fatal gun-related injuries". Work is ongoing to formally identify them.

The force had been treating the incident at the historic 150-year-old site as arson. They are receiving intense pressure to reveal the number of fatalities, citing "operation reasons" for remaining tight-lipped.

Hampshire Police said: "We've launched an active murder investigation following events at Point Grey. We are considering multiple lines of enquiry, including that the fire may not have resulted in the deaths of some of those at the hotel.

"There is evidence that some of the victims may have suffered fatal gun-related injuries. Post-mortems will be carried out to determine causes of death. This is a complex case as we are dealing with multiple bodies in challenging conditions. We understand it is distressing for the families and friends of the guests staying at the venue but we are currently unable to provide further details at this point for operational reasons."

The unique venue was being used for a summer party for employees of Buckinghamshire-based creative agency, Flavour.

Seven employees are confirmed to have been staying overnight at the former sea defence, which lies off the Portsmouth coast.

A Flavour spokesperson said: 'As a small company, we are devastated at this latest development. Our thoughts are with those involved. We continue to work closely with the police to assist in any way we can. We ask that if anyone has anything to share with the police they do so via the appropriate channels and not through social media.'

Comments:

Man_U_Dad: Tragic news for all involved. And so soon after what happened to that young graduate too. You don't expect this to happen on a work night out.

Beverley63: A shooting. It wasn't paranormal activity then.

StarfishX: My skinflint boss would never hire out a place like this for one of our nights out. Scrooge.

Kathrynnnnnn: Angels get their wings today 😇. ♡ #PointGreyVictims

The views expressed in the comments above are those of our users and do not necessarily reflect the views of News-Online.

28

Thursday 20th June

'Have you found help?' Nicole asks the moment Mel and Charlie come back into the residents' lounge.

Charlie shakes his head. 'Zander's right. The phone lines are down.'

Mel waits for him to tell the others about tomorrow's boat being cancelled but he doesn't.

'Here, this might help the swelling.' Charlie hands over the bag of frozen garden peas.

Bonnie has made a decent sling; it almost looks professional. Nicole is calmer now, the colour has come back to her cheeks slightly. But that might be thanks to the half-empty glass of whisky by her side.

'I just want to lie down in bed and wait there.' Nicole winces as she moves. 'Mel, will you come and help me get changed?'

Mel nods. She's also desperate to get out of her robe and into normal clothes.

Bonnie yawns. 'If it's ok with everyone, I'm going to call it a night. I'll come with you both.'

The women leave Zander and Charlie in the residents'

146

lounge with a bottle of whisky and instructions to come and get Nicole the moment the night manager shows up.

They wander through the hallway past eerie portraits of Victorian stern-faced soldiers in gilded frames, and past the lounge area where Mel noticed the missing gun earlier. Mel stops herself from pointing it out, she doesn't want to appear paranoid. Gus had told her not to worry. Staff were aware of it. The three women walk down the dark, silent corridor. Without any windows, the motion sensor light casts them in a warm glow, but throws shadows everywhere else. Mel makes sure to stick as close as she can to the others.

She curses the fact that she's been raised on jump scare nineties horror films, which mean her mind is sent into spirals whenever she hears a low creak or catches a flicker of movement in the gloom. You don't know what's lurking in the darkness and her first thought is never rational. Instead, her heartbeat quickens with her steps.

Nicole is cradling her arm and muttering about how she's going to sue the moment she can call a solicitor.

Mel carefully takes the room key from Nicole's robe pocket and opens the door to her bedroom. An icy blast of air hits them the second they step foot inside.

'Jesus,' Nicole gasps. 'It wasn't this cold in here earlier.'

'Ours were freezing when we arrived.' Mel shivers in her robe.

Bonnie says she'll try and adjust the settings whilst Nicole gets changed in the ensuite.

'Call me if you need a hand,' Mel offers through the closed door.

Nicole's bedroom is a little smaller than Mel's. Cans of

pre-mixed mojito cocktails that she must have brought with her are discarded by the flat-screen television. There are a couple of pairs of high heels thrown beside the wardrobe door. A glossy magazine is lying on the floor.

Mel almost steps on it and absently bends down to pick it up. She frowns as she sees what's on the front cover. *What's this doing here?*

It's a slim magazine created for the agency: 'A Flava of Flavour'. It had been another of Rohan's ideas, a way to build employee engagement by showcasing their achievements in print. In this digital age, he wanted something physical that staff could take home, share with their families, hold and touch. It's full of their performance targets, special mentions, shout-outs, etc. – a sort of printed blog. He only did two issues before he realised the costs of producing it were astronomical and most of the copies ended up in the recycling bin.

Mel turns it over in her hands. Is this a gesture from the hotel staff to welcome them here? But why not put a copy in everyone's room? It's a strange touch. And how did they get hold of it in the first place? Unless Nicole brought it with her? But why? This edition has got to be at least a year old.

'How come you brought this?' she asks as Nicole emerges from her ensuite. She's changed into a matching silky blush-pink pyjama set. Wide-leg palazzo trousers and a long-sleeved button-up shirt and piped cuffs. Mel's momentarily distracted by her perfect sleepwear combo.

'That? I didn't bring that. It was already here when I arrived.'

Bonnie looks over from the air-conditioning panel, to find out what the women are discussing. 'What didn't you bring?'

Mel holds up the employee magazine. Bonnie squints to

read the cover, her face blank. 'Maybe the hotel put one in every room?'

'Did you have one in yours?'

'No, not that I remember seeing but then I was too busy trying to get this damn thing to work.'

It's from May last year. Mel turns it over to the open page that it was on. It takes a second for her brain to work out what she's looking at. The familiar headshot image. The name stamped in thick block capitals. 'A Day in the Life of a Graduate: An interview with our newest recruit: Holly Mills.'

A prickle of unease zips up Mel's legs.

'Will you help me with these fiddly buttons please?' Nicole calls, interrupting Mel's thoughts.

Mel drops the magazine onto the perfectly pressed duvet. As she does, something falls out and hits the bedding with a soft thump.

She sees what fell from the pages of the magazine.

'What is this doing in here?' she breathes.

It's the photograph of the VIP guests – the Polaroid that was taken on the quayside. Mel scans the row of bodies. A bolt of ice shoots down her spine.

There's a mark over all the faces, made by a sharp object. Carefully. Precisely. One by one. The viciousness with which the marks were made means they almost leave holes in the paper. You can barely make out who is behind the cuts.

You can barely make out anything.

Every single face is brutally scratched out.

*

'Do you think she'll be ok?' Bonnie asks, gently shutting the door to Nicole's room.

149

Nicole had insisted repeatedly that she had nothing to do with the creepy defaced Polaroid. She had been almost hysterical about it. Once they finally managed to calm her down they left her to rest. Thankfully, Bonnie was able to set the room temperature to an acceptable level. They gave Nicole two paracetamols and helped her into bed, propping her injured arm up with a firm pillow. She looked exhausted.

'Something strange is happening,' Mel whispers.

'It's someone messing about.' Bonnie places a hand over her mouth and stifles a yawn. 'One of our other colleagues who had to leave, jealous about not being chosen to stay, that's all, don't worry.'

Mel wraps her arms around herself. 'I'd feel a hell of a lot better if we could speak to the night manager and call for help, especially as . . .' She pauses.

'As what?' Bonnie frowns.

Mel can't get the cancelled boat out of her mind.

'Well, there was something Charlie and I saw at reception. Perhaps it's nothing . . .' She takes a breath. 'According to the reservation system there's no return boat tomorrow. In fact, there's nothing in the diary for the whole of next week.'

Bonnie frowns, confused.

'It's weird, isn't it?' Mel says. She can't shake the unease building in her chest.

'Err yeah. I guess. Why didn't you say anything before?'

'Charlie thought it was nothing. A simple error. Perhaps I'm getting ahead of myself, worrying for no reason.'

Bonnie nods. 'It's got to be a mistake.'

Mel smiles but she's not as convinced. A yawn escapes.

Clearly, the night has come to an end . . . and not the way she wanted it. 'Right, well, night.'

There's a beat of silence.

'I don't feel comfortable going to bed and leaving Nicole without anyone checking in on her,' Bonnie says, chewing on a nail. 'I think we should go and look for the night manager. Will you come with me?'

'Oh, erm . . .' Mel stalls, her bedroom key in her hand. She wants to change into her pyjamas and lie down. To leave this night – and all of its drama – behind her.

'Please. I know you're tired but you said yourself that there are a few strange things that have been happening. I don't think I'll be able to sleep until I know what's going on.'

Mel doesn't want to roam the hotel looking for the night manager. It's dark, it's late, it's allegedly haunted and she's exhausted. But then, Bonnie's right, it's unfair to leave the others to look after Nicole. They should at least try and find out where this Edward guy is.

'Ok,' Mel says eventually. 'Should we get Charlie and Zander to come with us?'

'Why?' Bonnie asks.

Mel doesn't have an answer for that. She wants to say, 'Because it will make me feel less scared', but she knows that sounds pathetic. 'Ok. But let me get changed first.'

In her bedroom, as she takes off her swimwear and hurries back into her party dress, she tells herself that the phone lines are down because it's an old building. That the hot tub had a malfunction. That the boat cancellation is just a typo and that sinister Polaroid photo was done by someone messing about.

Yet, she's not sure she fully believes her excuses.

29

Thursday 20th June

Mel and Bonnie move silently past empty alcoves and deserted corridors. The only sound is their footsteps descending the stone steps, leading to the lower level where Gus took them on his tour. A sign reading 'Staff Only' separates it from the rest of the hotel. Mel tries to push away the sudden flutter of panic as the light changes, the brightness dims and the air turns colder. There's a strong smell of damp, rotten timber. It must be from the moss emerging in the cracks of exposed bricks. Clearly, the interior design budget went to the areas that guests use.

Mel can't help but feel that they shouldn't be here on their own.

'The night manager must be around here. I mean, imagine how old the phone lines are in this place,' Bonnie says. 'Once the phones are fixed we can call for help, sort Nicole out and go to bed.'

'What about the photograph?' Mel asks, shivering, picturing the ferocious scratches covering their smiling faces on the team Polaroid. 'Who would do such a thing?'

'Ach. I didn't want to say anything before . . . And I don't want this to sound like I'm blaming Nicole, but . . .' She takes a breath. 'At the party, I saw her show off her bedroom to loads of the younger lassies, rubbing their noses in it that she gets to stay and they don't.'

Classic Nicole. Mel can easily imagine her doing that.

'All it takes is for one of them to be jealous and leave it as a mean joke, you know?' Bonnie suggests.

They move past whitewashed brick alcoves and faded signs nailed to wooden doors. There are more hooks in the ceiling, but unlike the ones in her bedroom, these are threaded with thick cobwebs.

Mel remembers what Gus said about the supposed presence that haunts these corridors. She and Bonnie are now in the exact same place where he told the story about George the ghost. Her brain conjures up images that don't exist. A mutilated soldier stepping through the brick wall. A wailing scream. A sudden face thrust in front of hers. She wants to squish her eyes shut. Her legs tremble, willing her to head back to the safety of her bedroom.

'You ok, hen?' Bonnie asks. She's a couple of paces ahead of Mel.

She wraps her arms around herself and tries to keep it together. 'Yep, fine.'

Creepy dust sheets are thrown over jumbled pieces of furniture that she didn't notice on the earlier tour. It's not so much the sight of these ghostly objects but the shadows hiding further back in the alcoves that sends a shiver through her. From somewhere behind them comes a low creak. Mel tells herself it's the pipes, yet she quickens her pace.

153

'Ned said the staff rooms were around here, I think,' Mel says, praying they will soon get out of here.

Bonnie has stopped in front of a closed door. She raps a hand against the wood. Mel holds her breath. She can't hear anything except her heart beating and a faint dripping coming from further down the dimly lit corridor. Mel catches Bonnie's eye. She smiles tightly. She knocks again but there's still no answer.

Mel's head twitches with the sense of being watched, as if someone is behind them.

Come on, come on. Where the hell is this guy?

Bonnie moves to a different door and goes to knock it but when her hand makes contact the door swings open. It isn't locked.

'Oh . . .' She steps inside.

The room is lit by a single bulb. There are no windows. It's worse than a prison cell. There is a single bed pushed against the whitewashed stone wall. A framed abstract print hangs above a wicker headboard. A football scarf is draped across the top of a cheap IKEA wardrobe. There's a stack of note-pads and a dusty alarm clock that's showing the wrong time. On the desk is an empty Pot Noodle, half a bottle of mineral water and a couple of cans of budget men's deodorant. It smells of unwashed feet and damp ceilings.

'God,' Bonnie pinches her nose with her fingers, 'it's honkin' like my son's teenage bedroom in here.'

There's a tiny plug-in fan heater in the corner of the room and a couple of pairs of well-worn trainers lined up against the grubby skirting board. Mel shivers and rubs her arms around her for warmth. The decor is so different to the hotel guest bedrooms. The drastic contrast between opulence and cheap is unnerving.

'This must be the night manager's bedroom,' Mel says, pointing to the cork pinboard at the photo of Edward with an older man. It looks like it was taken recently. They're standing beside a lake proudly brandishing a large glistening fish.

On the desk, there's a washed-out soup can holding a selection of pens, next to a photo of a school-age boy and girl, both in their swimwear, sitting on a pebble-filled beach. The photo has faded with time, but you can make out that they share the same red hair and matching wide blue eyes. They're waving to someone off-camera. Not a care in the world. There's also a selection of loose change, a scrunched-up ten-pound note and some bank cards.

Mel picks one up. 'Oh my God.'

'What?' Bonnie asks, her nose still scrunched up at the smell.

Mel exhales slowly, 'Edward Mills.'

It's as if someone has placed an ice cube down her spine. Her mind whirs ten paces ahead of her.

'I don't understand?' Bonnie says, frowning at the bank card Mel is holding out.

'The night manager, Edward, has the same surname as Holly.'

'Well, I suppose it's a common name,' Bonnie says.

'No, they're related. I'm certain. Same eyes, same face shape. I thought I'd seen him before and now I remember why he looked familiar. He was at Holly's funeral.' *That's* where she remembers him from – not lurking outside the office, like Wesley insisted. She can picture him clearly now. He was stood at the front of the church, talking to the priest, shoulders hunched, the weight of grief visible on every part of his body. Back then he was a different person, wrung out and translucent, guiding an older man – the grandad – out to a waiting black car.

'Are you sure?' Bonnie frowns.

Mel nods. What are the chances that Holly's brother is in charge of them all overnight? Does he know his sister used to work at Flavour? Or that her colleagues were probably the last people she spoke to before she died?

'Well, it doesn't look like he's here,' Bonnie says, moving towards the doorway. 'What are we going to do about Nicole's arm?'

'I have no idea.'

Mel looks around for a phone. There are sheets of paper, piles of them, as if torn from a pad, cluttering the messy desk. Mel picks up a piece that's covered in crude drawings made with pencil-thin lines. Some of them are deeply disturbing. Bonnie pulls a face as Mel shows her one of a bleeding mouth, twisted in agony from a dagger thrust into the throat.

'That's so creepy.' She looks a little scared. She sweeps her eyes over the cluttered mess, swearing under her breath.

'What?' Mel asks.

Bonnie points to two small bags containing white powder that looks suspiciously like drugs, half-tucked under a brochure for the hotel.

There's an order of service for a man named Graham Mills, along with a photograph. It's the old man Mel had seen at Holly's funeral. *'Loving grandad and friend to all.'* He died three months ago. Edward Mills is listed as doing a reading at the church service.

'He's lost his grandad and his sister within six months,' Mel says, passing the card to Bonnie to read.

Mel takes one last look around the depressing room. *If he's not here, where is he?*

'Come on, let's get out of here,' Bonnie turns. 'He's got to be somewhere else.'

Mel is about to follow her out but something catches her eye. Underneath the drawings is an article roughly torn from a newspaper. Mel grips the jagged edges. She starts to read. A sickening sensation deepens in the pit of her stomach.

It's a newspaper article. A piece about Holly's inquest results. They've used Holly's headshot from Flavour's website. Mel remembers reading the same article online a few weeks ago, but instead of feeling unbearably sad, like she did then, there's something unsettling about seeing it again now. Here. In this depressingly dirty single room. On this remote hotel island. Cut off from the rest of the world.

A shiver dances down her spine as she stares at the page.

Something has been scrawled in pen over the top. Red ink bleeds through the newspaper.

A single word.

In thick block angry capitals, it reads: LIARS.

30

Tuesday 04 June

YOUNG GRADUATE FROZE TO DEATH ON WORK NIGHT OUT

London Daily Standard

A GRADUATE died from hypothermia after walking home from a work Christmas party on one of the coldest nights of the year, an inquest has heard.

Holly Mills, 23, was discovered partially covered in snow in Ashdale Woods, Marlow, after attending a company night-out on December 22 last year.

Her inquest was told that she died in temperatures of -5 Celsius after "becoming confused" while attempting to take a shortcut home.

Assistant Coroner Martin Moore recorded a verdict of 'accidental death' following a two-day hearing at Buckinghamshire Coroners Court in Beaconsfield.

The court heard that Ms Mills had been walking barefoot while wearing a thin, knee-length dress, on the night in question, when temperatures had plunged to eight-year lows across southern England.

Mr Moore said: 'There was evidence Holly had died because she became hypothermic as a result of being exposed on an extremely cold night.

158

There is nothing in this terrible sequence of events to lead me to the conclusion other than this was an accidental death and I hope that lessons will be learnt by young people, and that they will take heed of the tragic circumstances in which Holly died.'

Ms Mills was discovered by a dog walker hours after she was last seen at the Christmas party of her employer, Flavour Creative Design, at the Plaza Hotel in Marlow.

CCTV shown to the inquest captured Holly walking unsteadily away from the venue alone just after midnight.

She was found shortly after 9am. Emergency services were called to the scene where Ms Mills was pronounced dead.

Toxicology tests revealed her blood alcohol level was 173 microgrammes of alcohol in 100 millilitres of blood. The legal limit for driving is 80mg.

Pathologist Dr Priti Lau gave the cause of death as hypothermia and acute alcohol intoxication and said it was difficult to determine precisely when Holly had died.

Thames Valley Police said there were no suspicious circumstances and described the incident as a 'tragic accident'.

Her family, speaking through solicitor Arnold Morris, paid tribute to Ms Mills. They said: 'Our hearts will forever be broken as we try to come to terms with her sudden death. We cannot comprehend or accept life without her, and our world will never be the same again.'

A spokesperson for Flavour said: 'Our thoughts and deepest sympathy are with the family and Holly's loved ones. She was a rising star within our company after joining the graduate scheme just seven months before she died. We are shocked and devastated at her death.'

31

Thursday 20th June

Mel and Bonnie have called the others to the residents' lounge. Charlie and Zander pause their animated conversation about metrics and KPI's and top up their whisky glasses. Mel's heart thrums in her chest after racing up the stairs from the creepy lower level.

'Have you managed to get help for my arm?' Nicole asks, cradling her sling on the far sofa. They'd helped her out of bed, telling her they'd explain what was going on when everyone was together.

There's an awkward silence.

Bonnie stands up and starts to speak. 'We've discovered that—'

Zander interrupts. 'Hang on. Shouldn't we wait for Wesley and Jonty?'

'Yes, we probably should,' Mel says. Bonnie sits back down.

'Do you want me to go and try their rooms?' Charlie gets to his feet and goes to wake them up.

Nicole asks if they've found the night manager. All Mel can do is shake her head. She's trying to work out what it means.

160

Bonnie has gone even quieter than normal. She offers to get drinks, passing out bottles of mineral water, clearly wanting to do something whilst waiting to reveal the news.

Edward is Holly's brother.

LIARS.

It runs on repeat in Mel's mind.

They hear a rhythmic pounding on the bedroom doors. Charlie calls Jonty and Wesley's names. She wishes they would hurry up. Something is happening tonight that's starting to panic her.

'Maybe he's got earplugs in?' Zander says.

'Maybe . . .' Dread lies heavy in the pit of Mel's stomach.

She takes a sip of water. Her hand trembles as she puts down the glass. Neither of them are answering. Where are they? What's taking them so long?

'I bet Wesley has passed out. I mean, you all saw the state of him. I reckon he's—'

'GUYS,' Charlie yells, interrupting Zander. 'I need help!'

Mel's heart skips a beat at the fear in his voice. Bonnie and Mel share a wide-eyed look between them. Zander is first out of the room, the women not far behind. They sprint to the bedrooms.

The door to Wesley's room is wide open.

The covers on the large king-sized bed are messy, as though it's been slept in. His clothes are strewn across the floor. There is a strange smell in the air, but Mel can't put her finger on what it is.

She shivers as the chill of the air-conditioning hits her. It's been set extremely low, like it was in her room and Bonnie's room and Nicole's room.

'Wesley? Wesley?' Charlie yells. The intensity in his voice makes her stomach turn.

Her heartbeat thrums with each step closer to the closed ensuite.

Charlie swears loudly, pleading for a response, but from behind the bathroom door Wesley remains silent.

Mel doesn't know who managed to open the door. What she will never forget, however, is what she sees when she rushes in.

Breath catches in her lungs.

No.

Bile leaps into the back of her throat at the scene in the bathroom.

Oh, God. No.

Zander gasps. 'Is he d-d-dead?'

The whole room tilts.

Wesley is topless, slumped beside the toilet bowl, lying awkwardly on his back. His legs are bent, and his arms are flailed to the side. There is vomit puddled on the floor beside his limp body. A fuzziness seeps around the edges of Mel's mind. She clamps her fingers against her nostrils, blocking out the terrible smell. Her stomach painfully clenches with nausea.

Charlie has a hand against Wesley's neck, his fingers below a shaving rash. Under the bright bathroom lights, Wesley's blotchy skin has a sort of blue tinge.

His eyes are blank.

Bonnie screams, throwing a hand to her mouth, muffling the sound. Shock is stamped on Zander and Nicole's pale faces. One of them starts hyperventilating. A rush of light-headedness makes Mel's legs tremble. *This isn't happening. This isn't happening.*

Wesley lets out a low, pained groan.

'He's alive,' Charlie yells. 'Wesley, Wesley, can you hear me, mate?'

The next few moments are sheer panic and confusion.

'Turn him on his side. Quick!' Mel orders.

Charlie grabs Wesley and pushes him into the recovery position, his limbs flailing like a ragdoll's. Mel drops to her knees and thrusts the fingers of her right hand in his mouth to clear the airways, scooping out vomit, retching at the smell. Chunks of food from their dinner splatter to the tiles. The groaning sound has stopped. Now there's just the raspy trapped breath that's lodged in his throat. It's a sound that's hard to describe but she knows she'll never forget.

'Come on, Wesley. It's ok,' she soothes.

The stench of vomit splattered across his bare chest burns her nose. He is cold and clammy to the touch, like a packaged chicken pulled straight from the fridge.

'Wes, Wesley mate, can you hear us?' Charlie pants.

There's another gurgled sort of breath. Wesley's lips – the colour of blue marble – part. She presses her ear closer to try and make out what he's trying to say.

'Grrnnn.'

'What? I don't know what that is? Try again for me, Wesley?'

If he's trying to talk, trying to tell her something, that's a good sign, surely? For a brief second, she allows herself hope that somehow everything will be ok.

Wishful thinking.

'Grrnn Chrrlll.' He sounds like a drunk trying to talk underwater. White, frothy saliva dribbles down his lips.

'What's he saying?' Charlie is looking at her, eyes wide and darting about.

'I can't make anything out,' Mel swears. 'Someone call for help,' she shouts to the others.

'We can't, remember?' Zander yells from the doorway. Nicole and Bonnie are staring at the scene from behind him, holding one another up.

Charlie and Mel's eyes meet. This is pointless. They both know it. Wesley is getting limper. His breath slows, the sounds he makes raspy and strained.

Someone is crying in the background. A murmur of voices rolls around her. Mel tries to hold herself together. Charlie is still calling his name but Wesley's bloodshot eyes have a far-away stare. Mel cradles her injured wrist to her chest and leans her shaking right arm out to the sink to stop herself from collapsing.

'Stick your fingers down his throat. We need to make him sick again,' Mel cries.

But Charlie is shaking his head.

'He's gone, it's too late,' he says, sniffing back tears.

'Oh my God.' Bonnie spins, banging into a tall lamp in her haste.

Zander and Nicole are frozen to the spot in the doorway, looking on in horror.

Mel presses her trembling fingers to Wesley's cool neck.

Not a beat or flicker of life. She moves them around, trying to summon a non-existent pulse, willing him to come back.

But Charlie's right.

It's too late.

32

Friday 21st June

Someone has closed the door to Wesley's ensuite as a mark of respect. Before they left the room, Charlie covered him under a hotel-branded fluffy bath sheet. Bonnie and Nicole are on the king-sized bed, looking as white as the bedsheets. Zander has slumped to the chaise longue under the window, his head in his hands. Charlie is pacing back and forth across the bedroom. Mel rests against the cold brick wall and stares at the footprints he leaves in the plush carpet. Her breath is coming out too fast.

A clock chimes twelve. Midnight.

Wesley is dead. Twenty-six years old. The world at his feet. Dead.

'I can't believe it. It's not possible.' Zander sniffs the tears away. 'What the hell are we going to tell Rohan?'

'Rohan? You mean Wesley's family,' Charlie says.

'Yeah, I know, I'm thinking, well . . . another party, another death . . .' He trails out.

Despite the bathroom door being closed, the stomach-churning smell hangs in the air. Mel wishes she could scrub

165

herself clean but shock settles in her bones, pinning her to the ground.

'How the hell has this happened?' Nicole presses her thumbs to her temple. 'Charlie, you were the last one to see him alive. You took him to bed. How was he when you left him?'

'He was slurring his words but I figured he was high. I mean, you saw how drunk he was. I didn't expect this though. I'd never have left him if I thought he'd choke on his own vomit.'

Tears stream down his cheeks.

Mel wants to comfort him, let him know he's not to blame but she can't move.

'The PR is going to be terrible,' Nicole sniffs.

'What? Is that what you're really thinking of right now?' Charlie snaps. 'Have some respect.'

'Of course not. My head is everywhere, I can't believe it. I'm in shock like the rest of you. But we're going to have some questions to answer when the police get involved.'

'Police?' Mel looks up.

'Well yeah, a man has died.'

'He choked on his vomit . . . Why would the police need to get involved?'

'Because that's what happens. Until there's been an autopsy we don't know *exactly* how he died.'

Bonnie holds up a hand. 'Hang on, we need to go back. Charlie, you took him to his bedroom and then what?'

Charlie strides to the mini fridge and pulls the lid off a bottle of Coke, taking fast gulps of it. He wipes his mouth before he answers. 'I helped him take his shoes off.' He turns to the door, where they can all see that Wesley's designer trainers have been kicked to the side. 'He was babbling non-sense, singing football chants, just being drunk and annoying. He took his top off.'

They look where he's pointing. Wesley's shirt is lying crumpled in the corner.

'He got into bed, still in his trousers, and rolled over, mum-bling nonsense. I put a bottle of water on the bedside table.' The unopened mineral water is right where Charlie says he left it. 'And then I went back to join the rest of you ... Oh, first I went to the kitchen to get some frozen peas for Nicole's arm, thought it might help with the swelling, and I saw Mel at the reception where she was checking to see if the phones worked.'

'Now what do we do?' Zander picks up the phone on the bedside table, holds it to his ear for a second then slams it down in frustration. 'It's still not working. We need the night manager.'

Mel swallows.

'Err, so, we have some news about him . . .' Bonnie says, in a low voice, catching Mel's eye.

'We need to tell you about what we discovered in his room.' Mel's chest is tight.

'You went to his room?' Charlie stares at her.

'What? Has something else happened? I thought you said you haven't seen him,' Nicole asks, sitting up taller, cradling her arm.

Mel reaches into her pocket and unfolds the article they found in Edward's room.

'The night manager, Edward, he's . . . Holly's brother.'

A collective gasp and bewildered murmurs fill her ears.

With a trembling hand, she passes the newspaper cutting

around the group. A chill runs through her at the ferocity of the letters scribbled over the page. LIARS. It grows so quiet in the room that you can hear the waves slamming the concrete below. One by one, confusion tinged with uncertainty flashes across their faces.

'Are you sure? Just because they share the same surname? I mean, she had blonde hair, for one . . .' Charlie frowns.

'Obviously, she dyed it,' Mel says. 'I don't know how I didn't see the likeness earlier. He was the one who helped bandage my wrist.'

Her injury feels a lifetime ago.

'It has to be a coincidence. What are the chances that he's working here on the night of our summer party?' Charlie shakes his head.

'This is Holly's brother. I'm sure of it. I saw him at her funeral,' Mel says, frustrated that they don't believe her. Especially Charlie.

'Didn't Wesley say he saw him lurking around the office?' Nicole asks.

'Yeah, he did,' Zander gasps. 'Shit, what does that mean? Has he been stalking us?'

'Right, let's not get carried away. If he is related to Holly that doesn't mean anything ominous,' Bonnie says.

Mel clenches her jaw at the word *if*.

'Bonnie's right,' Charlie says, missing the look of surprise on Bonnie's face that he's backing her up. 'I mean, come on . . . if he is her brother he's probably grieving and expressing himself,' he adds, nodding to the graffitied newspaper cutting.

'But isn't it dodgy that he's here, especially after the strange

168

things that have been happening? It's got to be linked to our cancelled boat home—' Mel starts.

'Wait – what?' Nicole's eyes widen.

'When Charlie and I were looking for the phone at reception we discovered that according to the reservation system there are no boats scheduled to come to the hotel.'

'Why didn't you tell us that before?' Zander turns and asks Charlie directly.

'I didn't think it was important. Clearly, it's a mistake,' Charlie says.

'This might be some sick joke – leaving us stranded, to teach us a lesson? He clearly thinks that's what we did to Holly, that we abandoned her. What if we don't get off this place?' Nicole's words tumble out in a panic.

'Come on now, we're not going to be left here forever,' Charlie replies.

Zander takes off his glasses and rubs his eyes. 'So hang on, let me get this straight. The phones aren't working so we can't call for help, and apparently the boat isn't coming to get us in the morning as planned. There's also a guy who may, or may not be, a grieving relative with a serious grudge in charge and more importantly, Wesley is dead.'

'And someone sabotaged the hot tub and I've broken my arm!' Nicole adds.

'That was an accident. We don't know if it is broken, hen,' Bonnie speaks up.

'An accident? Oh, was it? Because plenty of things are not feeling very accidental right now,' Nicole snaps. 'What about the Polaroid photograph and the bloody staff magazine?'

'What is she talking about?' Zander asks.

'What photo?' Charlie asks.

Bonnie rummages in the pockets on her dress. Mel didn't realise she'd picked it up from Nicole's room. It's been such a blur. Time has slowed down and sped up at once. 'This.'

She passes the defaced Polaroid around the group. What they had believed to be a harmless prank is actually seriously twisted and possibly connected to everything else that has been going wrong.

'Who went into my room?' Zander asks, pulling himself up. 'This was in my bag.'

'Edward must have done it,' Charlie says, dropping his voice, starting to finally look concerned. 'He has the keys to every room.'

'But why?' Mel shivers as the ominous photograph is passed to her.

The silence speaks volumes.

'Did anyone else have a copy of *Flava* in their bedroom? This was tucked inside,' Nicole asks.

Mel remembers how the magazine was purposely folded open to the interview with Holly.

Zander picks up the newspaper cutting. 'What the hell does he mean – liars? Who is he calling liars? Us? The police? The coroner?'

'Who knows.' Bonnie shakes her head slowly. 'It's easier said than done but we all need to stay calm.'

'And if it *is* us, what does he think we lied about?' Zander repeats, ignoring Bonnie.

Nicole winces as she moves her arm slightly. 'Dominique told me that Holly . . . well, that she didn't walk to the woods by herself. No chance she could have got all that way alone. Someone put her there.' Her voice is small.

Mel sits up straighter. This is what Dominique said to her over pre-dinner drinks, she thought she had told her this in confidence. Clearly she has been working the room with this theory.

'I heard that too. No one knows for sure if someone gave her a lift that night.' Zander raises an eyebrow.

'Maybe that's what he means? He thinks one of us *knows* what happened to his sister,' Bonnie says.

'Well? Does anyone know anything?' Zander asks. 'Speak now or forever hold your peace.'

Mel freezes. Is it time for her to finally be honest?

Silence stretches out in the cool room.

Tell them what you did.

Confess.

She bites down on her bottom lip so hard that it hurts.

'I want to go home now.' Nicole's eyes are glassy with unshed tears.

Mel holds her breath. She can't admit what she did. How would she find the words to explain the part she played in Holly's death?

'See, we're all innocent.' Zander raises his arms in the air. 'Everything will be fine.'

Charlie holds up a hand. He's been quiet, taking everything in. 'So this guy is, like, wandering around the hotel some-where?'

'And he's planning on keeping us here . . .' Nicole is crying now.

'No one is keeping us here. We've got families and loved

ones who will miss us. We've got work, for God's sake. Don't you think the alarm would be raised if none of us showed up on Monday?' Charlie says, pacing. 'Bonnie's right. Let's not get carried away.'

'So you're not worried about this guy?' Mel asks him.

Charlie shakes his head firmly. 'No.'

'I need to see a doctor. Honestly, I can't describe to you how much this hurts,' Nicole says, wiping her tears on the sleeve of her pyjama top. 'And what are we going to do about Wesley?'

'He's dead. There's nothing we can do,' Zander says. 'Don't look at me like that, I know it sounds harsh but it's true.'

For a couple of minutes, the whir of the air-conditioning and sniffing back of tears is the only sound in Wesley's bedroom, as they each try to make sense of what's happened.

'Has anything else strange happened to anyone tonight?' Zander asks.

A bolt of adrenaline makes Mel's legs tremble. She raises an arm. If she's not ready to be honest about her part in Holly's death she can at least be honest about what's been happening here.

'I found Holly's perfume in my ensuite earlier. Well, not her actual perfume, the type she used to wear.' They turn to face her. 'Judging by the looks on your faces, I take it no one else did?'

'Do you also think Edward had something to do with the hot tub being a thousand degrees?' Nicole asks, dabbing her eyes.

Zander gets to his feet and glances at the closed bathroom door. 'What if this isn't an accident or coincidence?'

172

They turn to face him. 'What do you mean?' Mel asks, hesitantly.

'You've all heard the rumour that we were specifically chosen to be here? Right? That it wasn't the random *names from a hat* we were initially told it was?'

Mel remembers the comments at dinner about the VIPs being chosen for a reason.

'Well, what if Holly's brother is like, out for revenge? He's calling *us* liars.' He clears his throat, nodding to the newspaper clipping and the Polaroid photo.

'I think you're getting carried away.' Charlie makes a sound between his lips. 'Just because this guy thinks we're "liars",' he says, using his fingers as air quotes, 'doesn't mean he's out for revenge. The hot tub was hot. These things in your rooms are either coincidental or one of our other colleagues left them because they're jealous. I mean, why would anyone want to hurt Wesley on purpose? He was absolutely smashed and choked on his own vomit. It's tragic but accidents happen.' His chest rises and falls rapidly. 'Let's not lose our heads. Whatshisname must be fixing the phones, and if he's Holly's brother it doesn't mean anything dodgy. We're getting ahead of ourselves.'

'Hang on, we're forgetting someone . . . Where's Jonty? He could have done this.' Zander points to the photograph. 'It's his sort of humour.'

'Where *is* Jonty?' Nicole asks.

In the wake of everything that has happened, they've forgotten about him until now.

'The last time I saw him was when I was coming to the hot tub,' Mel says. 'But that was probably over an hour ago.'

And he said not to trust anyone, she remembers with a strange pull in her stomach.

'I don't know if he's in his room or not. He wasn't answering when I tried to get him and Wesley up,' Charlie says.

Zander folds his arms. 'If he's not in his room he'll be wrecking his lungs up on the roof terrace.'

'Still?' Mel chews her lip. 'Come on, let's go.'

'I can't face moving again, it's too painful,' Nicole says.

'You stay here,' Mel says.

'I'm not staying here with a dead body,' Nicole looks horrified at the suggestion.

'Well wait in the residents' lounge then. Whatever,' Zander snaps. 'Come on, let's get a move on.'

'While we're up there I think we should go and try our phones. Surely one of us will get a signal?' Mel suggests as they get to their feet. 'We're on different networks. And even if we just get one bar, that will be enough to call for help and speak to the police and find out what to do.'

Mel would feel a hell of a lot calmer if someone on the outside knew what they were dealing with.

'Great idea, Mel.' Charlie smiles at her. Normally this simple gesture would have her melting at his feet, buoyed by his validation, but she's irritated that he dismissed her belief that Edward and Holly are related so quickly.

On their way out of Wesley's bedroom, Mel sees an empty bottle of expensive Champagne sitting in a gleaming silver ice bucket, a starched white cloth folded over the edge to catch any drips. 'With our compliments' the printed note reads. It's tucked into the fold of the cloth. They must have rushed past it earlier.

'Wesley ordered room service?' Mel asks.

'That wasn't here when I put him to bed.' Charlie's eyes widen.

'Hang on, so that means the night manager has been here?' Bonnie tries to keep her voice measured but you can tell by her expression that she's struggling to remain calm.

A sudden heavy silence passes through the group.

'What were you saying about Edward being out for revenge? This is no accident,' Zander whispers, pointing to the bottle.

They all lean closer to it. The floor tilts. Someone swears.

There is crushed white powder around the lip.

33

Friday 21st June

Bonnie offers to stay with Nicole and take her to the residents' lounge. Everyone else grabs their phones and goes up to the roof terrace. Mel gulps at the dry night air – it smells like a sun-baked pavement – relieved to be outside. It felt like the walls were pressing in on her.

There is a slight breeze rustling through the reeds in the glazed planters. The strings of illuminated bulbs sway as if pushed by a phantom hand. But it's still exceptionally close. Something needs to break the pressure. It reminds Mel of staying up late, camping near the beach when she was young. Her dad would tell ghost stories while she pulled her sleeping bag around her head, burrowing away, blocking his words out. Her mum was the opposite. She always wanted to hear the ending. She was never afraid of anything. Mel is grateful to be reminded of these childhood memories amidst the panic that rolls over her.

Wesley's pained face flickers into view every time she closes her eyes.

What was the powder clinging to the edge of the bottle?

176

Who put it there? Was it the same powder from those tiny bags they found in Edward's room?

A rush of goosebumps spreads across her bare arms despite the warmth. Shock is settling in. The blankets beside the hot tub that Mel and Charlie sat on have been neatly folded.

'Edward has been out here at some point,' Mel says as she nods at the pile.

There's no sign of Jonty.

They peel off into separate areas: the bar, the hot tub area, the lighthouse, the edge of the fort walls. Arms raised to try and summon a signal to their collection of mobile phones. Mel catches sight of the image on her phone screen, it's one of her treasured photos of her and her mum, taken a few years ago on her birthday. A sudden longing to be back home over-whelms her. She pictures her mum, tucked up in bed, oblivious to what her only daughter is going through. To think, Leonora told her to enjoy herself. What a story she's going to have for her when they get off this place. *If they get off,* a voice at the back of her mind whispers ominously. She swallows, brushing it away.

'Anything?' they shout across the dark space to one another.

'No. You?'

'No. Zander?'

He's got the latest iPhone but it makes no difference. He shakes his head.

Charlie swears. 'Now what? We've got to find this guy.'

'And then what?' Zander asks, hands on his hips. 'What are you expecting to do, hey?'

Mel frowns, certain she can hear something. Over the sound of the waves crashing and the breeze rushing through

177

the potted palms, there's definitely another distinct noise. A slow methodical creak on a hinge. She steps away from the men arguing about what to do.

'Can anyone hear that?' she asks.

Neither of them is listening to her.

She notices the door to the wine cellar is half open, banging against the breeze that seems to be getting stronger. Jonty's packet of cigarettes is lying on a table nearby. His green lighter resting to the side of it.

'Did you go in here?' she calls over to Zander, pointing to the wine cellar.

He must have. He had two bottles in his arms when he found them in the residents' lounge after Nicole's fall. That was ages ago now. Tiredness envelops her. So much has happened since their other colleagues left. For one, Wesley was still alive. She shivers, remembering his limp, mottled body on the cold bathroom tiles.

The chalky powder residue on the lip of the bottle can't be explained. If Wesley was using something stronger than weed, why would he pour it into a bottle of Dom Pérignon? Someone else must have drugged him. Poisoned him. Those small bags full of white powder they saw in Edward's room zooms to the front of her mind. Until all the guests can be accounted for, there remain too many unanswered questions. It's the first time in her life that she's actually desperate to see Jonty and check he's ok.

'Zander?' she calls again.

Zander and Charlie are on the other side of the roof terrace, still arguing.

They must not have heard her.

She's about to shut the door when she realises there is a light on inside. The wooden door scrapes across the tiled floor once again. The sound shoots through her.

'Guys?' She waves her arms to try and catch their attention. Zander says something to Charlie and they start to head towards her.

The 'wine cellar' is more like a small bar. The narrow space is lit by dim bulbs in black gothic candle holders. Gus's ghost story rushes back as she steps inside. If there was ever a perfect setting for an apparition this would be it – the exposed crumbling brick, the faint smell of damp and briny water, the clunk of pipes, and the lone woman. More sinister hooks are bolted to the ceiling, menacing twisted clumps of iron hanging over her head.

Come on, Mel.

Uneven sandy-coloured bricks curve around what must be the centre of the fort. She remembers that Gus told them about the well that runs through the middle of this old building.

There are wooden shelves made up from wine crates stacked upon one another. A small bar area is tucked away at the back, unwashed wine glasses lined up, waiting to be cleaned. A couple of bar stools, in the shape of giant corks, sit under the bar top. There are no windows. The thing that surprises her the most is how utterly silent it is.

The quietness is unnerving.

'Hello?' she calls. Her voice is reed-thin.

Dust from the many vintage bottles makes her sneeze. The sound echoes.

179

There is a really strong smell. It must be the wood shavings, discarded corks and spilt rich red wine . . . but also something metallic.

The air is different here, staler. She takes one step further in. A rusty smell fills her nose, like someone has opened a jar full of copper pennies. She rubs her arms. Where are the others? She thought they were coming over. A wine fridge lets out a low humming noise.

She takes another step.

There is no one here. She turns to leave, relieved to get out of here when she sees something out of the corner of her eye. Her weight shifts on the ancient floorboard.

Creak.

She takes a step towards it.

Another louder creak.

Is that blood?

She freezes.

Zander and Charlie's voices grow louder from somewhere outside the room. They call her name and ask if she's ok but Mel can't reply.

Everything is distorted, even the sudden buzzing sound in her ears. She swallows sharply. Unable to take her eyes off the blood.

So much blood. Thick and syrupy blood.

This can't be happening.

'Mel? Are you ok?' Charlie shouts, alarm building in his voice at her continuing silence.

Clunks and thumps from hidden pipes bounce off the bricks around her. All she can do is try and control her breathing and not pass out. Heavy sounds of footsteps echo around the space as the men run in.

And then freeze.

'Is that? Oh fuck, is that . . .' Charlie can't finish his sentence, stopping still when he sees what Mel is looking at.

Her throat is clogged with fear. She can't begin to find any words to describe the scene in front of her eyes.

All she can do is lift up a trembling arm and point at the dead body.

34

Sunday 23rd June

Hampshire Constabulary: Interview started at 13.22

Officer O'Neal: For the purpose of the tape, please state your name and occupation.

Witness: Err, yeah. I'm Kirsten Jennifer Marie Brown. I work as a server on Point Grey.

OON: Thanks so much for coming down today. We appreciate your time.

KB: My DMs are on fire. Oh, God. Sorry. Not literally! I just mean that I've had loads of messages from journalists begging me to talk to them. I've told them all to F off. I'm not talking unless they want to pay.

OON: We would strongly encourage you not to communicate with any journalists directly especially as this is an ongoing investigation. If members of the media wish to interview you then we would suggest going through the Point Grey press team.

KB: Don't worry. I've not replied. Everyone I know's been posting about the shooting on TikTok. It's mad. I keep telling my mates that I work there. I mean, there have been times when I've wanted to set fire to the hotel . . . I'm joking, you know. We all have bad days at work, don't we? But I never imagined in a million years it actually would happen. Although, I'm not surprised. The whole place is filled with so much crap. History crap. Turning it into a sort of museum. The American guests love it but I hate the extra dusting we have to do at the start of our shifts. It wouldn't be difficult to set fire to the place. The smoke alarms probably never worked. It is crumbling to pieces in places. The staff rooms are a joke. If the paying guests could see the state of what it's like behind the scenes they'd get a shock.

Detective Inspector Hutchinson:	Please take a breath.
KB:	Sorry. I get nervous around the police . . .
DIH:	Well, you're not in any trouble. We want to get a round view of what might have happened from those who were there.
KB:	Yeah. Sweet. When do you reckon the hotel will open again? There are loads of weddings that are booked in. Gus is going to be gutted.
OON:	We don't yet know the structural damage the fire has caused. I'm sure your manager will let you know in due course how things will proceed. Now, you said to one of my colleagues that you wanted to talk to us about the manager. You have some concerns about Mr Raynor, is that correct?
KB:	Gus? No.
DIH:	He's the manager?
KB:	Yeah, but he's the best boss I've ever worked for. It's cash in hand, which is probably frowned upon, but he pays well and I get to keep all my tips. Some

183

previous places where I worked made you split them with everyone. Even the manager. I mean, I'm sorry, but why should the bigwigs get a share of my tips? They're nowhere to be seen when you're washing pots or lava hot cheese drips on your wrists from carrying too many plates. I've got the scars to prove it, you know.

OON: If we could get back to why you're here?

KB: Sorry. So Gus's a nice guy but doesn't exactly follow the rules. I mean there's never been any safety training or nothing like that. Now I think of it, it is a bit mad considering we are in the middle of the ocean.

OON: The sea.

KB: Sorry?

OON: It doesn't matter.

KB: Gus's not in trouble or anything, is he? He was on the boat home with me. We've both got alibis if that's what you're getting at.

OON: We're trying to piece together how the fire started and the events leading up to this incident. So, correct me if I'm wrong, but you came here to talk to us about the manager?

KB: Yeah. But not Gus. The other one. Eddie.

OON: Edward Mills?

KB: Yeah, him. The night manager. We call him Eddie. He was doing the night shift so he stayed over. Oh God, so that means . . . has he survived?

OON: We're not able to say anything about the situation at the moment, I'm afraid. (Clears throat). What can you tell us about him?

184

KB: He was always seen as a real rising star, everyone loved him. He was the life and soul of the party. He's quite fit too. But then it was a bit weird. He checked out.

OON: What do you mean?

KB: Like, he changed and I don't know how to describe it. He was . . . absent. I couldn't relax around him. There was an incident with another member of staff a few weeks ago, now I think of it. I don't remember what it was about. But man, Eddie can hold a grudge. He made sure this other guy was given the crap jobs on purpose. I think he ended up quitting. I presumed Eddie would have been fired for how he'd treated the other fella but well, once it came out that his sister died not that long ago and so did his grandad, who basically raised them. I know he had time off for a funeral. So he got away with it but was put on probation. Gus felt sorry for him, I think. Grief makes you do funny things, doesn't it? But it wasn't just grief. It was as if Eddie lost his mind.

OON: Was he aggressive? Mr Mills?

KB: No. More psychological stuff. It's sad. He was going places and then dropped to rock bottom. He became obsessed with monitoring the CCTV cameras. Hang on – can you not get the cameras and then just watch what happened at the hotel?

OON: It's not as simple as that.

DIH: Anything that can be salvaged will be.

KB: Ah yeah, I guess you might not be able to get to the recordings if the fire's spread. Well, the CCTV room was on the lower level, near the staff bedrooms. Hidden out of the way. Proper creepy. The lower deck gave me the chills and not just because of the ghost.

185

OON: The lower deck?

KB: Yeah, it's where the staff quarters are. Loads of
            random storage rooms too. I think they used to
            keep weapons down there back in the day. The
            creepiest one was the CCTV room. It used to be the
            cookhouse or something, where the soldiers made
            their food when they were based there. There's still
            the hooks they used for hanging meat and these
            dusty old antiques. I'd never go down there on my
            own. Never. It was freezing cold even on the hottest
            days. It used to freak me out to think that I was
            technically underwater. Anyway, it was during my
            shift on Thursday, the night of the fire, when I was
            told I needed to go and get some extra lightbulbs for
            the games room. It was urgent so I had to go alone.
            I was crapping myself as I raced down the stone
            steps. Seriously, it's so scary down on that lower
            deck.
            (Pause. Takes a sip of water)

KB: Anyway. Of course I can't find the sodding
            lightbulbs anywhere. I'm about to give up when I
            realise there's a light on in the CCTV room. Eddie
            was in there alone. He didn't hear me come in; he
            was completely transfixed. I asked him if he knew
            where the spare bulbs were kept and he nearly leapt
            out of his skin. No joke. Yelled at me for making
            him jump. Acted proper sheepish.

OON: Do you remember what he was looking at?

KB: Yeah . . . He was watching the guests eat their
            dinner. Staring at the screens. There was one man
            in particular that he couldn't take his eyes off.
            The tension radiated off him. It was the way he
            stared – as though he wanted to hurt the guy. It
            looked like he wanted to . . . kill him.

186

35

Friday 21st June

A pair of recognisable high-top trainers lie in a pool of blood. Mel's head pounds. *This isn't happening.* Her mouth is dry. No words will come out.

Zander races forward.

Propped against the bar, his feet jutting out before him, is Jonty.

His eyes have rolled back in his skull. His skin is a jaundiced yellow colour. His jaw is slack.

Syrupy blood has soaked through his shirt, glueing the fabric to his skin. There is a gaping bullet wound exactly where his heart lies.

An ice-cold grip of fear steals Mel's breath away. The tang of vomit burns the back of her throat as she takes in the bloodied scene.

'He's been shot,' Charlie swears.

Mel grips the bar, digging her nails into the wood, anchoring herself as her legs threaten to fail her.

Charlie is on his knees, his back to her, pressing his fingers against Jonty's waxy-looking neck searching for a pulse. He repeats his name, encouraging him to answer back.

There is no response.

Not a flicker of life in those dead, unblinking eyes.

Zander is making painful dry retching sounds from behind her.

She turns and races out of the claustrophobic 'wine cellar', pushing past him, making it up the stone steps in time to vomit over the wall of the fort.

Finished, Mel wipes her mouth and the strands of saliva trailing down her chin with a hand that shakes uncontrollably. Her face is wet with tears, the salty sea air stinging her eyes further. Her heart is racing.

No, it can't be possible. He can't be dead.

Like Wesley. Like Holly . . .

From further across the roof terrace she sees Bonnie running towards her, towards the open door from which Mel has emerged.

She wants to tell her to turn away. She doesn't want her to witness what she's just seen but she can't find her voice. Numbness chokes her.

When Bonnie's scream punctuates the night air Mel slumps to the cold ground. Her legs finally giving way.

*

The mood in the residents' lounge is one of complete shock. One by one the others join. No one says a word. All of them reliving the nightmare imprinted on their eyelids.

Zander drops to the sofa next to Mel, staring blankly at the floor, mumbling incoherently under his breath. Lingering shock fills the air-conditioned room.

There was so much blood.

She can smell iron and metal on her fingers and on her clothes. Her stomach swirls.

'Did you find him?' Nicole asks immediately. Mel swallows a pang of jealousy at her blissful innocence.

Bonnie trails in last. She sounds as if she's hyperventilating. Her breath comes out in snatched gasps as she moves towards the sofa on wobbly legs. There is blood on her dress. She must have also tried to find Jonty's pulse.

Mel gets to her feet. She knows a panic attack when she sees one, her mum used to get them when she was younger.

'Sit down, take a deep breath.'

She has a hand on the small of Bonnie's back and is gently rubbing it, telling her to inhale and exhale on a count of five. Her breath slowly starts to regulate. Mel can feel damp sweat through Bonnie's thin dress, her warm skin is almost vibrating with energy.

Charlie shuts the door behind them and leans against it, eyes closed, dry retching.

'W-w-what's going on?' Nicole presses, alarmed at the battle-scarred faces in front of her.

No one replies.

Nicole sits up taller, back straight, bracing herself. 'Guys? Did you find Edward? Will someone please answer me!'

Bonnie lets out a slow breath. 'No.'

There's a buzzing in Mel's head.

She wasn't Jonty's number one fan, not by any stretch, but she never in a million years wanted him dead. A rush of sorrow and remorse at how rude she's been to him in the past crashes over her. There's no chance to say sorry now.

'Jonty's dead,' Charlie says, his voice cracking slightly.

Hearing it spoken out loud doesn't make it any more real. Mel rubs her face, desperate to erase the images imprinted on her eyelids.

'Dead?' Nicole gasps.

Charlie unscrews the lid to the whisky decanter and the crystal pings as it catches the glass in his juddering hands. 'It looked like he's been shot.'

Mel remembers the missing gun, supposedly taken by a thieving guest.

Oh God.

Her breath quickens, her chest rising and falling rapidly. A sickening sensation rises. No, she tells herself. Gus told her they were display only and disarmed. He had no reason to lie to her. The weapon that was stolen from the wall of the lounge can't be the same one that's killed her colleague.

She bites her lip. Should she say something?

'What? Shot?' Nicole stares at him. 'No, no, no.'

Soft moans and cries swirl around Mel.

She lifts a shaking hand, her nail varnish chipped where her fingers gouged into the wooden bar top, and presses it hard against her gritty eyes. Black spots appear.

This is real. This isn't a nightmare she's going to wake up from.

Wesley is dead.

Jonty is dead.

Mel remembered what he told her about not trusting people. Her stomach tugs at the sudden memory.

She decides to keep her mouth shut. Nothing good will come from saying that she had concerns about a missing gun hours ago. It won't bring him back.

'Oh my God.' Nicole sits back, stunned. 'No. That can't be true. We would have heard a gunshot.'

Charlie shakes his head. 'Not necessarily. The walls are so thick, the gun could have a silencer. Have you ever heard a gunshot before? And who knows how long he's been there . . . It's been hours since any of us have seen him.'

'Zander. You went to the wine cellar . . .' Mel remembers.

'Yes, I took some wine but he wasn't in there then!' he replies.

Nicole makes the sign of the cross over her chest. 'And what about finding a phone signal? Please tell me you called for help?'

They shake their heads.

A sinister silence rolls around the room.

'Holly's brother did this? He killed Jonty?' Zander blinks.

'From now on we move around in pairs,' Charlie orders.

'We don't know that it was Edward. What about Wesley? He could have shot Jonty before he died . . .' Bonnie says, her voice small and uncertain.

'Wesley? The stoner?' Zander says, looking incredulous that Bonnie could even attempt to play devil's advocate right now. 'You saw the powder on the bottle in his room, didn't you? He wouldn't have put it there himself. Wake up! The night manager has killed them both.'

'But why?' Mel cries. Her cheeks are wet with tears that she didn't feel fall. She wants to scrub her brain clear of the images of Jonty's tortured face. The blood. The smell.

Nicole sniffs. 'He must have thought they both had something to do with his sister's death.'

'Oh my God.' Zander inhales. 'What did he write on that

article? He called us liars. What if he's taking us down . . . one by one?'

His haunting words land heavily on their shoulders. The numbness gives way to a steady thrum of panic, which swirls around the cool room.

'What the hell are we going to do?' Nicole's nails are bleeding from where she's been biting the skin.

More blood.

Mel's head thumps with tension. An uncontrollable shiver rolls across her. 'Is it me or is it getting colder in here?'

'I thought it was the shock,' Bonnie says, trembling.

'Listen.' Charlie silently throws back another glass of whisky in one, wincing as it hits the back of his throat. 'The main thing that's clear – or should that be the *only* thing that's clear? – is that we need to find the night manager.'

'Don't you mean we need to stay away from him?' Zander says.

'No,' Charlie says, mouth drawn in a hard line. 'We need to find this guy or else how the hell are we going to get off this fucking island?'

36

Mel can hear the others talking around her, but their words go over her head. She takes a thirsty gulp of whisky. Zander is pouring generous measures for Bonnie and Nicole as well. She hates the stuff but she's so desperate to blur the edges of her horrified mind that she would drink anything right now.

As soon as she's swallowed it, she rears back. A terrifying thought hits her.

'Stop!'

The others turn to look at her.

'We shouldn't drink anything. What if he's poisoned it all? Like he did to Wesley?'

Zander jumps away from the drinks cabinet as if he's been electrocuted. 'So we're trapped, in the middle of nowhere, with no way of calling for help, no way to escape, with a psychopathic murderer taking us down one by one?'

'Where is he? Why is he doing this to us?' Nicole sobs, pressing an ice-cold hand against Mel's arm.

She flinches at the unexpected contact.

It's as if she's been awoken from a spell.

'I think it's time we start being honest about what Edward thinks we've done to his sister . . .' Mel pants, breathless with a rush of adrenaline.

It's time. She needs to come clean.

There is a collective exhale of breath, no one wanting to be the first to acknowledge Mel's suggestion and implicate themselves.

'We were all there on the Christmas night out,' Mel encourages.

'So were a lot of people . . .' Charlie adds.

'I didn't know who Holly was until I read what happened to her in the news,' Bonnie says.

Nicole sniffs. 'I've obviously worked on projects with her but I've never had a problem with her and I certainly didn't do anything bad to her. But I also don't think Wesley or Jonty did either. I mean, why kill them?'

'I think I might know why Jonty might have been targeted,' Charlie says. 'Maybe Edward knew about Holly's complaint.'

'What complaint?' Bonnie asks.

'The fact that Jonty has been inappropriate with a few of the younger female members of staff. I think his sister might have been on the receiving end of one of his attempted advances. Isn't that right, Mel?'

Mel chews her lip. That was supposed to be confidential information.

'Holly put a meeting in my diary, which I presumed was to discuss Jonty and his *allegedly* less-than-professional actions, but she never made that meeting because, well . . .' She trails off and the others nod knowingly. 'But he told me he had no idea about upsetting her,' she reminds Charlie, biting down annoyance that he's shared this with the group. These people are meant to trust her. They need to know that she keeps her word.

Zander shakes his head. 'No, this is ridiculous. Holly's brother isn't going to have planned to murder because his sister may or may not have had beef with Jonty. Anyway, that doesn't give us a reason for him killing Wesley.'

From somewhere outside the room there is the toll of a grandfather clock. Its slow rhythmic chime announcing that it is now two o'clock in the morning echoes around the silent hotel.

'Hang on. Out of everyone in this room, *you* actually know Edward.' Zander spins to face Nicole. 'You're keeping that fact very quiet.'

'What?' Bonnie and Mel ask at the same time.

'I've just remembered that you won the pitch to rebrand this place,' Zander continues.

Nicole's cheeks flush with colour. She quickly burrows her head.

'Oh my God, I forgot. So, wait, you lied to us? You know him,' Charlie says.

Mel doesn't like the sudden change in atmosphere. Bonnie inches away from Nicole as if it was Edward himself was sitting there.

'No. I never met anyone called Edward.' Nicole stalls, chewing on a nail.

'Nicole?' There's something she's not telling them. Mel drops the volume of her voice. 'We need you to be honest. If you know anything then you have to share it with the group.

We need to work out who we're dealing with and what he might be planning next.'

Her heart pounds knowing she's also keeping a secret from them all. She just can't bring herself to say it out loud.

'I lied. Ok?' Nicole snaps.

'What do you mean?'

'Point Grey was actually Holly's client. She told me they wanted a rebrand and would like Flavour to do the work—'

'And you strolled into the meeting room and claimed the finder's fee as your own,' Charlie finishes off. 'You stole this project from her and took all the praise. I always wondered how you managed to persuade the hotel to come directly to Flavour and now we know. You didn't. Holly did, clearly because she had a contact here.'

'I know I shouldn't have but I did and I feel terrible.' She pauses. 'What if she told her brother and he's coming to punish me?' Nicole's voice is barely more than a scared whisper. 'What if I'm next?'

Seeing what he's done to Jonty and Wesley, there's no telling what Edward will do now.

Silence flows through the room. No one can bring themselves to soothe Nicole's worries. They have no idea what is going to happen next.

'What if Holly *was* killed?' Zander asks, lowering his voice. 'We've heard the rumours that she didn't walk to the woods herself. What if the police have made a mistake?'

Mel hasn't been able to stop thinking about this possibility since the results of the inquest were published. There was never any proof that Holly walked to the woods by herself. Mel remembers reading a line in the papers about the family not believing she'd made it there of her own accord, but the police had always maintained that her death wasn't being treated as suspicious. In their eyes, it was entirely possible that she walked there herself and there was no evidence to suggest otherwise.

'I found out this evening that Holly believed certain employees were stealing from the company. Pretty significant theft – fraud, in fact. She was preparing to become a whistleblower and expose the people behind it. Now I'm wondering if her death, and what she was working on, are linked?' Mel says. Her stomach tightens.

'Fraud?' Zander repeats.

'Who? Which employees?' Charlie frowns.

'I don't know. I've not seen the email. It was apparently sent before the party,' Mel replies, wishing she'd interrogated Tom a bit more about it all.

'I wonder if someone killed her to shut her up but made it look like an accident? Especially if Holly was about to uncover the truth . . .' Zander says, crossing his arms.

'What? You really think so?' Bonnie inhales.

'You might be onto something.' Nicole nods. 'The more I think about it, she wasn't alone that night. There's no way Holly would have been able to walk that far, no matter what the police said. Someone drove her to those woods and dumped her there to freeze to death.'

'Come on, I mean—' Charlie interrupts, scoffing.

'Shh, let her finish,' Bonnie says, giving Charlie a look.

Mel hadn't realised how short he could be with others. Clearly he's stressed, they all are.

'It makes sense it was someone at the Christmas party,'

Nicole continues. 'A colleague. Maybe her brother thinks that one of her work friends killed her. It would explain the red letters on the newspaper article. The "LIARS".'

'How many true crime podcasts do you listen to?' Charlie says. 'Come on, guys, this is Flavour we're talking about. Not some American crime documentary. There's no fraud and no whistleblowers. You said this email came yesterday before the party. From Holly?' Mel nods. 'But Holly's been dead for six months. Clearly, it's got to be bollocks.'

'Mel, who told you this?' Zander asks.

'Tom in IT.'

Charlie makes a noise between his lips as if that explains it all. 'Course. He's on a different planet half the time.'

Mel finds herself feeling protective of Tom. 'No he's not, he didn't come across that way to me.'

Charlie ignores her.

'I wonder which account it is. The one she's alleging is dodgy,' Nicole says, breaking the silence that follows. 'My money's on Westways. Like has anyone ever met anyone from that account?'

'Who are Westways?' Bonnie asks.

'Exactly, who indeed?' Nicole shrugs.

Zander sits up. 'I see their names crop up all the time, long lunches being booked out in the diary and tickets for sold-out concerts as part of their entertaining.' He frowns, his eyes dart to the side as if he is trying to think. 'But they're not on any of my records.'

Mel wrings her hands together, her heart thuds at what this means.

'Remind me, who looks after that account?' she asks.

'Oh my God. Jonty, Wesley and . . .' Zander trails out and swears under his breath.

Charlie slowly lifts his hand. 'Me too.'

Zander gives him a look of horror as if he is sitting beside a condemned man.

Mel swallows. Surely Charlie wouldn't do that. He wouldn't create a fake client in order to hide excessive expenses. Holly's got this wrong.

'This theory is nonsense,' Charlie says. 'Westways are property developers. They look after that new housing site, not far from the park. Just because they haven't been to the office yet doesn't mean they don't exist. I don't know why Jonty and Wesley have been targeted but it's got nothing to do with that. And Holly's death isn't suspicious. She died because she was pissed and out in the freezing cold without a coat on.' He shakes his head. 'This is ridiculous. None of us killed Holly, I mean—'

Suddenly, Nicole raises her good hand in the air. The movement stops him in his tracks. Her face is drawn. Her eyes bulge, a wide stare of horror. She presses a finger to her lips and turns her head to the side as if trying to hear something better.

Mel's heart leaps in her chest.

No one moves a muscle. Tension fills the air. Their eyes flick to the hallway.

What was that?

Is it him?

A long, slow creak comes from behind the closed door.

37

Sunday 23rd June

Hampshire Constabulary: Interview started at 16.45

Officer O'Neal:	Interview starting at sixteen forty-five. Thank you for coming back to speak with us, Mr Raynor.
Voice of Gus Raynor's lawyer:	I'd like to state for the record that my client has been fully cooperating with the police. He has some health issues and unfortunately, his health has taken a turn for the worse since the tragic incident at Point Grey.
OON:	I understand. We don't want to cause any undue stress, we simply want to get to the bottom of what happened. So, as I said, thank you for coming back to see us.
GR:	I didn't feel like I had much choice.
OON:	Since we saw you last, we've been given employee records by Cobalt Hotels and it makes for interesting reading. You were the one to personally hire Edward Mills, yes? (Pause)
Detective Inspector Hutchinson:	We need you to speak up for the tape.
GR:	I can't remember. Probably.

OON: Did you know about his previous conviction when you offered him the job? I have it here in front of me that Edward Mills is listed as having served time at HMP Seahurst for Grievous Bodily Harm. Were your employers aware of this when you hired him?

GR: Yes.

OON: That's not what they told us. According to them, hiring a member of staff who's served a prison sentence is against their employment criteria. Why did you lie about doing so?

GR: We needed workers. Brexit ruined everything for us. Eddie passed his probation period with flying colours and I believe in giving people second chances.

OON: You also told us that you were on the ten o'clock boat returning to Portsmouth Quays, as, in your words, *only one member of staff needs to stay at the hotel overnight.*

GR: Yes, that's correct.

OON: The thing is, your employer also informed me that you were meant to remain on the fort for the duration of your shift. That the two-person rule was in effect and not, as you stated, 'ignored because of cost-cutting measures'. Now, can you tell me, is there any reason you decided to jump ship on that particular night?

GR: They're wrong! Clearly, they're trying to cover their backs. One person *was* allowed to stay alone overnight. I did not jump ship.

Lawyer: OK, let's try and remain calm, please.

DIH: We would like to ask you again if you have anything to share about how the guest-list was created? To remind you, Flavour employees were told that eight

VIP guests would get to stay overnight. Apparently, staff at Point Grey picked these names from a hat. Previously you told us, and I quote: 'That's weird. Nothing to do with us.' Would you like to elaborate on this?

GR: No. I don't know anything about *choosing* guests . . .

OON: The man you left in charge was also the sibling of Miss Holly Mills, a young woman who tragically died after a work night out. Is it a coincidence that the party booking was for the company where Ms Mills had previously worked?

GR: What?

OON: You effectively left the group there, alone, miles from safety, with a person in charge who is known for having a violent past and a grudge against the company. Can you tell me your reasoning behind this decision?

Lawyer: (Whispers to client)

GR: No comment.

OON: You have worked in this industry for over thirty years, am I right? So it's fair to say that someone of your experience would be attuned to the different weather conditions. Possibly even have a sixth sense. The early hours of the twenty-first of June were full of quite extreme thunderstorms. The great big washout following the heatwave. I wonder if someone of your seafaring calibre would realise what was coming?

GR: No comment

OON: I have to warn you that these decisions are not painting you in the best light. You need to help us out here Mr Raynor.

GR: (Mumbles to his lawyer)

Lawyer: My client has requested to speak to me in private.

                 - (automated settings: interview paused at 16.51
                   hours)
                 - (automated settings: interview resumed at 17.35
                   hours)

DIH: Welcome back.

Voice of Gus   I have a brief statement to read on behalf of my client.
Raynor's   (Clears throat) *I don't know about the accusations*
lawyer: *concerning Mr Mills but I did forget to mention*
                 something in my previous interview. There were
                 three antique pistols on display in the lounge area
                 at the hotel. An overnight guest pointed out to me
                 that one had gone astray. I wasn't aware of it
                 missing prior to that night. I should have said
                 something sooner but I presumed it was merely for
                 display. However, I've since read that a gun was
                 used to kill at least one guest so I panicked and
                 thought I'd get in trouble for not telling you earlier.
                 I had no idea the antique pistol could be used to
                 kill, if this is what has happened. I want to come
                 clean about this now to avoid any confusion going
                 forward.

DIH: Ok. We appreciate you telling us that. Do you have
                 any idea what type of gun it was? Or when it was
                 last seen on display?

GR: No. I honestly didn't give it a second thought. I
                 presumed a guest had nicked it, we get a lot of that.
                 It baffles me considering the number of wealthy
                 people who stay, they're not shy about slipping a
                 little thing in their bags as a souvenir.

OON: I think you know more than you're letting on. Now I
                 have a theory that someone was paying you to leave
                 Point Grey effectively unauthorised. Did Edward

Mills pay you to leave him alone with those selected guests?

GR: No comment.

OON: We've been granted access to your bank accounts. We will be going through them with a fine tooth comb so if there is anything you'd like to tell us before that happens, then now would be a good time.

GR: No comment.

OON: Was he planning a punishment of some sort? Perhaps to teach these people a lesson? Because despite what he may have told you, it wasn't some childish prank. This was methodical and calculated and has ended with a number of people losing their lives. The fire was a cover-up. We've seen the bodies. This was no accident. This was murder.

GR: (Breaks into a coughing fit)

Lawyer: Gus? Are you ok?

OON: Mr Raynor? You've gone awfully red there. Gus?

Lawyer: We need to get him some water. I insist on taking a break.
(Sound of chairs scraping back)

GR: (Coughing stops)

OON: Gus? Gus? Can you hear us?
(Sound of thump)

Lawyer: We need to call for help! (Scraping of chairs. Static.)
(Continuous beep)

- (automated settings: interview terminated at 17:42)

38

Friday 21st June

'Is that him?' Nicole drops her voice to a whisper, eyes trained on the door of the residents' lounge where the ominous creaking sound came from.

They don't move an inch, as if in a macabre game of musical statues. The temperature in the room has plummeted.

Nicole leans forward. 'I'm sure I heard footsteps.'

'I heard it too,' Bonnie mouths. Silent tears run down her cheeks.

'Oh my God, what if it's him!' Zander hisses. He silently slinks to the carpet and cowers behind the sofa. 'He's found us.'

Mel can't hear anything over the pounding of her heart in her ears.

She copies Zander and slips to the floor. The scratchy carpet rubs against her knees. Her eyes remain trained on the closed door. Her shallow breath is trapped in her throat.

Breathe, just breathe.

Panic surges through her. They haven't got any weapons. Instead of sitting here drinking and trying to rationally work out what Edward's game plan might be, they should have been figuring out a way to attack him first.

At any moment this guy could burst in and open fire. She sends out a silent prayer that they will survive. Mel's teeth press into her quivering lips. Her bad choices weigh down on her. Smothering her. It takes her breath away. Her eyes dart around her colleagues. Horror mirrored on their faces.

She steals a glance around the room, catching sight of the CCTV camera tucked away in the corner of the ceiling. Her stomach plummets. He must be somewhere watching this play out. His sick entertainment. They are sitting ducks here.

Even if they hid he would find them. Mel has to swallow down the bubble of nausea that's risen to her throat.

Does he know what she did?

It was an innocent mistake. An accident.

There's another painfully slow creak. The sound jolts her. She definitely heard that one.

Or at least, she thinks she did over the blood rushing in her ears. Every second lasts a lifetime, waiting for him to burst in.

Her eyes catch Bonnie's and she mouths a silent message telling her it'll be ok. Pins and needles grow in her right foot. She tries to block out the fizzing sensation but she can't. It's only growing worse. She dares to stretch out her leg, wincing, but doesn't realise how close she is to the coffee table at this low angle and her foot bangs into the wood, knocking over an empty glass. She flinches. Holding her breath.

But nothing happens.

The door doesn't open. No crazed murderer races into the room pointing a loaded gun at their heads like she imagined.

Nicole is still straining to hear something but her shoulders have lowered ever so slightly.

'I think he's gone,' she whispers, turning to face them.

'How do you know that was even him?' Charlie hisses.

Nicole chews her lip. 'I'm sure it sounded like footsteps . . .' she says with growing uncertainty. 'Maybe it was in my head.'

'No. I definitely heard them too,' Bonnie says.

'Footsteps? Are you sure?' Charlie asks. 'It might just be the heat that's making things expand. This is an old building. Or maybe the wind is picking up. Didn't someone say there was going to be a storm?'

'A storm.' Zander widens his eyes. 'Are you kidding me?'

'It wasn't the wind. I heard a sound like someone was plodding past, slowly. Heavy tread. The wind can't make that sound. I heard footsteps,' Bonnie replies. She turns away, muttering under her breath.

Nicole roughly wipes the tears from her cheeks.

'Is it me or has it suddenly gone really cold in here?' Mel rubs her upper arms. Her fingertips are numb.

'No, look.' Zander points to the air-conditioning unit. The light is flashing blue. It's blasting out ice-cold air. 'I think this is part of his plan. He's trying to freeze us to death.'

Holly.

'Or he's trying to get us to leave this room,' Mel says. 'I think he's been watching us.'

The others follow her gaze and glance up at the security camera in the corner of the room.

'He's been watching and listening all along?' Nicole gasps.

'There's five of us and only one of him. We can overpower him, surely,' Zander says, dropping his voice.

'Well, apart from me,' Nicole adds.

'You're forgetting that he has a gun,' Mel says, pressing her thumbs to her temples, trying to ease the constant pounding in her skull.

'We can't hide in here forever,' Bonnie says firmly. 'I also *really* need the bathroom.'

'You can't go. He might be in the corridor, waiting,' Mel breathes.

'I don't know how much longer I can hold it in.' She shifts in her seat. 'Anyway, if this theory is right and he's focusing on avenging Holly's death then my conscience is clear.'

'Isn't everyone's? As long as the rest of us don't have anything to hide we'll be safe.' Mel is trying to sound authoritative but the tremor in her voice gives her away.

Bonnie looks up expectantly.

'I don't know. I'd feel a hell of a lot safer if I knew where this motherfucker was.' Charlie's eyes flick up at the camera.

'Same,' Zander says.

'Are you ok?' Mel asks Nicole.

She nods but she's not stopped shivering. Her teeth are chattering and her legs shake with coldness. There isn't a control panel in here for the air-con like in the bedrooms. There's no way of changing the temperature in this room without leaving and trying to find the central source.

'Hang on, I've got something that might help.' Zander points to a VIP goody bag which is slumped next to a coffee table on the far side of the room. 'There's a few extra Flavour jackets in there. I ordered too many by mistake. They're only thin but it's better than nothing.'

Bonnie pulls the branded jackets out, one by one, handing them round the group before putting one on.

'I'm fine, thanks,' Mel says, shaking her head when one is offered to her. The cold is actually helping to keep her alert. 'So now what?'

'We have two choices.' Charlie zips his jacket up. 'We either sprint to our rooms and lock the doors. Or we stay here together. Barricade ourselves in, maybe try and find a weapon, stay awake and wait until help comes.'

'Help isn't coming,' Mel says quietly.

'Tell me what weapons you see around you? He has a gun, remember.' Nicole sniffs. 'We need to get off this crazy hotel as soon as possible to get away from this maniac. Mel, did you say something?'

'I was going to say . . . if help isn't coming to us then we need to go and find help ourselves,' Mel suggests.

'You're literally talking in riddles,' Zander says.

'I mean, we need to get to the roof terrace. We need to do something that's going to get attention on the fort. Maybe if we turn our torches on our phones and stand as high as we can, a passing boat might—?'

Zander interrupts her. 'Or could we light a fire? There was a box with matches and kindling and stuff by the fire pit.'

'And what if it gets out of hand? Then what? It's not like the fire brigade are suddenly going to turn up. Plus, go outside and have a look out there. There's no one around for miles,' Charlie says.

Zander folds his arms. 'I'm trying to think about how to get us off this bloody man-made island. I don't see you coming up with any bright ideas.'

'What? Oh yeah, 'cause lighting a fire is such a good idea,' Charlie replies.

They begin to eyeball one another. The air crackles with tension.

'Stop. Can you stop,' Nicole cries. 'This is not helping. We need to focus on getting rescued, not falling out with one another.'

There's a pause.

'Wait – lifeboats. There are lifeboats! There was definitely one fixed to the outside wall, near the roof terrace. I'm sure of it,' Mel says as she shoots her head up, buoyed by the thought of taking back control and figuring out how to get off this place.

'She's right,' Zander says. 'Hang on, where's Bonnie?'

They turn around and realise her chair is empty.

'She said she needed the toilet so probably there?' Charlie says, muttering that 'she's got a death wish'.

Mel rubs her face. In an ideal world, they would all stay together, but nothing about this is ideal. 'Shall we wait here until she comes back?'

'No. You go and check the lifeboat situation with Charlie and we'll stay here and wait for Bonnie to come back,' Zander says, nodding to Nicole.

Charlie doesn't argue at this suggestion. It's a good idea for the two of them to be separated for a while.

'Fine but it's too cold to stay in here, go to a bedroom and lock the door. Zander's is the closest. Barricade yourselves in and don't open it for anyone but us,' Charlie orders.

Zander and Nicole lock scared eyes.

All of them are terrified. Mel fights the instinct to run to her own bedroom and lock the door too. But the only way this nightmare is going to end is if they work together to get away from this place before Edward kills again.

39

Friday 21st June

Mel's legs shake as she crosses the roof terrace. She wants to leave Point Grey and be safe in her own home but the only way that's going to happen is if they work together and find the courage to fight back.

It's almost half past two o'clock in the morning, there is a faint purple haze in the sky, the imposing clouds tinted with indigo. Charlie stays a respectable distance away from her. A flash of light comes from behind them and she turns, expecting to see someone walking over with a torch light on their phone. But the decking remains empty.

There's no one there.

It's the tiredness playing tricks on her, making her see flashes of lights that aren't there.

Mel rubs her tired and scratchy eyes.

Charlie must sense something's wrong. 'You ok?'

'Fine.'

There is a rumble of thunder overhead, as if someone is dragging a heavy wheelie bin across gravel. The air is so thick and humid you can almost taste it. Charlie picks up Jonty's cigarette packet, still on the side from when he last smoked one. Mel shivers at the memory. How is this still the same night as the party? A lifetime has passed since Jonty was issuing his cryptic warning. And yet, also, like no time has passed at all.

Then Charlie does something she doesn't expect. He pulls a cigarette out and places it against his lips. A click of Jonty's green lighter is followed by a heavy inhale.

'What? It's not like he's coming back for them,' he says, at the look Mel's giving him.

'I didn't know you smoked . . .'

'I don't. Well, only in highly stressful situations. And I'd say that right now qualifies.' He starts to pace.

There's something in his body language that's making her uneasy. Watching him take short, sharp lungfuls of smoke is wrong. The Charlie she thought she knew would never be a smoker. She wants to get on with their escape. Every second they delay gives Edward a chance to appear with a gun. She's about to tell Charlie to hurry up when he speaks.

'We had a row the night she died.' His voice is low, almost robotic.

'Who? Holly?'

'Yeah. I said some nasty things, which I regret, but I never got the chance to apologise.' He lets out a slow and measured exhale.

The smell makes her stomach turn. She wishes he'd put it out.

'What did you row about?' she asks.

He rubs the back of his neck. 'I honestly can't remember now. I was pissed. We both were. It was probably a load of nonsense and I felt bad after.'

She can't imagine him rowing with anyone. She's seeing a whole different side to him this evening.

'It got a little heated.' He inhales. 'I may . . . have threatened her.'

'What?'

It's as if someone has pressed a cold hand against the back of her neck. He drops his eyes to his feet, scuffing his shoes.

'I know. It was so out of character. I forgot all about it until the next day when I checked my phone and there was a voice memo I'd sent, apologising to her. But she, erm, never received it. It was unseen . . . so she wouldn't know how sorry I was.'

But someone else might have listened, Mel fills in the blanks.

'What if she told her brother about what I said, or he heard the voice note, and now he's after me?' Charlie looks ghostly pale. He stamps the cigarette butt under the sole of his shoe.

'I'm sure that's not true. We have to stay positive.'

Mel's brain is whirring. Hearing his confession makes her think of her own secret.

Charlie never spoke up when they were pressed on revealing anything that might be linked to Holly's death. When they were asked outright if they had anything to hide. But, a voice pipes up at the back of her mind, neither did she.

'Stay positive? Easier said than done when you're trapped in the middle of the sea with a complete nutjob, right?' He swallows, interrupting her thoughts. 'Come on, we'd better get a move on.'

Mel peers over the edge of the fort's walls. There is one lifeboat and it appears to be floating on the side of the building. Bulky metal beams are holding it in place. There is a dark grey tarpaulin cover over the top. She has never been in a life-boat before. She doesn't have a clue how to start one. Is it electric or petrol-powered? Or will they need to grab a set of oars and row? She doesn't care, together they will figure it out.

For the first time in a long time, she is hopeful.

This is a lifeline.

A chance for them to get off this godforsaken place and get help. And even if they can't work the lifeboat, there must be a radio they can use.

Of course, hope can be a dangerous thing.

'How do we get to it?' she asks.

Charlie cranes his neck to get a better view. 'Look, there's a ladder.' He doesn't waste a second before he has hold of a ladder, coaxing it from its holder. The sound of grinding metal shoots straight through her, like fingernails down a black-board.

'Careful,' she cries, watching as he climbs over the edge.

The ladder looks centuries old. Rust spots remain on the wall where it was fixed. If one of the rungs has corroded or he mistakes his footing, even slightly, then he could drop into the water below.

It feels like forever before he's descended and is safely on the small platform holding the lifeboat. Despite the warm air, she shivers being out here alone on the enormous roof terrace.

'You're not going to believe this,' Charlie calls.

His deflated tone makes her stomach fall.

'What?' she shouts back.

'It's fucked. Edward must have got here before us and van-dalised it.'

No, this can't be right. Despair rises up in her. They are always one step behind him. He's been out here already. He's made sure to cover all bases.

'I mean I'm no expert but take a look. He really wants us to stay.' There is a sound of Charlie slamming a hand against the side of the lifeboat. He calls to tell her he's climbing back up.

Once back on the roof terrace he wipes off the sheen of sweat from his forehead.

'Did you try the radio? See any flares? Alarms in lifejackets? Was there anything we could use?' she pleads, refusing to give up hope.

'Nothing. There's no way we can use that to get off here.' He shakes his head. 'It's a complete shell inside. Everything has been pulled out. There's loads of exposed wires, bird crap and rainwater. I should have known when I saw the cover. I thought the wind had pulled it off, but close up it looked like there were marks in the boat, slasher marks.'

Mel shivers. 'What?'

'There was a hole in the base so big you could see right through it. Even if we got it into the water, we'd sink immediately.'

Her breath catches as she inhales. 'Now what?' The desperation and panic in her voice is obvious.

Charlie swallows. He locks eyes with her. 'I have no idea.'

40

Friday 21st June

Panic ripples around Zander's bedroom as Mel and Charlie share the bad news with the others. Bonnie is thankfully back from the bathroom in one piece. She looks ill. No one speaks. They are all flagging now. The initial adrenaline that powered them is waning and the alcohol has worn off, leaving fear-filled exhaustion. Thankfully, it's not as cold as the residents' lounge.

'So what does this mean? Now there's no lifeboat? Did you definitely check that nothing could be used? Mel, did you have a good look too?' Zander asks, chewing a thumbnail.

'No, I was too high up,' Mel replies. 'I mean I could see the tarpaulin had been wrecked but there was only this one knack-ered old ladder and—'

'Go and look for yourself,' Charlie interrupts, scowling at him. 'You risk your life getting a good look at it if you don't trust me. Why would I lie? I want to get off here just as much as the rest of you.'

'It's a legitimate question. You don't need to be so defen-sive,' Mel says, snappier than she'd meant.

Charlie dips his head. 'Sorry, I'm just struggling.'

'Are you ok?' Mel asks Nicole who is lying on the bed, looking completely wiped out.

'She was sick when you were looking at the lifeboat. I think it's the shock of everything and the pain in her arm,' Zander explains.

'You haven't drunk anything, have you? We can't trust anything in this hotel. What if he's poisoned it all?' Mel says. Wesley's frothing mouth, face pinched in pain and agony rushes back. A pounding headache has settled behind her eyes. 'I don't think we should drink anything that might have been tampered with.'

Zander paces around the room. 'Where is he hiding? What's he planning? There must be something in the staff quarters on that lower level or . . . Wait! Remember how the old guy told us on the tour about the circular tunnel where the soldiers used to store stuff or hide or something?'

'What? Do you think there's going to be one-hundred-and-fifty-year-old gunpowder or some working World War Two cannons we can use to set off and bring attention to us?' Charlie says.

Zander bites his tongue, ignoring Charlie's roll of his eyes. 'No, but we've not looked there so perhaps we should? It might be a store cupboard full of crap or it might have something useful in it.'

'What about the horn that rings before dinner? Where do you reckon that is? That must be loud enough to call for help? Maybe another boat will hear it and . . .' Mel trails off, realising that perhaps she's clutching at straws.

'That's actually not a bad idea, it was down on the lower

218

level,' Zander says. 'But let's just think about this, that's also where Edward must be. Waiting. I mean, what if it's a trap?'

'What hope do we have?' Mel replies. 'It could be our only way of calling for help.'

Zander sighs deeply. 'Anyone want to volunteer to go down there?'

Even though she was the one to suggest it, the thought of that lower level sends shivers through Mel. 'I'm not good in tight spaces.' She swallows.

'I'll go,' Charlie says.

'Me too.' Bonnie raises a hand, her mouth set in a rigid line. Her hands are red from wringing them and her legs keep tapping the carpet thanks to the adrenaline of the evening.

'Fine. So will I. Safety in numbers, right? I have to get out of this room, it's making me go bloody bonkers. Why don't you stay with Nicole, Mel?' Zander suggests.

Nicole smiles gratefully.

'Ok. But please be careful,' Mel says, aware that her words are not much protection.

She watches the three of them trudge out of Zander's bedroom, praying they'll figure out a way to call for help.

41

Friday 21st June

Mel frowns at the small box that controls the temperature in Zander's room. It's flashing and emitting a low-level irritating beep. Edward's programmed this remotely. Earlier, Gus said all the rooms had these intelligent systems; this is what he must have meant.

Yet again he's in control.

She groans in frustration and gives up. Her tired eyes check the bedroom door one more time. She's already dragged the metal luggage rack, and the heavy leather buttoned-backed Victorian armchair over the carpet, pushing them right up against the wooden frame, to barricade her and Nicole in. He must have access to every single room in the hotel. They need to make it as hard as possible for him to get in.

'You ok? I mean, I know you're not ok but you do look pale. I would offer you a cup of sugary tea or a biscuit for the shock but I don't trust anything here,' Mel says to Nicole.

'I'm fine. Well, not fine. But I think Zander's right. It's the shock of it all. I still can't believe they're both dead.' Nicole shivers. 'Thanks though.'

Zander's bedroom has a similar creepy painting above his bed, like the one in Mel's room. Only, his is a portrait of a sailor, dressed in his finery with polished brass buttons and a peaked hat at an angle. He's looking away from the artist, the shadows of dark clouds behind him, casting him in an eerie light. There's something about his unsmiling expression that unnerves her. There is an air of going into battle on his pale tight face. As if he already knows his terrible fate.

There's a beat of silence.

'Did you definitely lock the door after they left?' Nicole asks again.

Mel nods. 'We're as safe as we can be in here.'

She scans the room to see if there's anything else heavy she could shove behind the door. The bedroom is filled with soft furnishings. There is a thick coarse rug in shades of deep blues, covering most of the polished wooden floor and a plush navy waffle throw on the king-sized bed. Zander's chic overnight bag is resting on a small table. It's not much, but she adds it to the pile.

She looks at the antique solid wood wardrobe.

'You won't be able to move that. But don't worry, we've already checked in there, and under the bed and in the shower, when you were at the lifeboat,' Nicole says, as if reading her mind. 'Edward isn't hiding in here. There's also no cameras . . . well, none that we can find.'

Mel wants to laugh at the absurdity of it all but she can't.

She doesn't know where to put herself. She hovers, shifting her weight from one foot to another. The two women have never hung out together, one-on-one like this, apart from the odd awkward lift journey.

'Come and sit down, you're making me uneasy. Here. Put this over you.' Nicole pats the bedspread.

They both get under the cover, pulling the soft duvet up to their chins, like frightened young children. It's comforting to know she's not here alone, even if being in bed with her colleague is slightly awkward.

'Who would have thought tonight would end like this? To think everyone else in the office was so jealous of us staying over, if only they could see us now,' Nicole says without a hint of irony. 'I keep thinking about Wesley. I've never seen a dead body before. I mean, I have on the telly but not in real life. Have you?'

Mel pauses. She doesn't want to alarm Nicole but she can't hide the fact that seeing Wesley's slumped lifeless body brought a whole load of unwanted memories rushing back.

'Yeah, once.'

Nicole blinks. 'Really? Who?'

'My dad. He took his own life when I was a teenager.' Mel picks at her thumbnail. 'I was the one to find him.'

'Sorry, I had no idea.'

'It was a long time ago, but you never forget.'

Mel tries to push down the memories that have bubbled to the surface since this nightmare began. She hasn't thought about that fateful Saturday afternoon in November, over twenty years ago, for a long time. Of course, it's been buried somewhere. She thought it was locked far enough away that it would never resurface, but flashes of that traumatic time have leapt to the front of her mind thanks to the events of tonight.

When she was twelve, her dad suddenly lost his job as a postman, which put even more pressure on her mum to find extra shifts at the care home. Her parents began arguing more than normal, and though they tried to brush it off as nothing, there was an atmosphere during every Sunday roast, a side serving of resentment and depression with the horseradish sauce. As an only child, Mel did her best to keep the peace but there was more to it than she could have ever known. It was finding him in the garage, the noose still swaying from the wooden beam, when she finally understood how in the dark she was being kept.

Bizarrely, she remembers his hands most clearly. His wide nail beds had turned white, almost translucent. The same hands that had held her as a baby, that safely guided her across busy roads on the way to school, that slammed on the dining table during another argument with Mum . . . Mel's eyes had remained glued to those veiny, hairy hands when the paramedics, and then the police, came.

Her dad had woken up that morning and decided he couldn't do it anymore. By dinnertime, he'd taken his own life, leaving a scrawled apology on the back of an unopened final notice envelope.

And that was that.

Her mum blamed herself. It broke her. Over the years that followed she drank her guilt away. The doctors told Mel her mum's stroke was a result of the alcohol abuse and that her mother was lucky to be alive. No one prepared her for the lasting effects. In time, her mum's body recovered but her brain was damaged worse than they initially thought. Dealing with her early onset dementia has been a full-time job. Every night Mel brushes her mum's teeth, bathes her, and tries to ease the tangles from her hair. She's given up her social life and any chance of romance to care for her mum. The only person at Flavour who knows anything about all of this is Rohan. And now Nicole.

'I had no idea,' Nicole sniffs, once Mel has finished. 'Why didn't you tell anyone what you've been going through at home?'

'At work, I can be a different person. My job is my escape.' Mel tucks her hair behind her ear. 'I wanted to keep the two worlds separate.'

Throughout it all, Mel had ploughed forward. Terrified that if she sat still and allowed herself to properly grieve then the illness that had stolen her father, the dark clouds which occasionally hovered at the periphery of her own mind, would consume her. She refuses to allow that to happen. Her mum needs her too much.

She refuses to be a victim. She's lost so much already.

But right now, trapped in this unfamiliar bedroom, miles away from help, with the weight of grief crushing her, she doesn't know if she can take any more, or if she can keep fighting. The easiest thing would be to crawl into the inviting Egyptian cotton sheets and give up. Await her fate, whatever it may be.

'But you're always so smiley. You act like you don't have a care in the world,' Nicole says, bringing her back to the present. 'In fact, I need to apologise to you.'

'Me? Why?'

'I may have said stuff behind your back.' Nicole shifts, wincing at the movement. 'But well, I'm not the only one . . .'

Was she one of the women in the ladies' bathroom? No, Mel would have recognised her voice, surely?

'I thought I'd only ever been nice to everyone.'

'Yes. Too nice. It's suffocating. You make the rest of us feel so inadequate at times. Here she is again, Sad Mel, with the organising and tea-making and raffles and sending round sponsorships forms on behalf of people and reminding us to donate to charity or whatever. I mean, have a day off.'

'Is that bad though? Life is hard enough. These moments of kindness matter or so I hoped.'

'I presumed you were doing it to be a suck-up, to get Rohan's attention or to prove you were better than us all.'

Mel blinks. Unsure where this sudden bolt of honesty has come from.

Mel has thrown herself into her job, embraced the routine, found comfort in the structure because her home life, her dating life and her family set-up has been riddled with loss and misery and mess. Dedicating herself to her work means she can forget all the hard things she faces. Is that so bad?

She hadn't realised her colleagues knew she didn't have a life outside of the office. Or that they resented her for it.

Nicole continues, 'You need a better work-life balance and realise that work isn't everything. Make some friends, go on dates, I don't know, download Tinder and swipe right on anyone and everyone. See what happens. Live a little.'

'But how do I do that?' Mel asks. 'You never seem to care what people think of you.'

Nicole laughs. 'Me? Yes, I do. I show it differently. I hide it better. With you it's so obvious, the desperation to be liked. But think about it, we're not your mates, we're your colleagues. Just because people are friendly doesn't mean they're your friends.'

Mel sits back. 'I guess I've always been like that. It's self-preservation.'

Of course she wants people to like her.

Before tonight, she thought her colleagues did.

'But who is the real Mel? I mean, have you ever got mad?'

'Yeah.'

'When?'

Mel sighs. 'Well, I mean, I've got draft emails where I've called people names. I sometimes type out my frustrations to get it out of my system. Not that I'd ever send them but it makes me feel better.'

Nicole shakes her head, her pale lips cracking into a smile. 'That's not what I mean. Maybe you should allow yourself to get mad and express your emotions instead of bottling it up all the time. I guess none of us know the real Mel, even after working together for all these years.'

'That's because no one has asked,' she replies, her voice quiet.

'I know, and I'm sorry. Well, I'm asking now. Who knows how long we're going to be trapped in here?' Nicole tries to raise a smile. 'So tell me about you . . .'

42

Friday 21st June

Mel tells Nicole how she worries she's always behind, in every aspect of her life. Whenever moments of self-doubt tap her subconscious, usually on Sunday mornings, she tries to tell herself she doesn't care but she does. Their unexpected heart-to-heart is punctuated with sudden pauses to listen for any unusual noises. They may be trying to take their minds away from the nightmare they are trapped in but they are both on high alert.

Nicole shifts in the bed, wincing as she does. Strands of sweaty blonde hair have stuck to her forehead in wispy lines.

It's so cold in here. Like the crisp snap of a winter's morning. She can see her breath. How long have they been here? The clock on the flat-screen television says it's been twenty minutes. What's taking the others so long to find this siren?

'You believe in that ask the universe stuff, don't you?' Mel remembers seeing a daily desk calendar with positive affirmations about manifesting a happy life on Nicole's desk.

Nicole smiles bashfully. 'Yeah.'

'Well, can you please manifest that we get off here safely, in one piece, and soon?'

'God, I wish it was that easy.' She sighs. 'I mean, where is this guy? I don't understand what sort of game he's playing. Is he waiting, trying to make us turn on one another?'

'I don't know. How the hell can we possibly try and begin to understand someone who is capable of killing another human being?' Mel shakes her head slowly. 'They'll find some way to call for help, I'm sure of it. We have to stay positive. You'll soon be dancing at your wedding and this will be a distant nightmare.'

'I thought that getting married with a broken arm would be the worst thing in the world.' Nicole sniffs. 'And then everything has happened since and, well, now all I want is to get off this place alive. I would give anything.'

Mel can't begin to process the rollercoaster she's been on since this day began. To think she came here hoping for nothing more than to find the confidence to flirt with Charlie. The woman who arrived at the quayside all those hours ago feels like someone she barely knew. How naive she now sees she was, thinking that this was just a fun work party. How did she think she'd ever be able to get away with it?

She shifts. A bolt of adrenaline erupts in the pit of her stomach.

It's time to tell Nicole what's been running through her mind ever since her name was pulled out of a hat to win a VIP place here.

Mel lowers her voice. 'I think I know the reason why I've been chosen to be here.' Her freezing fingers pull at a loose thread on the cushion beside her. Her mouth dries.

'What do you mean?' Nicole frowns.

She takes a long, slow breath. She's never told anyone this before.

'Did you do something to Holly, Mel?' Nicole presses when Mel doesn't answer, wariness laced through every word.

Mel drops her voice, 'It's been eating away at me.'

There's a creaking sound.

The night manager? Her scared eyes flit to the closed door, but it sounds as if it's coming from overhead. An old pipe perhaps. Where the hell are the others? What's taking so long?

'What did you do?' Nicole whispers.

Mel takes a deep breath. The words are just out of reach.

A flush of heat suddenly settles over her. This is difficult enough, and it's not helped by the intent way Nicole is looking at her, waiting for her confession.

That's why this is so painful, Mel realises. She needs to admit what she's been keeping so closely guarded to her chest for the past six months. She never, in a million years, expected to be spilling the truth to Nicole of all people.

'It was on the night of the Christmas party.' Mel casts her eyes down, fidgeting with the thread wound around her fingers. Tighter and tighter.

Another shaky inhale.

'I'd had a few too many to drink. We all had. I decided to call it a night and went to the cloakroom. It was dark. There weren't any members of staff around to ask. So I grabbed my coat from the rail and caught a taxi home. I didn't realise until the next morning when I saw it in the light of day. The coat I'd picked up wasn't mine.'

Nicole waits for her to continue. Her silence only adds more torture to this reveal she's kept secret for so long.

'It was by accident, I was drunk and didn't properly check to see if it was my coat or not. The one I picked up was so similar. Both were black, both the same sort of length, both with fluffy hoods. I took Holly's coat.' She swallows. 'I had no idea that she would go out in the freezing cold and walk home without one.' Tears leap to her eyes. Her stupid careless action played a part in Holly's untimely death.

'What?'

'As soon as I heard the news that she was discovered in only her little party dress I blamed myself. She might have survived if she had been wearing her coat. Oh God, you can't tell anyone. I thought about going to the police and telling them what I did but I was too scared. My mum needs me, I can't go to prison. Even though it was an innocent mistake you hear of people arrested for perverting the course of justice all the time.' Her words tumble over one another.

Wait, is she laughing?

Mel stares at Nicole, amazed by her reaction. The air is knocked from her lungs at the sound the younger woman is making. It's the first time she's heard her laugh in hours.

'It's not funny.'

'Sorry, no you're right. It's your face, I mean, I thought you were going to reveal something massive.'

'It is massive.'

'No, well not really, I mean, the fact she didn't have a coat wasn't ideal, but it didn't kill her, Mel. Even if she had been wearing one, she still was out in the freezing cold for far too long with hardly anything else on. You're not to blame for the weather or the fact she couldn't handle her drink! I honestly think you need to let it go.'

Mel holds Nicole's gaze, determined to confirm she's not winding her up. 'Really?'

'Seriously, don't beat yourself up. It was an innocent mistake; the police won't care. I blamed myself for taking the credit for securing the Point Grey account. Holly went mad at me the day before the Christmas party. Calling me names, threatening to escalate it and tell her line manager. She's not this innocent angel everyone's making her out to be you know. She knew her own mind. In fact, she was pretty vile at times. I hate it when people die and we can't talk about their faults. They were still human beings. No one is perfect.'

'I had no idea . . .'

'There were times when she was late for work or she turned up hungover for a meeting, and there was that stuff about the presents she was getting from her secret boyfriend. Showing off. Rubbing it in our faces just because her new man sent her flowers one time.'

'I didn't know she had a boyfriend?'

'Rumours were that she and Charlie had a fling . . . They were *particularly* close at the Christmas party. If that's true he should have been a gentleman and made sure she got home ok. He's got that on his conscience. Then again, so does Zander. He was supposed to be in charge of arranging taxis. What I'm saying is, you can't dwell on the past if you want to move forward.'

Mel sniffs. 'You're right, thank you. So, Charlie and Holly were together at the Christmas party?'

'We all know he goes after anything in a skirt that moves.'

Mel pushes off the duvet cover. Nicole complains at the shock of cold air which rushes in.

'Sorry, I'm desperate for the toilet.'

She checks the clock. Another ten minutes have passed. Where are they? A bleak flash of panic clutches her chest. *What if they don't come back?* She forces the thought away.

'He told me earlier he had a row with her that night,' she calls from the freezing-cold bathroom. A cloud of breath hangs in the air.

'A row? Over what?'

'He didn't say exactly.' Mel pauses, trying to remember. He was rattled. Smoking and pacing. Those weren't the actions of someone who has nothing to hide. 'He acted like he couldn't remember but it felt like he was lying. His body language said something different.'

'There you go,' Nicole says as if this confirms it.

Had Holly and Charlie been together? Was he her secret boyfriend? Mel remembers the girls in the ladies' bathroom saying something along those lines.

'Does anyone know if it's true?' she asks, drying her hands.

'He's like twelve years older than her, he's not going to be yelling it from the rooftops.'

Mel's heart aches. How has everyone else seen what's been going on but her? She absently folds the hand towel on the ice-cold towel rail and heads towards the bed, chastising herself for being so blinkered when it comes to Charlie. She has seen a different side to him tonight, picking up on how much he belittles people and ignores their ideas. It's a really unattractive quality. In fact, the more she's around him the more the shiny veneer cracks. Plus, she'd never date a smoker.

She's about to say all this to Nicole when the bedroom light above them suddenly flickers.

Their eyes lock.

'What the hell was that?' Nicole asks.

Adrenaline zips through Mel's body.

There's a brief moment when the bulb shines extremely bright.

The next moment, they are plunged into complete darkness.

43

Friday 21st June

The weak glow of the fire exit sign illuminated above the door casts the only light in the bedroom.

'Nicole?' Mel calls from the sudden terrifying shadows.

'I'm here.'

Mel moves and bangs her knee on something hard, a coffee table perhaps. A burst of white heat rushes through her leg. She hears the sound of rustling fabric and senses movement around her.

There is a whisper of a breeze that she's sure wasn't there a moment before – as if someone has opened a door but it must be her imagination as they barricaded themselves in.

She presses her eyelids shut, trying to block the escalating panic. Is it Edward? Has he been listening to them? Is this the next part of his plan? She swallows. Her fingernails dig into the wallpaper behind her, needing to hold on to something solid. It takes Mel's eyes a second to adjust once she opens them, but soon she can sort of make out the shapes around her.

'Nicole? Are you ok?' Mel asks, her voice is reed thin.

There's no response.

Mel's about to call her name again when, without warning, the main overhead emergency lights flicker on. The room is cast in an eerie green glow, it's like she's looking through night vision goggles.

Her insides turn cold.

Nicole's moved position.

She's out of bed.

'I was trying to find the light switch,' she says quickly, as if being caught doing something she shouldn't have. Her cheeks are streaked with make-up stains, marking the tracks of her tears. 'What the hell is going on?'

'Edward must have knocked the power out.'

The frosty chill and the whir of the air-conditioning has stopped. Her ears ring in the sudden silence.

Mel's confused at how pink Nicole's cheeks have gone. She looks guilty about something. *Where was she going?*

Nicole swears.

'Why did you move?' Mel asks quietly.

'Hmm?'

'Just then. You moved. Where were you going?'

'I told you. I was trying to find the light switch.' Her eyes flick to the side.

She's lying.

'Why are you looking at me like that?' Nicole asks, lifting her right hand to push her hair from her face. As she does the quick movement reveals something Mel hadn't seen before. Something that wasn't there before the blackout.

Beside Nicole, half tucked behind a cushion, is a tall, metal candlestick holder.

'Where did you get that?' She swallows.

'It was on the shelf. It's not to hurt you,' Nicole says, eyes widening as she sees the look on Mel's face. 'I thought I needed something to defend myself with, I thought Edward was about to burst in and attack us! Honestly, I wouldn't hurt you, Mel.'

Is she paranoid and looking for things that don't exist or is Nicole lying?

If this night has shown her anything, it's that she doesn't know her colleagues as well as she thought she did.

She remembers the vicious scratches over the Polaroid photo found in Nicole's room, supposedly planted by Edward. Did she take her word for it too easily? Mel eyes her warily. Right now, she doesn't have much choice but to believe her.

'Hang on. What was that?' Nicole whispers, interrupting Mel's spiralling thoughts.

They both strain to listen for a faint sound from outside the room that came a moment before.

'Mel? Did you hear that?'

'Shhh . . .'

'That was someone screaming. I'm sure of it. A woman screaming.'

Nicole and Mel swap terrified looks. 'Bonnie.'

44

Friday 21st June

They both sprint down the darkened corridor, towards the stairs leading down to the lower level of the hotel. In her rush, Mel nearly trips and hurriedly clasps on to the handrail, the shock of the ice-cold metal doing little to bring her to her senses. Nicole is right behind her. Pain etched on her face as she holds her injured arm. Mel's heart races, she feels light-headed with dizziness and panic.

'Help,' Charlie's voice echoes off the stone walls, coming from down below.

'We're coming!' Mel calls.

It's only afterwards she thinks how foolish they were to run towards their colleagues without knowing what they could be confronted with. But there was something so bloodcurdling about that scream they heard, they moved without thinking.

Mel prays that the emergency lights stay on. With no port-holes down here, if the power goes again it would be pitch black. It's like they're in an endless maze. Moans echo down the corridor. Confusion about where it's coming from makes her panic even more.

They rush down the narrow corridor, past the door marked private leading to the staff rooms. A network of pipes, tangled wires and sprinkler systems criss-crosses over their heads. Dusty metal tubes that were painted white decades ago, now stained with rust spots, are held with thick screws and rivets. It's impossible to see where they are heading.

'Hurry!' Charlie yells.

The thrum of blood pounds in her ears. Her heart is racing, not just from the exertion of racing down the steps, but also from the sheer terror of not knowing what new horror they're about to be faced with.

She turns the corner and is greeted with a scene that will stay with her in her nightmares. Bonnie is on the dusty stone floor, low groans of pain coming from her quivering lips. Her hands are pressed against her stomach. Blood is staining her fingers.

'Oh my God. Bonnie, are you ok?' Nicole gasps at the sight of her.

Charlie is crouched down, his head in his hands, panting.

'The lights went out. We found the generator. When it came back on . . . Zander, he, he, he . . .' Charlie can't get his words out. He lifts his traumatised face. His filthy hands trembling as he rubs them through his hair.

Bonnie is shaking uncontrollably. A stream of unintelligible words are flowing from her pale lips.

'Where's Zander?' Nicole cries. 'Where's Edward?'

They ignore her. Moans and swear words fill the cold air.

'Come on, we need to get out of here. She needs the first aid kit,' Mel says as she turns to Nicole.

'But what about Zander? Where the fuck is Zander?' Nicole

demands. 'Did Edward do this? Is he here?' Her head twists sharply as if expecting him to slip out from the shadows. 'Has he hurt you, Bonnie? Please talk to us!'

The longer it takes to get any sense out of the pair of them, the more the creeping dread envelops Mel. They're not safe down here. What if this is a trap?

'Can someone tell us what happened?' Mel cries, louder than she'd expected. 'Where's Zander?'

There is a harrowing moment of silence, only broken by a pained moan from Bonnie. Eventually, Charlie lifts his head to face them. Spittle dribbles beside his mouth. 'It's too late for him.'

'What?' Mel gasps. Her heartbeat pounds in her skull.

He hangs his head once more. 'Zander's dead.'

45

The Daily News Online

Monday 24th June

HOTEL OF HORRORS

<u>**Published: 14:02, 24 June**</u>

SOCIAL MEDIA trolls are being accused of hampering the investigation into the fatal fire at Point Grey hotel off the coast of Portsmouth.

The fire is believed to have been started deliberately in the early hours of Friday morning (21st June) at the 150-year-old luxury hotel in the Solent. Police have launched a murder inquiry after detectives revealed evidence of a shooting. Eight people were onboard at the time. The venue was being used as a corporate event by Flavour, a design agency from Buckinghamshire, for its annual summer party.

Hampshire Police last night attacked 'keyboard warriors' of hampering its enquiries and urged members of the public to stop speculating.

Detective Inspector Stephanie Hutchinson who is leading the investigation said: 'Please do not use social media to speculate, share false information, accusations and rumours.'

A source close to the investigation said, 'It's not helpful seeing armchair detectives come up with their theories about what's happened. Families are still waiting to find out if their loved ones survived. It's callous to read the things people are posting online.'

According to the source, at least one of the bodies had to be identified with dental records, and it is expected that further forensic examinations will need to take place.

These 'keyboard warriors' are also being warned by the Hampshire police to think before they post.

In a new statement, Flavour, the design agency which had hired the hotel for a summer party, has said: 'We are working closely with the emergency services. We do not intend to comment further and would ask people not to speculate on the circumstances. Anyone with any information is asked to contact Hampshire Police.'

It emerged today that the company was first hit by tragedy last year when one of its employees died following the company's Christmas party.

Holly Mills, 23, died in Ashdale Woods, Marlow, Buckinghamshire, on December 22nd last year. An inquest held last month concluded that she died from hypothermia after taking a short-cut on her way home from the Plaza Hotel, Marlow.

The fort is owned by luxury hotel brand Cobalt, which also owns several high-end hotels in the South East and on the Isle Of Wight. In 2022 the firm was fined £75k after admitting safety breaches in the infrastructure. Cobalt was approached for comment but declined.

Comments:

KezzLovesDan: You know it's never good when they're using dental records to identify a body. This must be heartbreaking for the families. I know social media can be harmful but the police have to understand that people are simply trying to help.

Nina89: That creative agency is clearly cursed.

KezzLovesDan: I heard they've banned all employees from speaking to the press.

Nina89: Sounds dodgy AF.

HugginsC: #RIPHollyMills

MerseysideMel: I stayed at Point Grey once. They couldn't poach an egg.

JohnM: But what about the other bodies? Why are the police taking so long to confirm what we all suspect? No one is surviving this.

The views expressed in the comments above are those of our users and do not necessarily reflect the views of News-Online.

46

Friday 21st June

He's dead. *Zander's dead.*

The words ring on repeat through Mel's mind as the grubby floor comes up to meet her.

A high-pitched buzzing sound starts at the back of her head. The beginnings of a migraine pulsating at the side of her brain. She blinks away the dark splodges creeping into the corners of her vision as Bonnie lets out a moan. The sight of Bonnie's blood cupped in her hands sparks her to take action.

'We need to get her out of here.' Mel turns to Nicole. 'Help me take her up the stairs. The first aid kit is up there.'

Eventually, they make their way back up to the surface, their progress hampered by Bonnie's wound, Nicole's broken arm, and Mel's injured wrist, which is starting to throb under the bandage Edward applied earlier. Bonnie flinches if Charlie goes anywhere near her. They manage to slowly make their way down the dark corridor to get to the residents' lounge. The hotel walls creak around them. Holding its breath. Guarding the truth. Keeping its sinister secrets.

Despite the air-conditioning not working, the room is still

freezing cold. Without the warm glow of the Tiffany lamps, it feels uninviting and haunting in here.

Nicole helps Bonnie carefully lean back on the sofa, she gasps in pain, eyes clenched shut. Mel shivers.

Charlie takes off his Flavour jacket. 'Here.'

Mel hesitates. 'Are you sure? I mean, you're not cold?'

'No. I can't feel anything.'

She silently takes the jacket. She thought it might smell of him but all she can smell is the plastic scent of the packaging it was wrapped in. She puts it on, gratefully. He sinks into an armchair and throws his head in his hands.

Nicole begins rummaging in the first aid box.

'Please can one of you tell us what happened? Did Edward shoot Zander?' Mel asks.

'No.' Charlie lets out a hacking cough.

Mel presses a thumb to her pounding temple. 'We need you to go back to the start. From when you left us.' *When Zander was alive,* she wants to add. When three went down, but only two came back. 'The three of you went to find the horn to call for help . . . was Edward hiding in there? Did you see him?'

'No. We went down to that secret passage, certain the horn would be operated from there.' Charlie shakes his head. 'I could hardly stand up in the tunnel, it was so low. Much lower than I thought. You had to crouch at this awkward angle. Well, I mean, I did. The others are shorter than me. So Zander went in first, then Bonnie, then me. Even before the power cut it was pretty dark down there, with only a few lights spaced far apart. Zander had the most battery on his phone so could use the torch. That's why he went first. So, he was leading the way, telling us to watch out as there were loose tiles on the floor and stuff, worried we might fall over. Suddenly he went quiet.' His Adam's apple bobs up and down. A tremor starts in his jawline.

Mel glances over at Bonnie, Nicole has found some gauze in the first aid kit to press against her waist. Blood has soaked through her dress. There is a smell of sweat in the charged air.

'It was eerie. I called his name. Bonnie did too, I think. But he didn't answer. I guess that's when I freaked out.'

'What do you mean *freaked out*?'

'I asked him to tell us what he could see. I was fucking terrified in case Edward was hiding down there.'

'Then what?' Nicole asks, looking up.

He dips his head. 'I pushed past Bonnie to get to Zander and see for myself what was wrong. I must have pushed too hard as Bonnie started screaming at me for stabbing her. I swear I didn't.'

'Yes, you did,' Bonnie gasps, finding her voice for the first time.

'What? No, I didn't.' Charlie lets out a wheezing cough. 'I only pushed her because Zander was acting really weird. He was completely silent. Perhaps she fell against a sharp pipe or something? There were loads of unsafe things down there. You can search me for a knife!' He holds his filthy hands up, covered in what looks like soot.

Judging by the speed of his breathing, he's getting worked up again. Mel needs him back on track with what happened.

'So you got to Zander and . . .' she prompts.

He shakes his head. 'No. I couldn't get to him. That was when the lights – the few lights there were – went out. I don't know if we knocked a switch or whether Edward did it from wherever he's hiding but it went pitch black. And I mean pitch black. You couldn't see a thing down there.'

So that was what caused the blackout across the entire hotel.

'Zander screamed. I've never heard anyone make a sound like that,' Charlie rubs his face. His trousers are blackened. There is plaster and dust in his hair. 'I fumbled around in the darkness, calling his name, begging him to answer me. Then the emergency lights powered up, and everything was this strange sort of orange colour.' That's when the generator must have kicked in. 'And that's when I notice Zander lying on the ground ahead, around the bend. Lifeless. I think he's been electrocuted.'

Electrocuted.

He gulps air. 'Bonnie was screaming. I couldn't breathe. That's when I yelled for you to come and help us.'

'So Edward wasn't in there?'

'No. I didn't see him. He didn't kill Zander.'

'Please tell me you at least found the horn to call for help before this happened?' Mel asks, her voice wobbling.

She already knows the answer.

'The only things down there were electrical cables, the generator, some random old tools and broken bits of furniture,' Charlie replies grimly. 'No horn.'

And now another body.

'That is bullshit,' Bonnie yells, her Scottish accent growing thicker in her fury. 'Charlie hurt Zander and attacked me.' She gets up, wobbling slightly and staggers towards the door of the residents' lounge.

'Wait – where are you going?' Mel calls. 'You need to rest, you're bleeding.'

'I'm not staying anywhere near him.' She looks genuinely terrified.

Nicole turns to face Charlie. 'Is it true? Did you kill Zander?'

'Me? No. I wouldn't do that—' Charlie starts.

'Did you stab Bonnie?' Nicole presses.

'No! I haven't hurt anyone.'

'Well why is she saying you have? Why is she so freaked out?' Nicole shares a look with Mel. Eyes wide, nostrils flared.

Mel was thinking the same thing. Subconsciously or not, both Mel and Nicole slowly inch away from Charlie. It's his word against Bonnie's and they both know he hasn't been completely honest tonight.

'I don't fucking know. None of you are listening to me, I told you what happened,' Charlie snaps.

Bonnie doesn't wait a second longer, she pulls open the door and lurches into the dark corridor.

'What happened to Zander was an accident and I swear I never hurt Bonnie, but there's some dude roaming this hotel who's legit killing people so if you want to chance it and bump into him, then be my guest. For all we know this could be his masterplan. Get us to turn on one another whilst he's just chilling somewhere,' Charlie yells behind her.

The door slams shut. Mel's heart hammers.

Nicole chews her thumbnail. Eyes flicking between Mel and Charlie. No one speaks. He mutters something under his breath.

After a moment of hesitation, Nicole leaps to her feet and rushes after Bonnie.

Leaving Mel and Charlie alone.

47

Mel has no idea where Nicole and Bonnie have gone. She shifts on the sofa, shivering despite wearing Charlie's jacket. He is hunched over in the chair opposite. He must sense her moving and looks at Mel with big watery eyes. There is no colour in his cheeks. In this dim light, he looks deathly ill.

'It was an accident. What happened to Zander, I mean. Any one of us could have touched the wrong thing. It was a death trap down there.' He pants, wringing his filthy hands. 'I didn't hurt Bonnie on purpose like she's making out. Maybe I was too rough when I pushed past to get to Zander but she's acting like I took a knife and stabbed her. I'm telling you the truth. Please, you have to believe me, Mel.'

Mel's legs zip with adrenaline. She struggles to look him in the eye. There's safety in numbers and right now she doesn't feel safe around him. He rubs his face. She sees the dried reddish blood stamped on the side of his hand. This isn't a terrible nightmare she will wake up from. This is real.

Something in her gut is telling her to go and find Bonnie and Nicole.

Just in case.

'I . . . I don't know what's going on,' Mel stutters.

Why would Bonnie lie about what happened? She looked genuinely terrified of being anywhere near him. But, if she is telling the truth then why have they both left her alone with him? She tentatively stands up, gripping on to the back of the chair for support.

'It's like you're forgetting about this night manager,' Charlie says, determinedly. His voice cuts through her spiralling anxiety. 'He's the one we should be afraid of. Not me.' He thumps a fist on the sofa arm.

Mel backs away. A moment ago, he was begging to be listened to. Now he's fired up. Gone is the distress, replaced by a steely resolve to prove his alleged innocence. Why switch from flight to fight mode so suddenly?

She's not sure what to do. Her body tells her to run, even if it means she risks bumping into Edward. She needs time alone to try and process things. Too much has happened too quickly. Three dead colleagues in a matter of hours and now accusations that Charlie is a dangerous liar. Worse than that. He stabbed Bonnie and killed Zander.

Her heart races.

'Come on, Mel. You can't think I would hurt anyone?' There's a desperate plea back in his voice. He must sense she's edging away.

Mel's never seen anyone look as scared of someone as Bonnie did with Charlie. You can't fake that. She thought she knew him but judging by tonight's revelations, she clearly knows nothing about this man.

She has to find Nicole and Bonnie immediately.

'I need a drink of w-water . . .' she stutters, backing away. Her calves connecting with the edge of the wooden bookcase, she bites down the heat of pain and heaves open the door. She races down the dimly lit hallway. Her breath escapes in jagged gasps with every step.

'Mel!' He calls after her but she doesn't stop.

She scrambles into the dark kitchen, her best bet to find a weapon. She needs to have something. Just as Nicole had that candlestick and Edward has the gun. The swing door lets out a gasp of air as it brushes across the tiled floor. She waits for the emergency light to come on.

An acidic taste burns the back of her dry throat from the sudden exertion. Her heart is pounding against her ribcage.

The harsh strip lights blink overhead. One of them isn't working and casts the cold, sterile room in a macabre cinematic flicker. There is a beeping noise coming from somewhere. Mel glances around nervously as if someone is going to leap out at her. She could be heading straight into Edward's clutch. Has he caught Bonnie and Nicole? Is this some sick game of hide and seek?

She tries to slow her breath as much as she can.

She's all alone.

There is a food preparation area to her left – a slab of stainless steel like a solitary autopsy table - cluttered with empty clear plastic trays, and breadcrumbs scattered across a scratched chopping board. Three tall silver cabinets with glass fronts holding neatly stacked crockery. Wipe-clean gun-metal grey surfaces jut out from the walls. It reminds her of a morgue. An imposing commercial oven sits in the shadow beneath an enormous steel hood and grill tops. Rhythmic drips from a tap clang against the stainless steel sink on the opposite side of the room. Instinctively she glances at the line of chef knives held up by a wide magnetic strip on the far wall.

One of them is missing.

Bile swirls in her stomach.

She dashes across the tiles and has a shaking hand on the handle of one of the other sharp butcher's knives when she hears something.

It's coming from the other side of the room, where the walk-in freezer is.

The repetitive dull beeping tone she noticed when she first entered the kitchen has grown louder. She realises it's a warning. An alarm to close a door that is ajar. Her own fridge makes the same noise if she's left it open too long. She picks up the knife, the cold chrome handle sending a jolt of adrenaline through her trembling palm.

Her eyes take in a dark stain on the floor. The light in here makes it difficult to see what colour it is. It's coming from the direction of the beeping. She takes a slow step closer to the noise.

Mel's heart leaps up into her throat. She lifts the knife higher in her quivering hand. Despite every fibre of her being yelling to run and hide, she has to see what's inside.

There's a buzzing in her ears. The ringing of the freezer alarm pounds against her skull. Louder and louder. A faint whimpering comes from her own cracked lips. She follows the deep stain on the tiles.

Her legs don't want to move any closer. Is this where Bonnie and Nicole are?

Mel swallows deeply, almost faint with light-headedness.

She reaches the enormous steel walk-in freezer and grips the large metal handle with her shaking free hand. The door creaks further open inch by inch. The sound travels through her bones. Her grip tightens around the knife. A gust of ice-cold air blows in her face as a bright white light flickers on, illuminating what's inside.

Darkness creeps to the edge of her vision, threatening to submerse her.

No . . . no . . . no.

Crash.

She drops the butcher's knife on the floor with a loud clang. Her knees buckle and she stumbles against a tall metal shelving unit. She closes her eyes, praying that when she opens them again things will be different. It won't be real. This nightmare will be nothing more than that. A horrific, terrible nightmare. She didn't think things could get any worse.

But no.

Her breath catches in her chest at what's in front of her.

The kitchen tilts.

Mel swallows down the sudden rush of bile that's leapt up to the back of her throat.

The black trousers, the light grey branded polo shirt, the flash of red hair.

There, in the walk-in freezer, amongst shelves full of frozen meat, is the night manager.

The very dead night manager. He's frozen solid.

48

Friday 21st June

Mel clamps both her hands to her open mouth and tries to stop herself from retching at the sight before her. Her body shakes with adrenaline, to the point that she doesn't register the sudden glacial drop in temperature or the bitterly cold air blasting out of the open freezer door.

Edward's bulging, veiny eyes stare back at her sightlessly.

He is lying on his back with his head tilted towards her.

Frost has formed on his pale, almost translucent eyelashes. His wax-like skin looks burnt, like those mountaineers who get caught out by an icy windstorm. At first, she thought he had frozen to death, trapped in the walk-in freezer, suffocated from lack of oxygen perhaps. But all it takes is a quick, second glance, to see what's really happened to him.

His legs are awkwardly bent in his smart suit trousers, and there's a flash of deep maroon pooling out around his head. Mel blinks. The wound, so deep that the fleshy, spongy inside is exposed to the icy elements. She sees the handle of a kitchen knife that someone has thrust in the side of his neck. Her stomach violently clenches. She has to swallow the vomit that's leapt to her throat.

There's no movement under his shirt, no hint of a breath, of his ribs expanding and falling. Hours ago he was with her bandaging her wrist, and now he's here.

Dead.

Murdered.

Freezing cold gusts of air blow across Mel's face. Holly immediately zooms to the front of her mind. Frozen like her brother.

She last saw Edward just after ten o'clock closing the hotel doors as the other party revellers went down to the pontoon to climb onboard the return boat. It's now almost four o'clock in the morning. At some point during these times someone has killed him and not told a soul.

She can't tell how long he's been here from the colour of his skin or how quickly he's bled out. She forces herself to look again at him. There is an icy layer on the blood from his neck wound, pooling around him. It hasn't frozen solid. This has happened recently.

She remembers the stain on the kitchen tiles. Smeared blood. Someone's killed him and dragged him in here. Hidden him from the others.

One of her colleagues has done this.

She stumbles out of the freezer, half aware of a noise behind her.

'Mel?' Charlie stops in his tracks.

Deep red circles are ringed around each eye. His hair is mussed up. His voice sounds distorted against the pounding in her head. The freezer is still beeping. A gust of arctic air blasts against her face.

'Are you . . . Fuck. Is that? . . . Is he alive?' he asks between heavy pants, moving closer to get a better look.

Mel can't speak. Her teeth are chattering. A cutting grip of panic has brought her skin out in goosebumps.

'No.' Charlie covers his mouth in shock.

She prays for him to close the freezer door. The beeping is incessant, warning them that the cold air is escaping. As if that's the worst thing that is happening in this kitchen. Charlie acts unaware of the noise or the ice-cold temperature gushing into the room.

This changes everything.

'Y-y-y-you got peas from the freezer,' Mel manages to say, her lips trembling, the words coming out in static bursts.

Hours ago, Charlie came here to get a bag of frozen peas for Nicole's swollen arm. A gentle touch that she had thought was so kind and considerate.

No one else has been in the kitchen, let alone the freezer since.

'Yes I did, but wait . . .' Charlie's eyes widen. 'Are you saying that *I* put him here? That I did this to him?'

'Well, someone did,' Mel shrieks.

Charlie tentatively steps towards her. The overhead kitchen light flickers ominously above them. 'Mel? Mel, come on. It wasn't me. I had nothing to do with this. Is this what you think of me? You know me. Come on!'

'I don't know you . . .' she stutters, her teeth chattering. 'You lied to me.'

'What? What are you talking about?' His posture has

changed. There's a frenetic charge of energy that pulsates off him.

She notices how his fists have curled by his side. A flicker in his strong jawline. A sudden rush of reality kicks in. Bonnie was so certain that Charlie hurt Zander and was coming after her. He can't be trusted. He lied. Mel presses herself against the wall to steady her trembling legs.

She needs to get as far away as possible from this man.

She spins and races out of the kitchen. Charlie's arm shoots out, trying to stop her. His hand almost grabs her but she's too quick. She catches sight of his shocked face, anger and confusion in his red eyes.

'Mel. Wait. Come back,' he yells.

She stumbles, her legs not working as quickly as she needs them to but she doesn't stop.

His voice echoes down the corridor after her. 'You've got this wrong. You're going to get yourself hurt!'

It's too dark, too difficult to see where she's going. The emergency lights offer little to show her the way to go. She hears him behind her, his heavy footsteps pounding after her.

Chasing her.

She tries to block out his desperate pleas for her to stop but she won't. Her breath is in her throat. Where is she going to go? Where are the others? There's nowhere to run to. No escape.

She pounds on closed bedroom doors, praying Bonnie and Nicole are hiding in one and will let her in. Lock this monster out.

The doors remain shut.

The grandfather clock chimes four from further down the

hotel. A heavy smoky smell wafts towards her. Something is burning. It's coming from outside. She races up the stairs from the courtyard to the roof terrace, praying the women are here and that they are safe.

It doesn't feel real at first. It takes a second for her brain to process the scene.

Her heavy breathing is drowned out by the hiss and spit of an open fire in the fire pit. Nicole is moving around it like some sort of sacrificial ceremony. Bonnie has something in her hand, throwing it into the growing flames. A blanket is wrapped around her stomach to stem the bleeding. Mel's overcome by their determination and skill but this fire might be too late. There isn't a boat to be seen on the horizon.

'The night manager . . . Edward . . .' Mel pants, a sickly buttery sort of taste at the back of her throat. Lactic acid pulses in her legs.

The women stop throwing paper on the fire when they see her.

'Where?' Nicole spins.

'He's dead . . . I found him in the freezer. He's been murdered.'

Bonnie snaps her head up, she starts to say something but is cut off by Nicole's screams.

She lifts her unbroken arm and points behind Mel.

Charlie has raced up the steps, following her.

Only now he's holding a gun.

49

Monday 24th June

*E*xhibit *number PG23: Messages retrieved from the Flavour creative design agency server. Evidence provided by Tom Beckett, IT Manager, for Flavour creative design agency on Monday 24th June.*

Date: Saturday 27th May 09.11
From: Holly Mills
To: Flavour Admin

Hey,

I just wanted to say thanks so much for helping me get home last night. I can't believe the rain. It was really kind of you to make sure I wasn't left stranded. I hope you had a good night and your head isn't too sore today. I had no idea the team was so wild – I mean, did you see Wesley on the dancefloor?

Being the new girl is always tricky but everyone has been friendly. Of course, there are some people – not naming any names – but you get them anywhere you work. At my last place, there was this guy who was so weird. We all had bets on when we would see his mug-shot on Crime Watch. You'll have to give me tips on who to keep an eye out for here.

Anyway, I'd better try and get some more sleep. See you at work on Monday and thanks again,

Holly x
[Sent via Powwow]

*

Date: Thursday 22nd June 22.03
From: Holly Mills
To: Flavour Admin

Hey,

Thanks for your help today. You didn't need to stay behind to help me clear up. I thought people might be asking questions about helping a junior employee given your job title. It was like herding cats, trying to get them all to sit down for that meal, wasn't it? Remind me never to volunteer to organise a dinner at a conference again. I had no idea how hard it would be!

I spent hours agonising over the menu. There's the gluten-free, vegetarians, vegans, lactose intolerants, and nut allergies. You name it, they work for the clients. I also had the seating plan to piece together, like one of those jigsaw puzzles where all the pieces look the same but are actually ever so slightly different. Usually with pictures of baked beans on.

When orders were sent to the wrong tables I freaked out it was all going to go wrong. As the newest starter in the room, I have the most to lose. Last in, first out, and all that.

Did you see how as soon as the wine was poured people started to unwind? You were right about that. I told myself that if I can get to the end of the meal then I can relax and enjoy myself. Sorry, you're the last person I should be moaning to but I wanted to say that your comments about how well it went made a difference. It's not often people praise the graduate for their hard work and I'm so happy you saw the effort I went to. I didn't want to let you down.

Anyway, I wondered if you still wanted to meet at the bar? Like you said earlier?

I'll wait for you, just in case.

Holly x
[Sent via Powwow]

*

Date: Friday 4th August 11.45
From: Holly Mills
To: Flavour Admin

That was so kind of you to drive me home. Don't worry I haven't told anyone.

[Sent via Powwow]

*

Date: Friday 13th October 11.45
From: Holly Mills
To: Flavour Admin

How many cocktails did you let me have last night? I didn't think I drank that much but I've been as sick as a dog all day. It was worth it though. ☺

Don't worry I'm sure no one saw us leave together. Nicole asked me how I got back and I said that I got an Uber.

You do not look hungover at all. In fact, you look great today. I keep walking past your desk; I'm sure Mel is going to notice. She's always hanging around wanting to talk to you about something. You're really kind to her, listening to her go on and on. That woman can talk for England. I bet she has a crush on you; most of the women here do. I shouldn't tell you that though, you'll get a big head.

I want to scream from the rooftops that I'm the one who is with you. Hands off, he's my man. Except, well, you're not, are you? I hate that you go back to her every night. When will you tell her? You promised me that I need to wait a little longer but it's killing me. I'm trying to be patient, baby, but when will you speak to her? I thought you said you had it all worked out. That you knew exactly how you were going to break it to her that it was over. So what's the hold-up?

I don't think I can wait. Keeping this secret between the two of us much longer is killing me.

> Love, H xx
> *[Sent via Powwow]*

*

Date: Friday 22nd December 19.47
From: Holly Mills
To: Flavour Admin

Answer your phone.
  Answer your phone.
  Answer your phone.

> *[Sent via Powwow]*

Date: Friday 22nd December 19.50
From: Holly Mills
To: Flavour Admin

I have to speak to you. I can see these messages are getting to you. I can forget those mean things you said the other day. I know you've been stressed and under pressure but please baby. You can't treat me like this.
  Please. We have to talk. It's URGENT.

> *[Sent via Powwow]*

Date: Friday 22nd December 19.52
From: Holly Mills
To: Flavour Admin

I really didn't want to tell you like this but you're acting like I don't exist.
  I'm pregnant.

[Sent via Powwow]

Date: Friday 22nd December 20.34
From: Flavour Admin
To: Holly Mills

If you don't get an abortion then I'll fucking kill you

[Sent via Powwow]

50

Friday 21st June

It's as if the world has stopped spinning. Mel forgets to breathe. Every muscle from her head to her toes is snapped taut. She is frozen at the sight of her colleague. Not any colleague, the man she has lusted after, dreamt about for so long. Her work crush is wielding a gun and the dark mouth of the weapon is trained on her.

The missing gun. One of the Victorian pistols that was on the wall of the lounge. But this one is different to the other two on display. It's been modified. A long, metal tube added to the barrel. She tells herself the weapon is a harmless antique like Gus told her. Except that's a lie. She saw the bullet hole in Jonty's chest.

'It was you,' Mel gasps, eyes fixed on the small but deadly weapon in Charlie's filthy hands. 'You killed Jonty!'

The fire flickers dramatically as the wind picks up.

The storm is on its way.

'No. No, I didn't kill anyone! This was lying next to Edward's body in the freezer,' he yells. 'I shouted to tell you, but you kept running.' His chest is vibrating, rising and falling as he pants. Sweat glistens off his forehead. Blood is on his

263

shirt. Plaster and dust sit on the tips of his messy hair from scurrying around the hotel's inner tunnel looking for the ship's horn. In this pre-dawn light, lit by the blaze of the fire, he appears maniacal.

Mel didn't see a gun in the walk-in freezer. But then again, she didn't wait long enough to examine the bloodied area once she realised that Edward was murdered tonight, like Jonty, Wesley and Zander.

'Why didn't you leave it there?' Bonnie asks, panic laced through every syllable.

'I took it to protect myself,' Charlie replies sharply.

'Protect yourself? We need to be protected from you,' Nicole screeches.

'I don't want to hurt anyone,' Charlie continues. 'There have been some crazy accusations thrown around and none of you are listening to me.'

He orders them over to the bench beside the lighthouse on the opposite side of the roof terrace. Away from the fire. They traipse over, following his demands, as quickly as they can. Mel steals a glance at Bonnie and Nicole. They are huddled together on the wooden bench, whimpering. She perches beside them. A smoky sea breeze lifts her hair.

'One of *you* killed Edward. It wasn't me. I should be congratulating you for taking out this psycho but judging by the state of him it's one of you who's the psycho. Not me.' Charlie arcs his arm, slowly moving the gun around. It lands on Nicole. 'Course, I've just realised . . . you get to be the hero.'

'What?' Nicole glances up slowly, mascara smudged around her terrified eyes.

'You literally organised this fucking party.'

'You're saying *I* killed him?'

'I mean, you knew the geezer, I can't be the only one to have put two and two together . . .'

'Yeah and got five,' Nicole gasps.

Charlie looks so angry. An angry man holding a firearm. The tendons in his neck are snapped taut.

'Please Charlie,' Mel says, gripping the wooden slats. They need him to calm down. 'Put down the gun and we can try to talk calmly—'

'You don't know what someone is capable of until you push them too far,' Charlie interrupts her.

'What's that supposed to mean?' Nicole asks. 'You're scaring us.'

'I'm saying that I don't trust you. Any of you. *Everyone* here is a suspect.' He flicks the weapon towards each of the women in turn.

'We could say the same to you,' Bonnie says quickly before casting her eyes away, flinching at being so sharp with him.

Charlie steps closer to her. Taunting her. Pulling himself taller. 'What?'

'You were the only person to go to the freezer,' Mel blurts out.

There's a stunned silence.

'Oh my God. She's right. Only one person has gone to the kitchen since we arrived . . .' Bonnie says.

'I told you. He wasn't in the freezer then,' Charlie says, sounding exasperated, clenching his jaw.

'Can you put the gun down, please?' Nicole begs.

He ignores her and starts to pace, muttering under his breath.

'What really happened to Zander?' Mel asks, using all her might to keep her voice as measured and normal sounding as possible. Too scared to blink.

'I told you. He must have touched a live wire or something,' Charlie says.

He drops to the bench opposite the women. Placing the gun beside him. Still too close for comfort but at least it's not in his hands anymore. Mel's mind whirs. He's claiming what happened to Zander was an accident like what happened to Holly.

'H-how did you get into Wesley's room?' Mel asks, she has been turning this over in her mind.

'What? It wasn't locked. Edward must have left it open when he drugged Wes. Oh Jesus. Don't try and pin that on me too.'

'I'm not trying to do anything,' she replies quickly, not wanting to provoke him further.

There's a tense, drawn-out silence. The only sound is a crack and spark of flame from the fire pit. Mel prays it won't go out.

'What was your argument with Holly about? On the night of the Christmas party?' Nicole asks. Mel stares at her, is she antagonising him on purpose?

'What?' The question throws him.

'Mel told me you rowed with her,' she says. 'What was it about?'

'I can't remember.' His eyes dart to the left.

He's lying.

He's lied about lots of things tonight.

'I think you can remember.'

Mel's about to say something to keep the peace when he speaks.

'Fine. She had been doing some extracurricular work, digging into certain accounts and she'd come up with a theory that something underhand was going on in the office.' He inhales. 'Apparently, the figures didn't match up for a certain client and she was basically accusing me of having something to do with it. I told her it was none of her business and she needed to focus on her own accounts.'

'Which client was it?' Mel asks, knowing what he's going to say.

'Westways.'

The email sent from Holly. The one where she says someone has been stealing from the company. It makes sense. She was onto him. Wes, Jonty and Charlie. The three people working for this fake client, passing off expenses and pocketing the money.

'So you rowed because she had worked out you were part of this racketeering ring. She was going to expose you all.'

'You're making it sound worse than it is. Things got heated. I'd had a drink.'

Away from the fire, the cool wind makes Mel shiver. She pulls her jacket closer around her, absently pushing her hands in her pockets for extra warmth.

'Holly was right,' Nicole says quietly.

'Yeah, ok. She was right. Me and Jonty and Wes were in on a thing. I didn't say anything to you lot as I have been shitting myself that Edward was clearly so obsessed with this nutjob theory that we killed his sister to shut her up. With Jonty and

Wes dead, he would be coming after me. So yes, that night, at the Christmas party I was mad at her for uncovering our set-up but not mad enough to kill her. It wasn't like we were making millions!'

Mel's fingers touch the edges of something hard, grazing a sharp corner that scratches her skin. There's something in the pocket.

'So it's a coincidence that she died that night? The same night she reveals what she had uncovered about the three of you,' Nicole asks. 'Edward was onto something here . . . you needed her silenced. If it came out about Westways and the thefts then all of you would have lost your jobs.'

'What?' Charlie stares at her. His chest is vibrating with pent-up energy. 'No. It wasn't like that.' He snatches up the gun and starts to pace. Head down. Mouth in a tight, pinched line. 'One of you lot is setting me up here.'

'Put the gun down and we can talk about this like adults,' Nicole pleads. 'There has to be an answer to everything. We can solve it together. If you say you didn't kill anyone we believe you.' She's changed her voice to the slow, steady tone a hostage negotiator would use.

'Shut up,' Charlie yells.

Mel pulls out whatever is in her pocket. A rush of nausea grips her chest. She has to remind herself to breathe, staring at what's in her trembling hands.

Nicole looks over and gasps, her eyes bulging wide. 'Is that . . . ? Oh my God, is that . . . blood?'

The space around Mel pulses and sways.

'Charlie?' Mel's voice cracks. 'Why is Edward's name badge in your pocket?'

Edward: Happy To Help

'What? I've never seen that before.'

'You gave me this jacket to wear in the residents' lounge, when you and Bonnie came back from the tunnel, after Zander . . .' She trails out, her heart pounds. 'You had been wearing it for hours . . .'

Charlie lets out a string of expletives. 'Someone's setting me up. I have never seen that in my life.' He points at the badge with the gun. 'For all I know YOU put it there!' Spittle flies off his lips. 'Why won't any of you listen to me? Edward was the psycho yet you're acting like I'm the bad guy. How many times? I didn't kill him. I didn't kill no one.'

Bonnie stands up and takes a bold step forward. This confuses Charlie as much as Mel and Nicole.

'What are you doing?' he shouts. 'Stay over there. I'm trying to talk to you all. I don't want to lose track of my train of thought. *You're* the one they need to watch.' He moves the gun up and down, eyes darting at Mel and Nicole. 'She has something to do with everything that happened here. I'm sure of it. She knows more than she's letting on. Don't trust a word she says. Back off.'

But Bonnie doesn't stop. Her hand is outstretched. She's trying to be brave and show him that she's not scared, but the tremor in her legs gives away the panic that must be tearing through her with every step.

'You feel like you're backed in a corner, I get it. But you need to put the gun down. We don't want anyone else to get hurt. Please listen to us.'

Mel watches her move as if in slow-motion.

Charlie ignores her.

'Put the gun down,' Bonnie says, a little firmer.

A crackle sparks from the fire, flickers of orange light shoot through the air.

He resists, his wild eyes darting from left to right like a threatened animal. 'Or what?'

Mel uses this moment of confusion to make her move. She surges forward. Her left shoulder connects with Charlie's chest, the sudden unexpected advance winding him. He thrusts his empty arm in front of him to protect his body. The gun in his other hand moves in the tussle. The barrel lifts into the air, towards the dark cloudy sky. He tries to push her away with his free hand, but she fights back, focused only on disarming him. She needs to get the gun over the fort wall and into the sea.

For a couple of frantic seconds, Mel can only see a blur of colour. She hears Nicole yelling something but can't make sense of it. She needs to get the weapon out of his hands.

Her rage boils over but he's fighting back. His size and height overshadow her. She can't catch her breath. A pain erupts in her side. The wind picks up, carrying smoke from the fire that chokes her. She's not strong enough, her energy wanes.

Then the gun goes off.

51

Mel's ears ring with the vibrations of the gunshot. A never-ending chime reverberates through her skull. She screams.

This isn't happening.

Wake up, wake up.

Charlie drops to the ground. Blood is oozing out of his throat through a fleshy hole that's ripped through his jaw. There is a sickening gurgling sound as thick sticky blood gushes to the open wound.

Blood.

More blood.

There is a microsecond or two before she realises what's happened. The gun, pointing upwards, must have moved towards him. The loaded barrel twisted so it aimed straight for his jaw. He stood no chance at close range like that.

Mel cries, 'I've killed him.'

She can't get enough air. Everything inside her is vibrating. Her muscles throb with pain.

'Oh my God.' Nicole dry heaves, turning around on the bench.

Bonnie's eyes are closed as she mutters under her breath. It sounds like the Lord's Prayer.

'I didn't mean to shoot him. I . . . I . . .' Mel stutters. 'I was just trying to get the gun off him . . .'

'You didn't load the gun,' Bonnie says eventually, breaking the silence. She starts to pace. Sweat beads on her forehead. 'You saved us.' Her voice is pitchy and it's clear she's trying her best to maintain some measure of calm composure.

'He was a liar.' Nicole shakes uncontrollably. 'He killed Edward. You saw how he had his name badge. He went to the freezer. I'm sure he had a part to play in Holly's death. He knew Edward was coming after him, that's why he was so scared . . .'

Mel tries to swallow the burning acidic bile that's leapt up her throat. She wasn't thinking. Something took over. Fight or flight. She only wanted him to drop the gun, not for it to go off! She can't bring herself to look at his body. The man she dreamt about, the person who was the brightness in her day, is dead.

She killed him.

An animalistic whine escapes from Mel's cracked lips.

'Holly was right,' Nicole says, wiping her nose on her sleeve. She wobbles towards Mel. 'She discovered who was stealing from the company . . . I just can't believe the lengths they went to shut her up. Do you think they killed her?'

Bonnie looks out at the dark empty water. 'He killed Edward. Of course he has it in him to kill Holly too. His downfall was thinking he could get away with it.'

Mel gulps lungfuls of air. The conversation between her

colleagues going on around her. There's a buzzing sound in her head. 'I was trying to get the gun off him . . .' she repeats.

The others make soothing voices, telling her it's not her fault, she's not to blame. The ringing in her ears swirls and sloshes around her brain.

'What the hell do we do now?' Nicole asks, wiping her wet cheeks. 'We still need to get help. We can't swim to the mainland or use the lifeboat. We don't know if we're going to be rescued.'

A sudden gust of wind moves across them. It's as if the sky is drawing its breath. A low rumble from the heavens gets louder, though it still sounds far away. There's a change in air pressure. A torrent of rain could fall at any moment.

'We need a bigger fire,' Bonnie says, leading the way to the fire pit. 'We need more things to burn. It's the only way to get attention from a passing boat and get off this place.'

'I don't know if I can do this,' Mel says, tasting blood in her mouth from biting her tongue.

'You have to do this,' Nicole orders. 'We're so close to this nightmare being over. And then we tell the police it was self-defence. Charlie was pointing a gun at us. Who knows what he'd have done if you two hadn't been so brave.'

Suddenly an inner strength Mel had long forgotten she owned presses behind her ribcage. She has to do this.

For all of them. They have to get out of here.

'Grab anything you can. We can't let this fire go out,' Nicole says.

Mel moves slowly, every limb aches from her slamming into Charlie, to try and help gather whatever she can to burn. A crack of lightning forks above their heads. Point Grey seems to shake with a thunderous bass. Her heartbeat is thudding against her ribcage, her armpits moist with sweat.

'We need to hurry. It's going to rain any second,' Bonnie cries.

This is their only chance to get a fire as high as possible for someone out there to see it, realise it's an SOS and respond before the storm hits. Time is against them. They move as fast as they can despite their various injuries. No one is leaving this place unharmed.

Mel can still hear the ringing of the gunshot. It's as if she's in some alternate reality.

She starts to shake uncontrollably. Her teeth chatter. She can't breathe. The pain of everything she's ever been through – losing her dad, of watching her mum disappear before her eyes, the guilt swirling around her part in Holly's death, and the terror of what she's witnessed here tonight, make her dizzy with sick disbelief. Everyone she's loved, she's lost. No, it can't be true. Charlie can't be dead. A gut punch of sorrow knocks the air from her lungs.

Nicole wobbles over and puts her good arm around Mel's shoulders, squeezing her tight. 'Breathe. Keep it together a little longer, you can do this.'

This spurs Mel on. Working on autopilot they sprint around the roof terrace in search of what they need to fuel the fire. No one goes anywhere near the dead body by the lighthouse.

Mel throws napkins, paper lanterns and cardboard menus onto the fire. The smell of melting plastic and wood makes her eyes water. The blanket she used as she sat next to Charlie and he popped open the bottle of champagne by the hot tub, is now crisp and black. Soon she is sweating from the effort, surprised at how strong Bonnie is, despite her injury. She manages to grab two massive bottles of vodka from behind the bar and sprays the neat alcohol over the flames.

A whoosh of heat and light takes Mel's breath away. The fire must be five feet tall. Surely someone will see this and realise it's a cry for help? *Please, God.*

'I think that's enough. We need to get down to the pontoon and wait for help. Any rescue boats will pick us up from there,' Mel shouts across the hiss and spit of sparks.

The fire is bordering on growing out of control. Metal is warping behind a hazy screen of fierce flames. Hot embers shoot out.

Bonnie is reluctant to leave. She keeps disappearing and returning with more and more things to throw on the fire. Mel marvels at her determination despite her stomach injury but she needs to stop now.

'This is enough. We don't want the whole place to burn down. Someone will see this and come to save us,' Mel shouts.

Bonnie acts like she can't hear her. She's dragging decorative cushions and dried flower displays to throw onto the bonfire. A picture in a thick frame. A wooden bar stool, grunting with the effort, and pulling it across to the flames. Billowing grey smoke plumes across the sky.

'It's not safe for us to be up here. We've done enough. Come on,' Nicole yells. They need to move away before it takes hold of the wooden decking.

'No, we need more,' Bonnie pants.

Sweat is glistening on her forehead, beading across her top lip. Her hair has frizzed up, loose strands fanning her red face, grainy black soot on her cheeks. Her chest vibrates. Mel sees something on her face, the orange glow reflected in her wide determined eyes, and it scares her.

'We don't. We need to get to the pontoon and wait for someone to come and rescue us. They can't get us from up here,' Mel repeats. 'The fire is too high, there's no hope of a helicopter coming over and dropping a ladder for us. We need to get to the water.'

The intense heat is pressing against her skin.

'Oh, God.' She panics.

They've gone too far.

Thunder rolls across their heads.

'Help us!' Nicole yells across the black waves to the tiny blinking lights of the coast, all the way in the distance.

Mel grabs Bonnie's arm, fingertips pressing firm and pulls her away. It's as if the trance is broken. Ominous gravel grey-coloured clouds press over them. Nicole runs ahead towards the brick archway and shoves open the unlocked wooden doors. She doesn't stop until she gets to the metal steps leading down to the pontoon, where they embarked over twelve hours earlier.

Before this nightmare began. It's like a different lifetime.

Only the three of them remain, fleeing for their safety. Mel prays that help is on the way. That they are doing the right thing. She hears the hiss and spit of the flames. A sudden bang makes them jump. Something must have exploded, but they don't stop.

Within seconds the first raindrops start to fall.

'The fire is going to go out!' Bonnie cries.

'It's fine. Keep walking. We did as much as we could. Some-one will have seen it, I'm sure,' Mel says.

There are buoys in the distance, she can see small lights bobbing on the water. Soon a boat will pick up on their SOS and come and save them. She has to believe this is going to work.

Nicole is at the front, descending the steps, slightly ahead of the other two. She's gone quiet. The shock of the past few hours must be kicking in. Bonnie is in the middle. Mel is at the rear, to make sure Bonnie doesn't turn and return to the fire once more. She knows she's got their best interests at heart, but something was unnerving about her sheer determination to continue to stoke the flames.

The rain is falling heavier with every second. Mel's spirit crumbles. She doesn't want to alarm the others, but what if the fire does go out before catching anyone's attention? What if nobody realises it's a cry for help? What if the storm prevents any help from getting to them? She blinks these thoughts away and concentrates on holding on to the cold handrail and carefully making her way down the wet steps towards the pontoon. All they need is one fishing boat to see the fire and rescue them, take them away from here.

'Watch out. It's going to be slippery,' Mel calls from the back. She has to raise her voice as the rain splatters loudly against the metal.

She can see the lifeboat pinned to the side of the fort, their earlier chance of escape so near yet so far.

'I can't believe it,' Nicole says, cradling her arm. The homemade sling is covered in dirt, soot and blood. The fabric is turning translucent as it gets soaked with rain.

'What?' Mel asks.

'How could Charlie have fooled us all, acting like he was as scared as the rest of us, knowing what he'd done? I mean, *when* did he kill Edward?'

'I don't know—' Mel starts to answer but Nicole talks over her.

'He could have attacked him when he got those peas from the freezer but something doesn't feel right about that.' Her hair is stuck to the back of her neck. 'And the name badge . . .'

'Well—' Mel is cut off from saying anything else as suddenly there's a blur of movement followed by a high-pitched scream.

It's so fast that Mel can't work out what's happening.

Nicole tumbles forward. She flies in the air.

Bonnie reaches out a hand to stop her from falling but she isn't quick enough.

Nicole's leg twists and her arms flail as she lets out a strange, terrified sound.

Mel can only watch in horror from behind the two women as Nicole falls forward.

Her slim body crashes loudly against the metal and there's a sickening crack and a yelp of pain as she clatters down the rain-soaked steps. She lands in a heap on the bobbing pontoon.

'Nicole!' Mel screams.

But Nicole doesn't move.

52

Friday 21st June

Mel and Bonnie race as quickly as they can to Nicole, who is lying still in a crumpled heap at the base of the pontoon. She must have cut herself during the fall. There is a bloody trail marking her trajectory.

The sudden rainfall is getting heavier. There's nowhere to shelter. The roar of the waves fills their ears. The platform moves and sways and lifts with the tide. It wasn't this unsafe when they disembarked the boat but, without the collective weight of their colleagues, it's like being on a flimsy life raft. At least a railing lines the edge to stop anyone from falling into the water. Chunky black metal posts keep them contained.

'Oh my God,' Mel cries, blinking the rain off her lashes. 'I think she's knocked herself out.'

Nicole's not moving. A bruise is deepening around her right eye socket and there's a nasty gash on the side of her forehead but it's her leg in her grubby palazzo pyjama bottoms that looks the most worrying. It's jutting out at an unnatural angle.

'What happened?' Mel yells over the sound of water drumming against the metal base.

'She tripped . . . I tried to catch her but . . . but . . .' Bonnie stutters, bending down to their colleague. Her sodden Flavour branded jacket is slick against her small frame. 'She fell so fast and I . . . I couldn't help her.'

'Nicole? Nicole, can you hear us?' Mel asks loudly. She picks up Nicole's limp wrist and searches for a pulse. It's growing weaker. Her hands are covered in soot and scratches.

'Nicole?' Bonnie calls her name. 'Christ. This place is cursed.'

Salty sea air whips their wet hair. Mel scans the horizon. If a rescue boat comes, they will pick them up from here.

When, not *if*, Mel tells herself. It's only a matter of time before the fire draws people's attention and someone comes. As long as it stays alight.

This is their only chance of escape.

'Help will come. Someone will have seen the fire,' Mel says with as much conviction as she can muster.

'No boats are out in this weather. What if it's hours until anyone comes?' Bonnie cries.

'We've got to stay positive.'

The pontoon sways with each sudden wave. Nausea rolls through Mel. Her head is a jumble of thoughts. How has tonight ended like this?

The minutes pass.

The two women rest against the metal railing in numb silence, both locked in their own shell-shocked worlds. Eventually, Mel swallows the lump in her throat, to speak. She has to shout to be heard over the slapping waves.

'What was she saying before she fell?'

'Hmm?' Bonnie looks up. She reminds Mel of the images

she's seen in the news, of women in war-torn countries who stare at the camera lens with blank, dead eyes the only glimpse into the horror they've witnessed.

'Nicole. She said something about the name badge . . .'

'I think she said she can't believe that Charlie had it.'

Mel takes a breath. 'She's right. If he killed Edward, why would he take it and then carelessly leave it in his pocket for me to find?'

Bonnie shrugs and massages her temples.

'Things don't add up,' Mel croaks. 'Little things, like, I don't know . . . Charlie was so believable. He was adamant he didn't kill anyone. He looked as shocked as I was when we found Edward in the freezer.'

'He's been stealing from the company for God knows how long and got away with it. He's a good liar.'

Mel wraps her arms around herself. 'But why didn't he just admit to killing Edward, even if it was in self-defence?'

'Maybe we'll never know why.'

Mel tries to think straight. She needs to work out what's not adding up. She's missing a piece of the puzzle.

When did Charlie get the chance to kill Edward? He had an alibi for most of the night. He was never alone apart from when he went to get the peas from the freezer but he couldn't have killed Edward then. There wouldn't have been time. Plus Edward went on to kill Wesley with the drug-laced room service wine after that.

Think. A painful thudding sensation strikes up at the base of her skull. Exhaustion and dehydration kicking in.

Bonnie looks as if she's about to say something but in the distance there's a faint sound that lifts Mel's spirits. She's certain it's the honk of a ship's horn. She stands up straight, wobbling slightly.

It's the best sound she's ever heard.

'Look. I think someone is coming,' Bonnie starts to yell for help.

Mel holds a hand across her eyes, squinting against the rain, trying to peer across the water, to see if she can make out the boat that's on its way over to them. A rescue lifeboat? A fisherman? She doesn't care, she just needs them to hurry up.

Her brain ticks as the seconds drag by.

Why would Charlie offer his hoodie to her with the badge inside? Did he forget about it?

If it wasn't Charlie, then who did kill Edward?

'We're going to be saved!' Bonnie claps her hands. 'Nicole, help is coming. Hang in there a little longer, hen.'

Mel's eyes are fixed on the vessel coming towards them.

The only person who was ever alone for a longer period was Bonnie. She left the group in the residents' lounge to 'go to the bathroom'. Mel went to check on the lifeboats with Charlie so, really, she has no idea how long Bonnie was gone. Enough time to kill? Her mind whirs. Bonnie looks over at her. Mel tries to muster a genuine smile back.

Mel's heart thuds in her chest.

Things are slotting into place.

Bonnie stops waving her arms for the captain of the boat to see. 'Mel? Is something wrong?'

Mel gulps. She needs to act like everything is fine. If Bonnie's capable of violently killing Edward, then what's she capable of doing to Mel?

'No . . . I mean, I'm just in shock.'

A flash of darkness flickers across Bonnie's wide brown eyes, picked up by the faint beam of light, momentarily stuns Mel. Bonnie doesn't seem happy. In fact, she looks the complete opposite. Although Bonnie has been acting like a victim, she's equally capable of being the villain.

Bonnie stares at her as if reading her mind. 'This wasn't the plan . . .'

53

Friday 21st June

Mel tries to calm the building panic thrumming inside her chest. 'What do you mean it wasn't the plan?'

Bonnie stares at the rescue boat, which is still a fair distance away. Unaware of the things running through Mel's mind.

'What do you mean about a plan?' Mel pushes again, the lashing rain momentarily forgotten.

Bonnie continues to ignore her.

'Bonnie?' Mel presses, wiping rain from her eyes. She needs to see Bonnie clearly. 'What plan? Talk to me, please.'

'I knew Eddie.' Her voice has this otherworldly nature to it.

'Edward? What? What do you mean?' A prickle of unease runs down Mel's spine. She tries to keep her voice measured despite her rising fear.

She doesn't want to break eye contact with Bonnie to see how far off the boat is, but every second she's forced to wait lasts a lifetime. She's overwhelmed with adrenaline and uncertainty. She's learnt tonight that she doesn't know any of her colleagues and she certainly doesn't know anything about Bonnie.

'Bonnie?'

'You won't understand.'

'Please, I will.'

Eventually Bonnie takes a long, shaky, slow breath. 'I was coming out of work one night and a man stopped me. He said he needed me to help him with a task. At first, I wondered why he'd picked me but then it twigged, he'd seen my work uniform and knew that I had access to the office when no one else was around.'

'Edward?'

'Yes.'

'What did he want you to do?'

'He took me for a coffee, his grief filled the entire cafe. He made it sound so simple. He said he'd pay me to look for his sister's lost necklace.'

'Oh?'

'It was some family heirloom that Holly never took off, but it wasn't in her belongings that the police bagged up. So he scoured the woods where she died looking for it, in case it came off by accident but he couldn't find it. He'd also checked her flat and her car and he knew she'd never sell it so that's when he came to me, thinking perhaps it was at work. Maybe in her desk drawer. I said I'd hunt around to see if I could find it. If I did, he would pay and even if I didn't find it, he would still pay me. Win-win. It was the easiest money I'd ever make. All I had to do was look for this necklace.'

Bonnie swallows, shivering in the bitterly cold sea spray. The pontoon lurches. They both grip the railing.

'Did you find it?'

'No.'

Jonty was right when he accused Bonnie of going through his things. Searching, not stealing.

'I did, however, find something else . . .'

'What?'

'It was around the time you asked me to clear Holly's desk. Inside was her journal. It was full of accusations of bullying – spiteful comments, mean jokes, and things that others brushed off as office banter. It explained about the finances not adding up, the Westways account and the people she believed were stealing from the company.'

There is a twist of dread in Mel's chest and thoughts of the approaching boat – of the possibility of being saved – are momentarily forgotten.

Bonnie knew all of this? Every revelation that has shocked Mel this evening, Bonnie already knew and had known for some time.

'What did you do with this journal?' Mel asks, her voice doesn't sound like her own.

'I gave it to Eddie.'

Mel bristles at the familiarity of his name. 'Why didn't you come to me?' Any complaints about the company or employees should go to HR.

'What? And you'd do what with it? It was her diary. She was dead. I didn't want to be involved. Whatever she had going on, was not my battle to fight. I presumed Eddie would take it up with you if he thought it was important.' She swallows. 'It wasn't the necklace but he paid me anyway and we said goodbye and that was it. I didn't expect to see him again.'

'But then . . .'

She clears her throat. 'One evening he was waiting outside

for me. He claimed pages were missing. I told him his sister must have torn them out. But he didn't believe me, said I was hiding something. He quickly apologised for snapping and said his grandad had recently died. Then he asked for another favour.'

Mel's stomach clenches.

'You have to understand I needed the money for Dylan, to save my son's life.'

'What? What are you talking about?' Mel's head spins. 'You said he was working away in Italy?'

'I lied. He's in a rehab centre in Wandsworth. My wee boy is an addict. Heroin. I've tried everything to get him clean. But it's so expensive. This is my last shot at saving his life. You'd do the same if it was your child.' She bites her lip, tears shine in her glassy wide eyes. 'At first, Eddie appeared like an angel, offering this money when I needed it the most. He said he would pay even more, and that's how it started. The demands grew.' She dries her face with her sleeve.

'Like what?'

'He wanted me to listen to gossip. Record conversations. Jam the printer on purpose so I could clear documents at the end of the day and give them to him. I drew the line at stealing a laptop. He was fixated on the fact he believed there had been a cover-up around his sister's death and these people named in her journal were behind it. The fact Holly was onto something with Westways, was about to hand in the evidence she'd gathered but then she *died* . . . Well, he obsessed over it.'

Mel sags back against the metal railings, they wobble against her weight, unable to believe what she's hearing.

She thinks of the many conversations that Bonnie must

have overheard every single day. The things she's seen in the wastepaper bins. The printouts carelessly tossed by the printer. She has been watching, listening, taking it in without any of them realising.

Mel glances over at Nicole as the storm rages around them. She thinks she can see her chest rising and falling.

Bonnie takes a shaky breath. 'One evening Eddie turned up. We went for coffee and he explained where he worked and how he had suggested his venue for Flavour's annual summer party. He told me that he wanted to meet everyone who was named in Holly's journal. The VIPs. It was an opportunity to find out the truth. He hoped that one of you would tell him something – anything – which might help bring him closure.'

So they *were* all chosen.

'I honestly thought I was being helpful. If I'd known he was so crazed with grief I would never have let him continue with this party idea. I don't know how he managed to rig the draw so your names were chosen . . . I didn't want to know.'

All of them here tonight were named in this mysterious journal. They'd hurt Holly. Completely ignorant to the fact she had taken things so badly and had written it all down. Mel is desperate to know why her name was included.

Bonnie doesn't give Mel time to think, she raises her voice over the wind. 'It was only when the boat left and the taunts started that I began to worry. It was so subtle at first, I didn't pick up on it. Things like setting the air-con too cold, or leaving that magazine I'd given him in Nicole's room, or cutting the phone lines and damaging the lifeboat. But it was seeing that he'd poisoned Wesley, that's when I realised that he was here to get revenge.'

Revenge.

Mel almost tumbles as a strong wave lifts the pontoon. Wobbling she shifts her weight on the uneven decking. A white beam of light bounces over the waves. It's hard to tell how far away the boat is. How much longer does she have to wait?

'Where are these notes now? This hate-filled journal?'

Bonnie looks down at her soot-stained fingers. 'I don't know. That's why I went to his room with you. It would look too suspicious if I went alone. I wanted to search for it to show you.'

Mel blinks and wipes the salt spray from her face. Her hands smell of bonfire.

'As soon as Jonty was discovered, I realised exactly what a monster Eddie was. He would have gone on killing if Charlie hadn't killed him.'

Cold raindrops trickle down her face.

Mel clenches her jaw. 'That's a lie. Charlie didn't kill Edward . . .'

'Yes he did!'

She doesn't need Bonnie to finish her sentence. Mel is finally one step ahead of her. 'He didn't, did he? You know because *you* killed Edward.'

54

Friday 21st June

Bonnie loses her footing as the waves swell. She drops to her knees on the pontoon beside Nicole; she's not moved but she's still breathing.

'It was self-defence. Like you and Charlie,' Bonnie says.

'No.' Mel shakes her head. Her wet hair clumped together. 'No, this is nothing like me and Charlie. That was an accident!'

'So was this! Edward was coming for me. I was about to be his next victim. I knew too much. This was the end game. We *all* would have been murdered by him. Think about it. He planned for none of us to survive or get off this place alive. Himself included.'

Bonnie pulls herself back to her feet, wobbling as the pontoon lifts.

Mel listens in horror as she continues.

'Once I realised what he was up to I knew I had to try and reason with him. Maybe he'd listen to me, see sense. So, on the way to the bathroom, I saw him head into the kitchen. I followed him and begged him to stop. But he went mad and started coming at me. That's when I saw the gun in his hand. The one he'd used to shoot Jonty.'

Mel holds her breath.

'I tried to run away and must have knocked something on the floor. The tiles were wet. He chased after me and slipped. It happened in slow motion. He put his hand out to stop himself but there was a knife on the counter. He fell into it. Hit his head on the sharp edge of the kitchen surface and dropped to the floor. Blood was spurting out! I kept calling his name but there was no answer. So, I dragged him to the freezer and thought I'd closed the door. I don't know what I was thinking, honest. I didn't know what to do.' She's working herself up reliving this, her eyes blaze. Spit flies from her mouth.

'Why drag him into a freezer? Why not leave him in the kitchen?'

'I wasn't thinking straight.'

Mel's eyes flick to the boat behind Bonnie, growing ever closer. She wills it onward. A sudden wave lifts them both. She clings on to the railings.

'What about Zander? You said Charlie killed Zander and he stabbed you.'

'I lied. I think Zander *was* electrocuted. I watched as he pulled a low-hanging wire. I think he was moving it out of the way so we could get past, but he didn't realise it was a live cable. Charlie pushed me so hard to get to him that it felt like I'd been stabbed, but it was an accident. I wasn't thinking straight. I was in shock. My words came out jumbled.'

Mel stares at her. 'But if you knew Edward was dead, you went down to the tunnel for no reason . . .'

291

'I wanted to find the horn and call for help. I want us to be saved!'

'You could have come clean, we would have believed you, but you didn't. And then Zander died, needlessly.'

'I couldn't tell anyone what had happened without revealing everything. Without you all blaming me. That's why I kept it quiet.'

'But you let us believe that Charlie killed Edward.' Mel spreads her arms, the rain beats against her. 'His name badge . . .'

'I put his name badge in Charlie's pocket,' Bonnie says, her voice barely more than a whisper.

Bonnie had convinced them that Charlie was responsible for Zander's death, her injury, that he'd killed Edward. That he had something to do with Holly's death in revenge for her catching him stealing. That they had to be afraid of him. Charlie had pleaded for them to listen to him – he warned them about Bonnie – and they chose to ignore him.

Mel can't breathe.

She saw the hilt of the handle sticking out of Edward's neck. He didn't 'fall onto a knife'. Despite the believable theatrics, Bonnie viciously stabbed him to death. She might be petite but she's a powerhouse, she was able to drag his body into the walk-in freezer and lied to cover her back.

A lie that cost two innocent men their lives.

There's a loud honk of the boat's horn but it momentarily disappears from view beyond the swells. Mel's fingers have gone numb from the adrenaline coursing around her body. The platform sways dangerously under their feet, lifted by the rough waves. The salty smells of the water, petrol oil and bonfire trapped in her blood-stained clothes rush up her nose.

Another blast of the boat's horn. They're close. They must be able to see them here, surely? See them shivering in the spray of the crashing waves. See the blood splattered all over their corporate hoodies. Mel's heartbeat speeds up in her chest. For a split second, she debates whether she could make a jump for it, dive into the water and swim across to the boat. But she can't leave Nicole.

'It's all Eddie's fault. He's the one to blame. He planned this summer party. I had no idea he wanted to kill us all.' Bonnie lets out a gut-wrenching cry. 'He was going to kill me – it was self-defence.'

There's a low groaning noise from Nicole that pulls both their attention.

'You let us blame Charlie . . .' The white heat of anger rises in Mel's chest.

'I didn't think you'd shoot him. I was trying to get him to put the gun down.'

'Charlie is dead because of you.'

A rage swells in Mel like never before. She raises her fists, frantic and sharp. Pent-up frustration that she has been holding on to for far too long comes flooding out.

She scrambles towards Bonnie and pushes her.

Bonnie's elbow catches the side of Mel's head. Despite her size, she is strong, much stronger than Mel is. She yanks her arm back and delivers a better blow, one which stuns Mel for a few seconds. She never saw the wound to her stomach. She has no idea where that blood, or what looked like blood, came from. Mel realises as the blows come again and again that this woman wasn't badly injured. Another lie.

Everything blurs. She scratches her face and tugs her hair.

She sees the look of pain and alarm in Bonnie's eyes as she fights back. Mel's hands are sore. Her skull is on fire. Her ribcage rattles with every breath she takes. Another crack of a fist, this time against Mel's stomach. Bending her double. She drops to the rising and falling pontoon base. Close enough to Nicole's still frame to see she's still breathing.

'Enough!' Bonnie spits into the waves. She pants with exhaustion.

Mel can taste blood in her mouth. Her eyes flutter shut to stop the dizziness from overpowering her. She wants to be sick. Motion sickness engulfs her. She senses movement and forces her heavy eyelids open.

'I'm sorry . . .' Bonnie's throat sounds clogged with emotion, but there's a steeliness in her dark eyes. She stands above Mel. Her chiffon hem plastered to her bare legs. 'I didn't want to have to do this.'

Her voice catches on the wind. Mel tries to work out what she's saying.

She doesn't get a second before something hard suddenly flies towards her head. It comes out of nowhere.

The metallic taste of blood gushes in her mouth. White flashing lights appear. A searing pain shoots through her skull eclipsing the trauma she's already caused.

And then everything goes dark.

55

Friday 21st June

Transcript taken from comms onboard Atlantic B-802. RNLI Poole. Recording taken at 04.40 hours on Friday 21st June.

Crew member 1: Can you hear me? Hello? What's your name?

(Muffled sound of beeping)

(Long pause)

(Static)

Crew member 1: Sorry, Dominique, did you say? Keep talking to me, Dominique. You're ok now. Everything's going to be ok. We're going to get you to safety.

Crew member 2: What's happened here? Who else is at the hotel?

Crew member 1: (Clears throat). Operator we need backup. Request urgent backup. The police, the coast guard, the fire brigade, everyone up here. Something terrible has happened at Point Grey. We've managed to rescue one female. She looks in severe shock. She's injured and—

Crew member 2: Wait. What's that in the water?

Crew member 1: There's a body. And another one! [Expletive] Quick, help me try and get them out.

(Sounds of movement and swearing)

Crew member 1: Dominique, is there anyone else on Point Grey? Are there any other survivors? Dominique?

(Silence broken by intermittent beeping)

Dominique: [muffled]

Coastguard 2: What did she say?

Coastguard 1: Everyone is dead.

(Expletives drowned out by the engine revving)

56

The second Mel wakes everything hurts. It's as if a searing red hot needle is being scraped along the inside of her skull. The persistent pounding is almost too much to bear.

'Mel? Oh Mel.'

She can hear Rohan's voice. But that's not possible. Why would Rohan be in her bedroom? She hears the unfamiliar beeps. A clinical antiseptic smell hits her.

This isn't her bedroom.

'I'll call for the doctor. Oh, I can't believe it, we didn't know if you'd wake up so soon.' His voice is crackly as if layered with tears. 'We've all been so worried about you.'

Mel tries to lift her heavy eyelids but it's too exhausting. She manages to force one open for a split second but the crack of bright white lights pierces her retina, bringing a wave of sudden nausea. She hurriedly clamps it shut again.

'Take it slow, don't rush. Ah great, here's the doctor now.'

Mel listens as he tells someone – the doctor she presumes – that she just flicked her left eye open. Every word is drenched with relief.

There is movement beside her. A patter of rubber-soled shoes across a plastic floor. The brush of a person as they lean across the bed, their bodyweight pulling the bed sheet tighter across Mel's legs.

Her legs. She can feel her legs! What else can she feel? She tries to move her fingers. Turn her head. Open her eyes again. But it's too difficult. She liked it better before. The soft space, the gentle sleep. This is too bright, too loud, and too painful. She wants to go back.

'Her obs are dropping,' a woman's voice rings beside her.

An ear-splitting beep starts ringing somewhere above her head.

'Mel. Mel?' There's panic in Rohan's voice.

Mel wants to tell him that it's fine, she's ok. She needs to sleep. Hands start pulling and tugging across her, cold plastic wires are pressed against her skin. The beeping sound doesn't stop. It gets louder and louder until everything goes silent.

*

The smell wakes her. A cheesy smell that makes her nose wrinkle up.

'You're awake. Thank God,' Rohan says over a rustling sound. 'Let me wipe my fingers, I don't want to get crumbs over your sheets.'

'Where am I?' Mel croaks. Her throat is thick and bone dry. Every word is a gargantuan effort.

'You're in hospital. You've had a bit of an accident. But you're OK now. The doctors are looking after you. How are you feeling? Sorry, silly question.'

He looks like he's not slept. His beard is long and flecked with grey, his hair is messy, which comes as a shock as he's

298

usually so polished. There are creases in his dark checked shirt. The empty bottles of Coke and crumpled food wrappers lying on the table beside him, suggest he's been here for a while. Waiting for her to wake up. A rush of emotion squeezes her heart. The fact he is at her bedside means the world.

'Your mum will be so relieved. We all are. Leonora and I decided it would be too difficult and confusing for your mum to come and see you here, but I've been keeping them updated.'

Mel nods. Every muscle in her neck is stiff.

The summer party.

Those terrifying final moments come rushing back. The blood. The fire. The screams. The cold dark water. She swallows and tries to blink them away. She needs to listen to Rohan's soothing voice, not submerge into a panic attack.

He must sense something's wrong as he offers her a drink of water. A paper straw touches her cracked lips. With an enormous amount of effort, she manages to suck the room-temperature water into her mouth. It tastes of blood. She wants to spit it out but she can't.

'The others?' she croaks, swallowing sharply.

'Don't worry about anyone else, the main thing is that you're ok. The police want to talk to you, but they can wait. I told them that you need to get your strength back first. It sounds like you've been through one hell of an ordeal.' His voice breaks. 'None of us can believe it. It's been all over the news, of course. The press are desperate for information but . . .' He shakes his head as if stopping himself from saying something. 'Like I said, we can talk about everything soon. You focus on recovering.'

It's too much for Mel to take in. Pain swirls and pulsates

through her skull. She instinctively lifts a hand to touch her head where Bonnie hit her. Her fingers find bandages and the scratch of sterile tape.

'You got quite a nasty head injury from falling that way, they put you into an induced coma for a few days, to relieve the swelling,' Rohan says, gently moving her hand back by her side. 'Try not to touch it.'

Falling? What is he talking about?

Mel can't move her lips to speak. They crust and crack as she tries. The skin splits with the effort. There is a constant thudding pain in her temples. The room is too bright and loud. Everything is slightly out of focus. It's as if she's here but not here.

'Don't move. It must be scary but you're going to be ok. You need to rest and recover. Your spine was hurt so the doctors decided it was best to put you in a neck brace. It's going to feel pretty sore, but the main thing is that you're going to be ok, Mel.'

He starts tidying up the empty packets, a rustle of cellophane loud in her ears.

I didn't fall. Bonnie hit me across the side of my head with something.

'Nicole?' Mel manages to ask.

'Nicole is fine. Well, not fine, exactly. I mean I can't imagine the trauma from all you've witnessed. But erm, physically she's doing ok. An impressive cast on her left leg, a sprained arm and a bit of a mild concussion but she's ok. She's down the ward.'

Oh, thank God.

'Bonnie?' Mel rasps.

'There was a fire, do you remember that?' Rohan absently picks up an empty energy drink bottle and turns it in his hands. 'In the fire pit. Not far from the DJ booth. It spread quickly, by all accounts, so, erm . . . well, it might take the police some time to get to the bottom of it.' He rubs his beard, eyes flicking around, avoiding contact with Mel.

So many questions dance on the edge of Mel's swollen tongue but she can't summon the words to come out. She needs to try and explain what happened. 'Bonnie . . . she did this.'

'What?' Rohan frowns. 'Erm, ok. Well listen, don't worry about that right now.' He shushes her softly, as a father would if talking to their confused child. 'I'm sure you can tell the police everything that you remember when you're ready to talk to them.'

'Soon,' Mel says, the heavy call of sleep tugs at her eyelids. 'Soon.'

57

Wednesday 26th June

Nicole is at Mel's bedside. A nurse wheeled her in. Her left leg is in an impressive cast, her cheeks are covered in grazes and bruises, a thick plaster covers the deep cut to her forehead, and her blonde hair is pulled back into a low ponytail. The wide smile on her bare face shows how happy she is to see Mel. It's comforting to see her looking less than perfect for once. It also means that what happened, happened.

Although it was terrifying for Mel to be trapped on the pontoon hearing Bonnie's confession, it must be equally as scary for Nicole not to remember a thing from when she fell down the wet steps. It's a miracle that neither of them drowned after Bonnie pushed them into the water. The lifeguard crew arrived in the nick of time.

Nicole is absently stroking Mel's arm. One of her acrylics is missing. Her thin bird-like wrists tremble.

'Does anyone have any idea where Bonnie is?' Mel croaks.

Her neck brace has been removed but she's still nervous about moving too suddenly.

Nicole shakes her head. 'She's vanished. She lied to the

rescuers, said her name was Dominique, and told them that we fell from the top of the fort, a good fifty-feet drop.' Nicole winces. 'She said that Edward went on a rampage, Charlie eventually killed him and then shot himself, and we leapt overboard to escape it all.'

Tears spring to Mel's eyes.

'Charlie didn't kill Edward.' Mel clears her throat. It's scratched from the number of tubes which have been down there. It hurts every time she swallows. 'Bonnie did.'

Nicole's mouth drops. 'What?'

'She confessed it all to me.' Mel takes a laboured breath. It's as if something heavy is pressing down on her chest.

She explains about Holly's missing necklace, Edward's innocent request that spiralled.

'Edward was working his way through the list, killing anyone in Holly's journal. It happened to be Wesley and Jonty first. Who knows who else he would have gone after if she hadn't killed him.'

Nicole sits dumbfounded. 'So the search for some family heirloom started this whole thing?'

Mel wishes she'd seen this journal. If she'd cleared Holly's desk herself she would have found it and perhaps this whole thing could have been avoided. She stops herself from thinking like that. She's carried enough unnecessary guilt about Holly's tragic death. For so long she believed she was part of the reason Holly died. She can't replace that burden with this one now.

'Yep . . . Oh and I don't think you fell down the steps. Bonnie pushed you,' Mel says, her voice barely more than a whisper.

It wouldn't have been difficult for Bonnie to trip Nicole up from behind without Mel seeing, to stick out an elbow or dig Nicole in the ribs with some force.

'Oh . . . my . . . God . . .'

'You rattled her with that comment about the name badge. She must have panicked that you were onto her.'

Mel has been turning the whole sequence of events from the party over and over in her mind at every opportunity when she's been left alone in between sleeping. Her energy levels are non-existent. She's never experienced fatigue like this. Thankfully she's got enough drugs in her system to mute the nightmares.

For now.

Nicole chews a nail. 'So it was a coincidence that the stuff came out about Westways? With Jonty and Wes being killed first?'

'Yes,' Mel replies. 'Charlie was telling the truth, he didn't kill Edward. It was just bad luck that he happened to be in the tunnel when Zander was electrocuted and Bonnie was able to convince us Charlie had caused it. She planted Edward's name badge in his pocket. She lied. She told me it was self-defence. But I saw Edward's injuries . . . the knife in his neck was no accident.'

Nicole blinks, taking it all in. 'So she used Dominique's name because she knew she needed to get away? She panicked.'

Mel attempts to nod but it's too painful. Even saying it all out loud, it still doesn't feel real.

Nicole swears. She shifts in her wheelchair. 'I've already spoken to the police and given my view on events.'

The police are waiting for Mel to speak to them. She's been putting it off, wanting to see Nicole first. What if they don't believe her? A heavy nausea has been sloshing in her stomach ever since she woke up. She's been utterly terrified that she will be arrested. In black-and-white terms, her actions caused a man to die. If she hadn't tried to be the hero and get Charlie to drop the gun it would never have gone off and killed him.

Mel tries to get comfy but the sheets scratch and her brain won't slow down. Will there be a trial? Will she be sent to prison? What will happen to her mum? Will anyone believe her version of events?

Nicole clears her throat. 'I told the police that Charlie shot himself. Coincidentally, what Bonnie told the rescuers too.'

Mel looks at her. 'But—'

'He shot himself, Mel,' she repeats, firmer.

Mel nods, letting her know she understands. She thanks her just as the door opens.

The smell of freshly brewed coffee enters the room before he does. It makes Mel's stomach rumble.

'Hello, you two. How did you sleep, Mel?' Rohan asks.

He passes them each a takeaway coffee. She takes a sip. It's bitter and burns her tongue. He's forgotten that she takes one sugar.

'Not great.'

The smell of bonfire in her hair brought on a mild panic attack earlier this morning. The scent must be trapped in her unwashed hair, because, as soon as she moved her head she was back there again. It was as if she could hear the screams over the waves, taste the blood, smell the death and see the crazed look on Bonnie's face. A kind nurse gently washed her hair and now synthetic coconut masks the burning smell. Mel tries to push the memory away. Bonnie could have killed her with that metal pipe, one of the loose railings from around the pontoon that she used to knock her out, once she realised that Mel didn't buy her lies.

'I can't imagine what it's been like for you both. I'm still trying to understand what the press and the police are saying.' Rohan rubs his tired-looking eyes with the heel of his palm. Deep bags weigh them down.

Mel hasn't seen a newspaper or watched television and her phone is still somewhere on Point Grey – but Rohan has been updating her with developments.

'The sooner we get you home the better. You must be desperate to see your mum.'

Mel blinks back the tears that have sprung to her eyes. Rohan is distracted with his phone, which hasn't stopped beeping in his pocket since he walked in.

'You've had a lot of people interested in talking to you and asking about your visiting hours. I wanted to let you know that everyone is thinking about you. Tom has been calling every day.'

'Tom?' Mel repeats, catching Nicole raising her eyebrows.

'You're clearly very popular,' Rohan smiles.

Mel would laugh if it didn't hurt so much. Her ribs have a constant dull ache.

His phone buzzes again and he swears under his breath.

'What?' Nicole asks.

'The press have had a field day covering this and dredging up all the Holly stuff too. Bloody parasites.'

'God, you should see my DMs,' Nicole says.

A nurse raps on the door interrupting whatever Rohan was about to say. 'I've got the police here to see you, Mel. An

Officer O'Neal and a Detective Inspector Hutchinson. They've asked for the room to be cleared so I'm going to have to bring this party to an end, I'm afraid.'

Rohan stands up, preparing to wheel Nicole out of the room, telling Mel they'll visit again tomorrow if she's feeling up to it. There is a moment of silence before the nurse smiles at her.

'Ok if I let them in, love?'

There's a twist in her gut.

Rohan's phone rings, he quickly moves to silence it when the nurse gives him a fierce look. Nicole turns to Mel and smiles at her, encouraging her to be brave.

'Shall I let them in, Mel?' the nurse asks again.

Despite her subconscious screaming at her, she nods. 'Sure.'

58

Wednesday 26th June

It's not long before two police officers enter her private hospital room. The man introduces himself as Officer Martin O'Neal. He must be way over six foot tall. An angry red light on his body cam blinks on his broad chest. Despite his intimidating stature he has a kind face with bushy black eyebrows. A female officer slips in behind him, she is half his size and dressed in a smart grey trouser suit. She gives Mel a smile drenched in sympathy, introducing herself as Detective Inspector Stephanie Hutchinson as she rubs her hands. The tang of antiseptic gel wafting with the movement.

Mel wishes they would sit down.

'Hello, Mel. We appreciate you've been through the most extraordinary ordeal. As a key witness to what happened on Point Grey, we have been anxiously waiting to hear your side of the story,' Detective Inspector Hutchinson begins.

'If you don't mind, I'll be recording this conversation. Is that ok?' Officer O'Neal asks, his voice low.

Mel nods, watching Detective Inspector Hutchinson pull out a notepad.

'DI Hutchinson will jump in with any questions she may have. Please don't be alarmed, this is just a chat to get your version of events.'

She doesn't want to relive it all. She doesn't want to be reminded of the night from hell. Do they know what she did to Charlie? Have they found Bonnie? Her skin prickles with sweat under their fixed gaze. A plastic pulse oximeter is clasped over the tip of her left index finger. She expects an alarm to ring as her blood pressure rises.

'Sure.'

The plastic chair opposite Mel's bed creaks as Officer O'Neal rests his full weight on it. He smells of peppermints. DI Hutchinson stands by the small window overlooking the hospital car park.

'So, Mel, we want to get your take on the events from the party. We appreciate this is a very upsetting time but anything you can give us will really help our investigation,' O'Neal says.

The coffee that Rohan bought her swishes around in her stomach, threatening to come back up.

'I suppose I should start at the beginning.' Her throat feels like it's been set on fire, she knows she'll need to stop to take regular water breaks, prolonging this agony.

It all comes pouring out. She tells them about Edward. About Holly. About Westways. She's purposely vague about exactly how Charlie died, wanting to make sure her and Nicole's stories match. The officer listens and takes notes, his expression hardening with each revelation of every grim death. She tells him everything she knows up to the moment when Bonnie hits her with one of the metal railings and it goes black. The next thing she remembers is waking up in the hospital and being told she's lost five days of her life whilst being so heavily sedated.

Officer O'Neal looks up from his notepad. 'So Bonnie told you that she was chosen by Edward to search for a *necklace*?'

'Yes.'

DI Hutchinson has come to sit opposite her bed. 'But this has never been found?'

'No.'

Mel still can't believe Bonnie's involvement in the office party. She was so naive to believe that the VIP names were picked out of a hat. The signs were there all along. Bonnie had access to the office at unusual hours. She held the master keys – able to access every inch of the space. Everyone expected someone else to tidy up after them and Bonnie took advantage of this complacency. She also knew how to clean away evidence.

'Have you found her yet?' Mel asks.

'No. She was admitted under your colleague's name – Dominique. She was treated for a minor wound to her stomach – the doctor believed it to be self-inflicted – and left. We don't know where she went after she discharged herself on Friday lunchtime.'

DI Hutchinson replenishes Mel's water glass and encourages her to take small sips.

Officer O'Neal clears his throat. 'Since you've been here, we've established that Holly was right, there was theft in the company. Westways was a fictional client and money for expenses and elaborate "client entertainment" had been syphoned off, going to a separate account for at least ten months. We're pretty confident it was being split three ways – Wesley, Jonty and Charlie all taking a cut. They were effectively stealing from Flavour.'

Mel blinks. No wonder Holly wanted to speak to her so urgently. She had somehow uncovered this deceit was going on and was collecting evidence in order to blow the whistle on the whole thing. Her journal was an evidence log.

Mel finds her voice. 'Edward was convinced that someone from the office was responsible for Holly's death.'

The police officer shakes his head. 'The coroner ruled it an accident. We have no reason to dispute that.'

Mel presses her thumb to her temple. A pounding headache has started at the back of her eyes. Edward was torn apart by grief, unable to believe his young sister's choices caused her to die, but, like the judge ruled in his verdict, no one was to blame but Holly herself. She put herself in danger by drinking too much, wearing inappropriate clothing in the depths of winter and getting lost whilst taking a short-cut home. There was no maliciousness to her death. The three men she accused of stealing – Jonty, Charlie and Wesley – didn't kill her to cover up their deceit. No matter how convinced Edward was otherwise.

He clears his throat. 'Our colleagues have managed to recover some items from the hotel. I thought you might want this back.' He hands over her mobile phone, it's sealed in a police evidence bag, and his business card. 'If you remember anything else to tell us please don't hesitate to give me a call.'

The first thing she does, once the officers leave, is open the plastic Ziploc bag.

A puff of smoky air escapes and turns her stomach.

She wipes the tears from her cheeks and tries to push the nightmare away. She puts her phone on charge and as soon as there is enough battery, she calls Leonora and asks if she can speak to her mum.

59

Wednesday 26th June

The nurses have asked if Mel wants medication to help her sleep but she refuses. She's seen what those pills do to her mum, how easy it is to rely on them. If a temporary dose of insomnia is the price she has to pay, she'll pay it. Her injuries are healing as well as can be expected, she just needs to be patient. It's only much later, after her interview with the police, once she's alone and lying in her bed, the relative hush of the hospital at night-time washing over her, that she's able to run through things in her wide-awake mind.

Holly's missing necklace. Where did it go?

She tries to get comfortable. Her ribs ache and she's covered in bruises that press against the hard mattress. Something is niggling her. Something she can't put her finger on.

She had to turn her phone off as the notifications buzzing through were overwhelming. Since the news of her survival, her number of Instagram followers has shot up. She's been sent direct messages from strangers asking if she's okay, some heart-felt and selfless, others . . . less so. There have been journalists wanting to know if she'll speak to so-and-so at the *Daily Mail* and sell her story. Rohan asked her not to speak to anyone in the press. He's hired an external PR consultant who specialises in crisis management, any enquiries need to go through them.

It's started raining. She can hear it hitting the dark windowpane. She thinks of the movement, the thrashing waves. She remembers the driving rain pelting her back and has to blink the rush of panic away. She's safe now.

Perhaps Mel should buzz the nurse and ask for some earplugs? There's no point trying to sleep. She turns her phone back on wanting a mindless distraction but for some reason, Googles Point Grey. She doesn't know what comes over her, a desperate need for this to be a horrific nightmare, perhaps? It hasn't sunk in that this is her life, she's now one of the 'Point Grey Survivors' as one of the tabloids has named this tragedy.

She clicks on a news article.

Her serious-looking headshot from the Flavour website stares back at her. She's smiling but it's forced, and anyone looking at this will be able to tell she is uncomfortable being in front of the camera. It's unnerving to think that so many people now know her name.

Charlie's face leaps out of the lineup of photographs. His deep dimples and smiling brown eyes make her stomach clench. Tears rush to her tired eyes. She prays that how Charlie really died will never come to light, she still can't believe it's true.

Her fingers scroll faster and faster. She inhales one article after another.

The TikTok clip that Wesley persuaded her to do has been shared everywhere. The footage of her, red-faced and slightly out of time, now seen by millions of people.

But it's the images of the burnt-out rooftop at Point Grey

that take her breath away. It's a miracle that rescue workers were able to get on board and sift through the wreckage. The fire they started, the one that was supposed to be a cry for help, has utterly destroyed the entire roof terrace leaving a blackened mangled shell behind. It looks as if a bomb has gone off. The metal staircase is almost unidentifiable. The spindles are twisted and unnaturally bent. Someone has started to sweep up the debris judging from the soot-covered footprints left in the ash. Mel only has to close her eyes to picture it as it was before. The luxurious space with ambient music and smiling members of staff serving them drinks.

According to 'unnamed sources' Point Grey is likely to be demolished as it is structurally unsafe. Readers have commented what a travesty it is that a piece of history has to be destroyed because a work party 'got out of hand'. There are many angry comments. People looking for someone to blame. The company that owns the hotel have come under scrutiny for not having more rigorous safety and recruitment policies in place.

The papers have named Edward Mills as being behind it all.

She reads an update that says the bodies of Wesley, Jonty, Edward, Charlie and Zander have been removed from the hotel. There's yet to be an announcement of when their funerals will take place.

She clicks on another article. Snippets of text leap out.

'This isn't the first time the agency has been struck with bad luck. Just six months ago graduate, Holly Mills, 23, was discovered frozen to death following a Christmas night out with the agency.'

Rohan is right. The press were obviously going to dredge up what happened at the last party. Mel scrolls on. She knows she should turn her phone off and go to sleep but she can't help herself. It's as if she's seeing everything in a new light. The stories that appeared in the press when Holly died are now different somehow because of Edward's desperation for revenge.

She wishes she could read Holly's journal. Discover what Holly wrote about her. Find out exactly why Dominique, Zander, Nicole and Mel were also targeted.

There's a photo that has been lifted from Holly's Facebook. In it she's smiling at the camera and holding up a cocktail. In another she's snapped with a friend, both wearing matching pink gym wear. Her Instagram user handle is linked. Mel clicks through. Holly's page fills her screen. A life frozen in time.

Relaxing on a boat in the glittering Mediterranean sea. Pumpkin picking in a field with a couple of her friends. A bonfire party where she's raising a lit sparkler in the air. She looks so happy and carefree, young and full of life. There is a photo of a bunch of flowers and a box of personalised brownies on her desk at Flavour. The caption is a line of red hearts. Mel remembers what Nicole said about Holly having a boyfriend. She hasn't tagged anyone in the post though, and the comments don't reveal who she was dating. Mel was naive to these gifts. She must have walked past her desk and assumed it was deliveries made by grateful clients.

She scrolls some more looking for signs of this mystery man. There's a couple of pictures of the view from her desk on a frosty morning, snaps of her protein bowls she brought to work, and of Holly at the launch of a health club that Flavour did the campaign for. Charlie is amongst those standing behind her, grinning at the camera. Mel's heart clenches. Was he her secret boyfriend?

Catching sight of the time, Mel's about to put her phone down – trawling through her dead colleague's inactive social media when she should be sleeping is not healthy – then she sees something that sends a chill down her spine.

Further down her page, Holly has posted a photo of herself at someone's wedding. She's dressed in a stunning floor-length navy gown. Her hair is curled and pinned up. She looks like a Hollywood starlet. But it's her jewellery that catches Mel's eye. More importantly, the necklace she's wearing.

A blue azure teardrop hangs around her neck.

This must be the necklace that Edward asked Bonnie to search for all those months ago. The priceless family heirloom that he desperately wanted back. The one that's still missing. Mel brings her phone screen closer to her tired gritty eyes, zooming in on the image to get a better look.

She frowns.

She's seen this necklace before.

Not only that, she thinks she knows where it is.

A sudden dart of pain shoots across her side as she twists and leans over to the bedside table. Wincing, she rummages in the stack of magazines that Rohan brought in for her, ones that Rumi loves – catwalk fashion and high society gossip – not the sort Mel would normally pick up, still, she appreciated the thought. Earlier, she'd tucked Officer O'Neal's business card inside as a bookmark. A terrible sinking feeling claws her stomach as she scrambles to find it.

She pulls it out and despite the late hour calls the number. Mel holds her breath.

She prays that he picks up.

60

Thursday 27th June

Hampshire Constabulary: Interview started at 15.33

Rohan Ali:	Will this take long? I've got shareholders demanding answers. Members of staff asking when the agency will properly reopen. You guys said you had a warrant to search the offices but I'm still waiting to find out what it is you were looking for. Six days ago, I woke up to the news that my business is on fire and I'm trying to keep all of this afloat.
Officer O'Neal:	Like I said on the phone sir, we thought it would be easier to talk at the station rather than in front of your employees.
RA:	Sure, I mean I've got nothing to hide.
Detective Inspector Hutchinson:	Is that why you've declined the opportunity of having a solicitor present?
RA:	(Sigh). Can someone please tell me what this is about? If I had a clue why you've dragged me here then I might be able to decide if I need legal help or not.
OON:	Ok, well, firstly I will apologise for keeping you in the dark somewhat. As you know, this is an ongoing investigation, which has garnered some heavy media

and public interest to find out exactly what happened at the Point Grey Fort on the night of the 20th of June when your company had exclusive hire of the hotel.

RA: Of course, That's all everyone wants, myself included, to get to the bottom of what happened and how Edward Mills was able to kill. I told the other officer all I know. I left on the 10pm boat along with the majority of my employees. I'm sorry but there's nothing further I can offer that will help explain what happened on Point Grey in the hours that followed.

DIH: My team have been working day and night to piece things together. We've already spoken to key witnesses and I know you gave a brief version of events to a colleague of ours. However, we would like to dig a little deeper given some new evidence that has recently come to light.

OON: What can you tell us about his sister, Holly Mills?

RA: Holly? Erm, well, probably nothing that you don't know already. She was a bright, professional graduate who was at Flavour for around seven months. During that time she proved herself to be well-liked by her colleagues and clients. She was full of ideas for new campaigns and was always eager to share these in meetings. For someone so young, she had a mature and level head on her shoulders.

OON: So you would say she had a bright future ahead of her.

RA: Yes. Absolutely.

OON: How well did you know her?

318

RA: Oh, not very well. I mean our paths didn't cross that often in the office but when they did I always found her to be friendly and polite. Why?

DIH: And how about outside the office?

RA: I'm confused. What does this have to do with the events at Point Grey?
(Rustling in the background)

OON: For the purpose of the tape I am now showing the witness exhibit number PG38. This is a silver necklace with a blue teardrop in the centre. We believe it to be a sapphire. What can you tell me about this piece of jewellery, Mr Ali? Please take your time.'

RA: (silence followed by an inaudible mumble)

DIH: We are going to need you to speak up, I'm afraid.

RA: I said (long pause) . . . I need to speak to my lawyer.

61

The police officers have returned to Mel's hospital room. She is preparing to move to the ward today, a sign of her continuing improvement. Mel is propped up in bed with pillows behind her back, her heart races at the looks on their faces as they walk in. She's been waiting for an update ever since she called Officer O'Neal and told him what she suspected. She was so confident but, since she put the phone down, she's been doubting herself. Perhaps she got it wrong?

Seeing them file in around her hospital bed makes this suddenly very real. They say a brief hello. She expects them to pull out chairs but they remain standing. She doesn't know if that's a good sign or not.

Detective Inspector Hutchinson comments on how well she's looking. Mel has seen her reflection so she knows that she's being kind, but she thanks her anyway.

'So, it turns out that you were right when you said you'd seen that necklace before,' Officer O'Neal says.

Mel holds her breath, her eyes scanning his face for any sign

320

that this is some sort of joke. She desperately hadn't wanted it to be true.

Detective Inspector Hutchinson has a matching grave expression. 'We spoke to Rohan's wife who told us she was given the necklace as a Christmas gift. Rumi handed it over to our forensics team and we can confirm that it belonged to Holly Mills.'

Mel swallows. 'Rohan had Holly's necklace . . . but why?'

'He told us she sold it to him, but his story didn't add up. So we dug deeper . . .' The police officer shifts on his feet. 'What can you tell me about Powwow?'

Mel frowns, confused about the change in subject. 'The employee chat system?'

It was some corporate software they'd trialled last summer. Rohan had the idea to create an online suggestions box. A safe place for employees to submit ideas about different ways the company could work smarter. The thinking behind it was that it would allow anonymous suggestions as 'no idea is a dumb idea', however, this backfired as people started to use it as a space to be silly. Not long after, the 'message all' function was turned off and any non-anonymous legitimate questions directed into Mel's and Rohan's inboxes. The inability to talk to the whole office soon meant people got bored and only a trickle of genuine suggestions ever came through – that a breastfeeding area should be set up, and switching to eco-friendly washing up liquid or using better quality toilet roll, are some of the things she remembers.

'What about it? We cancelled it as it was a waste of money.'

He shakes his head. 'Not according to our searches. It's still a live system. But you've been taken off as an admin, so you haven't been getting any notifications.'

Mel frowns. 'What?'

'We believe that Rohan didn't want you to know he was still actively using it.'

Mel's about to interrupt and tell him that Rohan was hardly going to send work ideas to himself when Officer O'Neal speaks again.

'There were all sorts of images of Holly on there. Sexy images that she'd sent of herself.'

Mel's breath catches in her throat.

'Clearly she was using it as a sort of private chat . . . with Rohan,' Detective Inspector Hutchinson adds.

'What . . . wait, so you mean . . .?'

She clasps her hands together. 'We believe they were having an affair. There are hundreds of messages between them, spanning multiple months. But then, in December, it gets ugly. He calls it off and she threatens to tell his wife everything. We suspect they used the system to communicate because if his wife happened to see any notifications on his phone she would have assumed it was work stuff. Clever, really.'

Mel's head is spinning trying to keep up with what they're saying.

'The last message Holly sent was on the day she died, at the Christmas party. She tells Rohan that she urgently needs to talk to him. That she's expecting his baby,' DI Hutchinson says. Her voice is measured.

'She was pregnant?' Mel blinks rapidly. 'I had no idea.'

'No one did. Because it wasn't true. There was no mention of a pregnancy in the forensic examination.'

'She lied?'

'We believe so. Possibly as a way of getting his attention.'

Mel's eyes flick between the police officers, her mind races.

'Holly had a taxi booked for after the party but for whatever reason she chose not to take it. The last sighting of her before she was discovered in the woods the following morning was her walking unsteadily away from the Plaza hotel.'

Mel remembers the haunting CCTV that was shown in the media, a warning to youngsters on nights out to be better prepared for the freezing winter weather. She thinks of the unsuspecting early morning dog walker who stumbled upon Holly's frozen body and shivers.

'Rohan wasn't drinking at the party. He drove home. The journey should have taken twenty minutes. He told us he left around eleven but when we checked with his wife, she said that Rohan didn't return home until three o'clock in the morning. He can't account for this lost time,' the detective continues. 'His wife remembers when he returned because he woke the dogs, which in turn woke her. He gave her the necklace on Christmas morning. He told her it was an antique.'

Mel's head thumps. She had no idea about this web of lies. She had only remembered the necklace because Rumi wore it to Buckingham Palace. It was there in the photo of the two of them behind Rohan's office desk. She admired it every time she went into his office, with no idea of the history behind the jewellery. Hidden in plain sight.

'It wasn't widely reported but the pathologist found evidence that Holly had hit her head, and though initially it was thought that she stumbled of her own accord, we now believe she was pushed in the woods. I think when Rohan confronted her about the pregnancy, rage consumed him and he knocked her over with such force he killed her. She was tiny compared to him, intoxicated and probably already suffering from early-onset hypothermia so she could never have fought back. He left her for dead and took her jewellery. We presume it was some sort of trophy, who knows? This may have been a crime of passion but he still had the presence of mind to take the valuable piece.'

Mel tries to remember what she read in the papers about exactly how Holly died. There was mention of a head injury from tumbling down a wooded embankment but it was believed to be the hypothermia which had killed her. But actually, it was the other way around. She was pushed and left for dead. Edward was right when he feared someone else was to blame. Her stomach clenches.

'Rohan deleted all evidence of their online chat, especially as the last message he sent her threatened murder, but the digital footprint was already there.'

Mel fills in the rest as silence falls in her warm hospital room. He believed no one would check. Her lovely gentle boss, the man who had a life many envied, had lied to everyone. She closes her eyes, trying to digest what she's been told. Goose-bumps have broken out across her skin.

'He confessed to her murder, under pressure,' DI Hutchinson concludes.

'Have you managed to track down Bonnie yet?' Mel asks, a headache making itself known.

Officer O'Neal shakes his head slowly. 'No.'

Without warning, an unexpected yawn escapes Mel's lips.

'We need to be on our way and you need to get back to full

strength. We'll be in touch if we need any more. Take care, Mel,' DI Hutchinson smiles.

Mel watches the officers leave. She closes her eyes to try and come to terms with what they have told her, but she is in too much shock to process anything.

62

One Month Later

It's been difficult watching this play out online. The posts and memes going around her social media feeds have felt endless.

'The boss from hell.'

'I thought my boss was bad but this is another level – imagine working for him!'

'Surely someone knew what he was up to?'

Mel's head spins with the shockwaves Rohan's arrest has caused. She turns her phone to silent and puts it on the table in front of her. The constant buzzing of notifications is giving her yet another headache.

A week ago, Mel was discharged from the hospital and had an emotional reunion with her mum. Leonora has been working overtime to ensure her mum's routine wasn't too disturbed as Mel recovered, and Mel is immensely grateful.

She's taking things slow but for the first time is hopeful that everything will be ok. Everyone says she is recovering well, considering what happened that night, just over a month ago. The flashbacks are lessening. She's not having as many nightmares. However, just a waft of smoke makes her stomach turn.

Today is the first day she's been out since returning home. She cradles her hands around her oversized mug, the soothing smell of roasted beans and mundane conversations in the busy chain coffee shop goes on around her.

Nicole hobbles on crutches from the bathroom to join her. Her leg is still in a cast but luckily her arm has healed. It was a nasty sprain after all. The cuts and grazes have vanished under a layer of flawlessly applied foundation. Her hair has been professionally blow-dried and her fingernails are a polished maroon colour. Mel now wishes she'd taken more time to get ready.

'You look great,' Nicole says, gently touching Mel's arm as she fidgets in her black cardigan, as if reading her mind.

'Thank you. I didn't know what to wear.'

The great British weather is back to normal. It's not stopped raining for days. The heatwave is a heady memory. 'Well, you can't go wrong with a little black dress. Right, I think we need to make a move in a minute. Are you ready?'

Mel glances at her watch. They don't want to be late for the memorials being held for the four men: Jonty, Wesley, Zander and Charlie. They are both dressed in muted shades of black and grey for the sombre occasion.

'I wonder if Bonnie will turn up?' Nicole says, finishing her oat latte and pulling out a compact to check her lipstick.

'Imagine.' Mel shudders.

There has been no sighting of her since she discharged herself from hospital. The police have put out numerous appeals for her to come forward as a 'person of interest' but nothing. It's as if she has vanished into thin air.

'No, we will never see her again. I'm sure.'

Mel tries not to think about her too much. Bonnie believed in her 'caring mother' image, taking Edward's money to help save her son's life, clearly desperate to get her family back on its feet. Mel doesn't doubt that was true but she'll never forget that steeliness in her eyes on the pontoon. The ferocity of that kitchen knife in Edward's his neck. The fatal lies she told.

That woman is dangerous.

Another notification lights up her phone, and her eyes instinctively trail over it. It's a request from an Australian podcast company who are preparing to launch a series about what happened on Point Grey. They want to interview Mel. Nicole's phone chirps to life with the same request, a few seconds later.

'You going to do it?' Mel asks, glancing up from her screen.

'I can't. I signed that media contract, remember?' she says, flashing her engagement ring that glints under the lights.

In the end, Nicole and her fiancé, Tristan, decided to postpone their big day. She's done a deal with a tabloid newspaper to feature their wedding in an exclusive double-page spread in return for an in-depth interview. Mel has received her invite for her and a plus one. At first, she wasn't sure how she'd feel going to a party, the first gathering since Point Grey, but she can't let her life pass by anymore. She needs to be brave. In fact, she's already chosen the floaty floral dress she'll wear for the occasion and has someone in mind to ask but hasn't plucked up the courage yet.

'What about you?' Nicole asks.

'No way.'

Mel has declined every press opportunity. Despite the money being offered for a no-holds-barred interview and knowing how that would help her mum out, she couldn't bring herself to talk about that night to a stranger and profit from Charlie's death. She wants to get on with her life. Any time Point Grey is mentioned her stomach drops. In her opinion there is nothing more to be said.

Rohan is awaiting sentencing and, according to the detectives, on the advice of his lawyers, he's pleading guilty to Holly's murder. The papers have turned him over. Deep dived into his background and dredged up all manner of skeletons from his closet. Every day there's a new angle, a new sordid secret, a different person from his past speaking out for the first time.

'Rumi has sold the company, Flavour will be dissolved and merged with a larger agency. It was her money bankrolling it all along. Not his. His rags to riches story was bollocks,' Nicole says, absently dabbing a thumb to pick up fallen crumbs from a pain au chocolat she's been picking at. 'An email went round to say there would be a restructure process etc but I know loads of the team are taking the package to leave. I've not made my mind up yet.'

Rohan stood to lose everything if the affair came out – his wife, their children, the business, his reputation. The public perception he'd carefully crafted of a charitable family man would come crashing down.

Nicole sighs deeply. 'I should have known the constant "we are family" crap he loved to go on about was a huge red flag when I joined Flavour. Seriously, any company that proudly says that when no one is genetically related needs to have a word with themselves. It's controlling, like they expect you to be emotionally tied to them, but we're not family.'

'Thank God. Have the police given you any news on Bonnie?'

'No. I'm guessing they still can't find her. At first, I couldn't sleep thinking she might come back for us, finish the job, but surely she knows they're looking for her so must be lying low.' She offers Mel a mint. 'Right, come on.'

'I'll catch you up,' Mel says to Nicole.

She spots Tom walk through the door of the coffee shop, glancing around hopefully.

'Oh . . .' Nicole smiles.

'It's not like that.' Mel flushes.

'Hey, Tom. Lovely to see you again,' Nicole says, throwing Mel a knowing look.

'Hey,' he replies, bashfully.

'Well, I'll see you both there. Don't be too late,' Nicole instructs, raising a perfectly defined eyebrow.

Tom clearly picks up on her unsubtle signals as his freshly shaven cheeks turn bright pink. His dark curls dance around his head as he nods.

'We'll be right behind you.'

Once she's gone, Tom gives Mel a light kiss on the cheek. He's actually very handsome, especially in his dark suit. They struck up a friendship after Mel left the hospital. When she'd felt strong enough, she'd messaged to thank him for the fruit hamper he'd sent her – she remembers his thoughtful hand-written get well soon note, it wasn't full of generic well wishes like other cards she received, he appeared genuinely concerned about her – and they haven't stopped talking since.

This is the first time they've met up in person since the night of the summer party and she was expecting it to be awkward, especially given where they are about to go. But knowing he will be by her side fills Mel with a comforting lightness.

For the first time in a long time she feels like she is someone's priority. They end each day with a good night text, and they start each morning with a chirpy 'How did you sleep?' message. Who knows where it will go – she's trying not to overthink anything.

She finishes her coffee. 'So, erm I wondered what you were doing on the twenty-first of September . . .?'

He takes out his phone and swipes to the calendar. 'Nothing. Why?'

Mel takes a deep breath. 'It's Nic's wedding and if you've not got anything else on then, well, I wondered if you wanted to be my plus one?'

The smile that erupts on his face gives her the answer she needs.

63

Wednesday 11th September

The job interview is today. Mel thought she had given herself enough time to get ready but somehow she's still running late. Tom has been texting her all morning, helping her come up with snappy answers, quizzing her on imagined topics the interviewer may ask. She's more comfortable asking the questions than answering them.

As much as Nicole teases her, Mel loves working in HR. She's good at it. And this new role for a national charity feels like it's the right thing to do. She's ready to get some structure back into her life.

If she gets this job, her increased salary will more than cover the fees at Silverdale. Rohan put a word in for her mum, like he said he would, he must have done it before the summer party as it wasn't long before a place became available. Mel had been unsure about taking it, not wanting to accept anything from this man who had wrecked so many lives but she couldn't miss this opportunity to bring some 'normality' back into her and her mum's life.

She opens her wardrobe to pull out her trusted suit, praying it still fits. There is a screech of metal as her coat hangers run along the rail. She scans the rows of colour, looking for the smart navy blazer.

She wore it to Charlie's memorial all those weeks ago. It was hell sitting through the service knowing what she'd done. Nicole had squeezed her hand so tight she thought she would draw blood. Mel has buried a lot of what happened at Point Grey. Charlie is dead. Nothing will change that. She can't keep living in the past no matter how much she wishes she could change things.

Her eyes land on the bin bag burrowed at the back of the wardrobe.

Mel is struck with a sudden clarity.

Today is the right day. This is about new beginnings and fresh starts.

She drops to her knees to pull out the hidden package. Out of sight but not out of mind – her terrible secret. Holly's coat. She runs her hands over the soft, faux fur hood. She had hidden it here all that time ago, terrified that she would be blamed for Holly's death. Now it is time to let the guilt go.

Rohan was to blame. He killed her.

Mel places the winter coat on her bed, carefully folding it. She will donate it to charity. Since coming to terms with what happened, a steeliness has been lit inside her. She doesn't need to ask for permission anymore.

Holly's signature smell, which was once woven into the fabric, has faded. Mel remembers smelling it in her bedroom at the hotel, convinced that someone knew about the coat. That someone had seen her walking off with it and was tormenting her.

She had no idea it would be so much worse than that.

She picks it up to put into a plastic bag when she feels something she hadn't noticed before. Inside the cream silk lining, there is a lump. Her fingers trace the hem, finding a hole in the pocket. Something has fallen through it and is lodged in the lining. Mel manages to manipulate the fabric so she can guide whatever it is around.

It's crunchy. An old receipt or dry-cleaning stub perhaps?

She pulls out a yellowing piece of paper. It's cheap quality. Looks as though it's been torn from a notebook.

Mel's stomach flips. She recognises the handwriting.

This must be one of the pages from Holly's journal, the ones Bonnie said Edward claimed were missing.

Her fingers tremble as she flattens it, smooths out the curled edges. It's been scrunched up, folded in two, and forgotten. On one side there is a scribbled drawing, childish biro lines. A picture of a pregnant woman, the giant swollen belly taking up much of the page. Is this supposed to be Holly? Was she planning on giving this to Rohan that night? Or is it idle doodling? She's written some dates. It looks like a series of numbers but is this her working out her last period? Has she tried to figure out when her fictional due date would be?

Her eyes trail down the sentences. Lying about being pregnant cost her her life.

Mel turns the paper over. This is a longer chunk of text, written like a diary. There's no date. Mel's name leaps out. This is about her. She starts to read, immediately hearing Holly's voice in her mind.

'There's something different about Mel. She's like this calmness amongst the creative chaos ... Perhaps I've been

334

too harsh on her. Today, for example, I watched her hand out all the teas and coffees. Not one person said thank you. But she didn't appear to expect it either. Maybe she's nicer than people say she is. Perhaps I jumped to conclusions about her . . .'

Mel re-reads it.

She doesn't know what to do with this information. She always wondered what she'd done to warrant her VIP invitation to Point Grey. At first, she presumed it was because someone knew she took the wrong coat, then she wondered if it was because she didn't act sooner on Holly's complaints but whatever she did, it looks as if Holly had a change of heart about Mel.

Tears glaze her eyes, blurring Holly's words until they vanish.

What if she hadn't been one of the chosen guests? Maybe Charlie would still be alive? She swallows. Then again, maybe Edward would have killed them all, who knows? She can't change the past.

Her trembling fingers tear the note into pieces. Tiny pieces of confetti scatter her bedroom floor. Life moves on.

64

The Daily News Online

Thursday 12th December

KILLER BOSS JAILED

Published: 17.33, 12 December

A COMPANY boss who murdered a young female worker in a bid to cover up a marital affair has been jailed for life.

Rohan Ali, 51, attacked Holly Mills, 23, before leaving her lifeless body in a woodland.

The young woman, a graduate at Ali's design agency Flavour in Marlow, Bucks, was killed "to keep their affair secret", a court heard.

Ms Mills was the sister of Point Grey Hotel killer Edward Mills, whose crimes triggered a fresh police examination into the circumstances of her death.

Passing sentence at the Old Bailey in London, Mr Justice Knowles said married Ali was determined "to protect his reputation as a loyal family man at all costs".

He had been in a romance with Ms Mills for around five months at the time of her death.

In court, Mr Ali sobbed as the judge told how he drove Ms Mills to Ashdale Woods in Marlow on December 22.

He killed her by pushing her down an embankment, causing her to sustain a fatal head injury.

Ali "staged the death to look like a tragic accident", said Mr Justice Knowles, and claimed she had "walked there alone following a company Christmas party".

Police initially treated Ms Mills death as non-suspicious after she was discovered by a dog walker, with the coroner ruling death by hypothermia as forensic evidence suggested she had fallen while trying to walk home in freezing winter temperatures.

But fresh pathologist tests were ordered in the wake of events at Point Grey Hotel on Thursday 20th and Friday 21st June, a luxury hotel venue based in a repurposed maritime sea fort, where four people were killed by Holly's brother, hotel night manager Edward Mills, who then died from self-inflicted injuries.

Detectives believe Mr Mills was acting in revenge over his younger sister's death but that he targeted the wrong suspects.

It was evidence which came to light during the murder probe that unmasked Ali's involvement in Holly Mills' death. He has pleaded guilty to murder and perverting the course of justice. He has been stripped of his MBE following sentencing.

Mr Justice Knowles described the killing as "callous and despicable".

He said Ali was "an entitled man with no care for the lives of others" adding: "You have taken not only Miss Mills' life, but also ruined countless others with your unimaginable actions. You will serve at least twenty years before you will be eligible for parole."

Speaking after the sentence was passed, senior investigating officer DI Stephanie Hutchison, said: "Rohan Ali has today been rightfully jailed for the senseless and tragic murder of Holly Mills. Holly was a young woman with her whole life ahead of her and the cowardly actions of Ali that night, believing he could get away with her murder, show the arrogance and contempt he had for everyone else. Holly's life was tragically cut short because of his pride and ego. Her family, friends and those who knew her have been left devastated by her loss."

Police still urgently want to speak to Bonnie McCulloch, one of three employees who survived the tragedy.

Flavour has since gone into administration.

Comments:

Carly_lashes: Horrendous. Poor girl. I remember reading that story and thinking there was more to it. The police need to take a long hard look at themselves. Shoddy detective work.

JoeStephenson: Bring back the ultimate penalty. He makes my boss look like a saint.

ToniRrrr: So good to see that Point Grey survivors are starting to move on. Nicole looked amazing on her wedding day! I wish them all well.

The views expressed in the comments above are those of our users and do not necessarily reflect the views of News-Online.

65

Thursday 12th December

'Joanna? Did you manage to clean the ground floor gents?'

Bonnie is about to reply when her phone buzzes with an alert. She instinctively pulls it from her pocket. It's a breaking news notification from a news app.

'I'm afraid there's a no-phone rule until break time, Jo,' her new line manager, a woman with mild halitosis, says in a simpering Welsh accent.

'Of course, sorry.'

A quick glance at the headline told her all she needed to know anyway. Rohan Ali has been jailed for the murder of Holly Mills. Twenty years before he will taste freedom.

'Jo . . .?'

'Erm, yes, the gents are all done,' Bonnie replies.

'You're a quick learner, aren't you.' Her boss grins, revealing crooked yellow teeth, stained from years of cigarette and tea breaks. 'I'll have to tell the agency how well you're doing.'

Bonnie says something in polite response, waiting until she's waddled off to pull her phone out and properly pore over the article to see if her name is mentioned. Well, her real name.

338

She saw those grainy CCTV shots that were released to the media of her leaving the hospital after her, Nicole and Mel were rescued. It scared her to death that she'd be recognised.

After what happened five months ago at Point Grey she knew she needed to lie low so discharged herself and caught a taxi home to pack and escape as quickly as she could. She cut and dyed her hair, changed her clothes and now wears glasses and hats so she looks different to any photo that might have been shared with the general public of her from 'before'.

Perhaps fleeing was a bad idea but she was too scared to stay and face the music.

She holds her phone closer and reads the line about how the police urgently want to speak to Bonnie McCulloch. *Why haven't they let this go?*

She's travelled around a bit since then and now finds herself in Cardiff. She wanted a big capital city full of nameless people like her. She needs to replenish her funds, which is why she's signed up to a temporary cleaning agency. The identity checks they did were laughable.

Her eyes trail the news article, her stomach turns at the sight of Rohan's face staring back at her from her screen.

She knew Holly had a boyfriend. She remembers cleaning her desk and seeing the chocolates, the flowers and a simpering note signed off with a million kisses, no name. She had no idea who the lucky guy was. Her money had been on Charlie. His eyes roamed over every young woman at the office. Never in a million years had she imagined it was Rohan. Eurgh.

It is unbelievable that the night at Point Grey, the 'hotel of horrors' as the papers refer to it turned out the way it did.

It was a weak moment when she told Mel everything. Perhaps she needed to clear her conscience.

Well, not *everything*.

Some things she couldn't put into words.

She casts her mind back to the beginning.

Finding that little yellow notebook hidden at the back of Holly's desk drawer was the start. She snuck it into her tabard. Pored over every hand-written page. It was a log-book of issues. A catalogue of errors that Holly had been keeping ever since she started working at Flavour. Clearly, someone had advised her to write it all down, possibly as evidence for a tribunal. It was a goldmine of bullying, catty remarks, sexist comments and borderline gaslighting. It also contained detailed notes that Holly had taken on her suspicions of theft in the office, namely a fake account being used by Jonty, Charlie and Wesley, she was working on bringing the injustice to light.

Eddie paid Bonnie well for this discovery.

But despite his requests to look into each of these accusations, he was never quite as quick to pay.

In fact, Bonnie spent most of the party trying to find Eddie, needing to ask about the last instalment he'd promised. Time was running out. The rehab centre was chasing her for payment. She'd kept up her side of the bargain and was losing patience that he was avoiding her on purpose.

Earlier on at the party, they'd bumped into each other in a corridor as she was heading to her bedroom.

'Where's my money?' she demanded.

'What?' He looked different. She couldn't put her finger on what had changed. Something flickered across his eyes.

'You said you'd pay me more,' she hissed, needing to keep her voice low but the anger bubbled up inside her.

'There is no more. Now get out of my way.' He barged past her.

She was furious. Eddie had never spoken to her like that before. He wasn't the man she met for coffee all those months ago. What did he mean, no money? He'd promised her. She was trying to make sense of what had happened when Wesley emerged from the shadows. He must have heard the whole thing.

Her stomach flipped. He gave her a look and carried on walking.

She couldn't relax in case Wesley told someone what he'd overheard. She was secretly relieved when he pulled out that joint on the roof terrace. At least if he was stoned he would forget the suspicious incident.

However, as the hours ticked on it became clear how Eddie was going after everyone mentioned in his sister's journal. The men were involved in the company theft or, in Zander's case, just for being vile and treating the graduates like dirt. Mel, Nicole and Dominique had been picked because they either ignored Holly's concerns, dismissed her ideas or stole praise for projects she'd worked on.

Bonnie's name wasn't included anywhere in this little yellow book, she'd checked, but she was guilty by association. So she couldn't say a thing.

Edward wasn't going to let her walk away. It was kill or be killed. Of course, she can understand the fierce love of a sibling but still, it's no match to that of a protective mother. She had to bide her time.

Bonnie went to the kitchen and waited behind the larder as Eddie walked in. She caught sight of the gun in his hand and for a split second froze, fearing that her plan wouldn't work.

When she sprung out, praying that the element of surprise would buy her a few precious seconds, he fell back, startled just as she hoped. She launched herself at him and thrust the kitchen knife into his freckled flesh, meeting a grinding resistance from the tendons in his pale neck. Possessed by a manic energy to wedge the blade further. Deeper.

It was over in seconds.

She somehow managed to drag him into the walk-in freezer. She doesn't know why. She wasn't thinking straight, she just needed him hidden. She quickly wiped the blood from her hands, the splatters from her cheeks, and cleaned up the messy floor tiles as best she could.

That's when she saw his name badge glinting up at her. She knew she had to pin this on someone. There would be too many questions otherwise. Questions she couldn't answer. She needed to save herself. She wouldn't let her son inject himself to death with no one on the outside to care for him.

She joined the others, trying to calm her breath, hide her trembling hands, and act as though nothing had happened. Zander and Nicole were in the residents' lounge, arguing about something, neither of them gave her a second glance when she slipped in. They all headed to Zander's room to wait for Charlie and Mel to tell them if the lifeboat was an option to escape. Bonnie couldn't tell them they were no longer under threat.

It was in the tunnel that she had the idea to plant Eddie's name badge on Charlie, slip it into his pocket. But Zander saw.

The pause felt like an eternity.

He turned to say something, stretched an arm against the wall to steady himself. He didn't see the tangled web of exposed live wires. She watched as his eyes bulged with a microsecond of realisation before his limbs jolted and he cut the power.

The smell. Charred flesh. Cooked from the inside.

She screamed as his body convulsed. Charlie tried to move in the dark to help Zander, which gave her the opportunity she needed. She hid the name badge in his pocket then picked up a sharp metal sign that had been dumped in the tunnel and sliced her stomach. Charlie could take the blame for this too.

Everything was falling into place.

She needed Charlie to be blamed. It was unfortunate that he was shot in the end.

But she underestimated Mel, that's for sure.

Every day in the Flavour office, Mel always looked as if she was about to apologise for something, more often than not for something someone else had done. Bonnie wanted to snap her straight. Slam a palm against the hunched back and stooped shoulders and strengthen her backbone. Turns out she didn't need to do a thing. Mel found her voice on her own.

How the lifeboat crew didn't see her knock Mel out with one of the railings she'd managed to prise free is beyond her. Luckily, neither did they see her push the women into the water.

But she didn't kill them.

Bonnie picks up a bottle of bleach and silently makes her way through the empty office block, passing an artificial Christmas tree with cheap flashing fairy lights that someone wrongly thought would add some festive cheer. This is an investment firm, not Santa's Grotto. It's a lot more boring than Flavour, but has a lot more potential too. She sees halitosis breath at the far end on her phone, back turned. Clearly the no-phone policy doesn't extend to those higher up the ranks.

Bonnie won't be here long.

People's workspaces reveal so much, more than you think. When she cleans she is very careful to put things back as she found them. She has a photographic memory that way. It's a skill to be able to look at something and memorise it exactly.

But she's tired. The past six months have taken it out of her.

All the lying, responding when someone calls her new name, constantly being on the move, remembering her fabricated backstory has been tough, but the worst part of all is not being able to go and visit her son.

Her manager loudly clears her throat bringing Bonnie back to the present. She hadn't heard her come up behind her.

'So, Joanna, if you could move to the gents on the first floor? I can only apologise for the state of them . . .'

'Not a problem.' Bonnie grabs her cleaning equipment, making sure her phone is safely tucked in her tabard, and gets to work.

The lift is out of order so she trudges up the stairs, the bannister is wrapped in tacky silver tinsel. Her mind is elsewhere as she turns the corner. She doesn't hear it at first.

The wiry carpet tiles muffle the sound of their rubber-soled boots. Their arrival escapes her notice.

'Bonnie McCulloch?' A deep no-nonsense male voice calls out.

Her yellow duster cloth flutters to the floor as she sees the uniform. Her eyes dart about, searching for any form of escape.

Nothing.

It's over.

ACKNOWLEDGEMENTS

The Summer Party wasn't the easiest book to write, especially as the story predominantly takes place in one location on one night. Trying to keep track of where all the characters were was like carrying a Cluedo board in my head! So I owe a huge thank you to those around me during every edit as I grappled with the plot and structure to make sure it made sense. Point Grey is loosely based on one of the real-life naval forts in the Solent but I took artistic licence with many exact details.

My 'colleagues' are spread all across the country. Thank you to my friends for pressing my books into the hands of strangers and telling them to buy a copy! Especially Emma, Claire, Jenna, Nicola, Sarah, Helen, Laura, Desiree (and JJ!), and Rachel. Special shout out to Jen Atkinson for her agency knowledge – all mistakes are entirely my own – and Jo Huggins for supportive chats over (many) glasses of Sauvignon.

Thank you to my author friends for their advice, encouragement and for organising brilliant writing retreats: Cesca M, Izzy B, Kirsty G, Katie M, Cress M, Cathy B, and the Harrogate crew, also to everyone in Anstey's Writers Group, which has quickly become a highlight of my writing week.

To my agent Juliet Mushens who inspires me more than she

knows. Her unwavering belief in my writing fuels the fire. Thanks also to the rest of the Mushens Entertainment dream team, especially Rachel for stepping in whilst Juliet was on mat leave for reading a messy first draft and giving great encouraging feedback. Thanks also to Eve Hall, Caroline Hogg and Bethany Wickington for their priceless editing advice.

Thanks to Tracey and her family at Low Costa Mill for a quiet place to write, and to the staff at Gladstone's Library for a slice of silent heaven.

Thank you Mountain Leopard Press for their enthusiasm and professionalism, including the editing minds of Beth Wickington and Jenni Edgecombe. Rebecca Bader, Izzy Smith, Jess Harvey, and Sinead White in Sales. Katrina Smedley in Marketing, Isabelle Wilson in Publicity, Ellie Wheeldon in control of Audio and Louise Rothwell in Production.

Thanks to the many booksellers, book bloggers and librarians who champion my stories across the world. Your tireless hard work in spreading the word is so appreciated.

Special thanks to my family – including Mum and Steve, my siblings, my Ukrainian family, my children, and my husband, John – for always being consistently supportive of my writing. I wouldn't be able to do any of this without you.

Finally, thank **you** for picking up this book. I appreciate your support whether that's buying, loaning, reviewing or cheerleading my writing, it all helps!

You can get in touch with me via my website www.kategrayauthor.com, where you can also sign up to my newsletter, so you don't miss any updates on my books, and offers or competitions. You can also find me on social media: @KateGrayAuthor or tag me on Instagram @kate_gray_author.